Lost Souls

Of

Cypress Hill

Laura Litkea

ROYAL MEDIA
& PUBLISHING

Royal Media & Publishing
www.royalmediaandpublishing.com
royalmediapublishing@gmail.com

Cover and Layout: Elite Book Covers

Paperback ISBN: 978-1-955501-23-1
Hardback ISBN: 978-1-955501-24-8

LCCN: 2025900742

Printed in the United States of America

Dedication

To Kentucky, where Midwest values and Southern charm mingle with history, haunting tales, and the timeless spirit of the past. May the stories of this land continue to inspire and enchant all who walk its paths.

Acknowledgements

Writing this book has been an incredible journey, and I have so many people to thank for their support and inspiration along the way.

First and foremost, I'd like to express my heartfelt gratitude to my family and friends. Your unwavering belief in my dreams kept me going during the late nights and long writing sessions. Thank you for listening to my plotting and planning while at work, at church, in the grocery, and while walking our dogs.

To the brave spirits who continue to show themselves at some of the most haunted places on earth, whose stories live on through whispers in the wind and shadows in the night—thank you for the inspiration.

Finally, to the young readers out there, I hope this book sparks your imagination and takes you on a thrilling adventure. May you always seek the magic in the world around you, even if it lies in the unexplained.

With all my gratitude,
Laura Litkea

Table of Contents

Prologue

After a long journey home from Europe, Colonel Adalbert Sommer sipped iced tea on the veranda with his friend, Isaac Lewis. The stifling summer days were much easier for elderly men like them to tolerate, doing nothing with a chilled glass of sweetness in their hand, rocking in their wooden chairs. Adeline nodded to them as she stepped outside and seemingly floated down the stairs to the lawn.

"Your daughter-in-law sho seems happy here." Isaac gestured towards the young woman strolling to the rose garden, wearing a light blue gown and white lace parasol. "She likes that gazebo ya built them, doesn't she?"

"I think that was the best addition to this old house since the solarium."

"And that new addition on the side, for Henry's family. If he ever get one."

"Now, you know Henry ain't right in the head, Isaac. No woman gonna wanna marry that fool. He's talkin' about wasting money on some automated tractor."

"Suppose ya right." Isaac nodded. "Franz will keep him in place."

"He ain't right, either." Adalbert drank from his glass, took a cigar from his pocket, clipped the butt, and fired it up. To him, Franz and Henry didn't have a lick of sense in them. Now, Raymond, he's the one Adalbert chose to run the farm. He puffed until his cigar burned, then took it out of his mouth to examine the smoke. "You want one, Isaac?"

"No thank you, sir. I don't smoke."

"I forget that."

They sat in silence for a while, watching a young housemaid walk down to join the other in the garden. They clipped budding roses and fresh mint, carrying a basket full around to the back of the house.

"Remember in the spring, how we'd have an Easter egg hunt at the church, then everyone would come up the hill for a picnic with ham and all the fixin's?"

"Sho do. Them's some good times."

"And we'd have a big pumpkin patch, every fall everyone'd gather for hot cider, candied apples, and they'd take a pumpkin home with them." The colonel sighed. "Cypress Hill was once the finest home in the county, but Franz stopped the activities that brought us together as a community while we's in Europe."

"You do have a lovely home, but times are changing. We the old generation. They the next generation." Isaac knew better than to speak about money matters to the boss and chose his words carefully. "They'll be okay, ya know."

"There is some insurance, Isaac, but I haven't told them. A treasure. I've hid it in plain sight, right under those trees. Remember?"

"Yessir, I remember well." It was all Adalbert talked about lately.

"I'll need to tell them about the treasure, seein's how my memory seems to be fading. I can barely remember that woman's name. The one Raymond married."

"Adeline."

"Adeline. If I forget, tell her about the treasure, Isaac. She'll do what's right."

Chapter One

Raine Sommer awoke at the break of dawn to a symphony of crowing roosters and squawking hens from the barnyard. The sun warmed a dark sky behind the budding branches of maple, sycamore, and locust trees. She stretched her arms above the heavy quilt her great-grandmother had made and pulled the mass of curls into a knot on top her head.

It was mid-March, and the world was shrouded in a bittersweet mist, memories of her childhood lingering like a delicate melody in the early morning air. The pale light filtering through her bedroom window seemed to cast a gentle embrace, as if the universe itself acknowledged the weight of the day.

The room, with delicate, pink-flowered wallpaper and traces of her mother's spirit, was a sanctuary of both comfort and sorrow. The scent of lavender, her mother's favorite fragrance, lingered in the air. Her best friend, Eva, had gifted her a bottle of the flower water from the local apothecary, and Raine sprayed some on her pillow every night before bed. Raine lay in bed for a moment, her thoughts a mosaic of love and loss. She inhaled deeply into the pillow, savoring the lingering aroma.

Her gaze drifted towards a framed photograph of her parents on her nightstand—a snapshot frozen in time, capturing the warmth of a love that transcended the physical realm. She traced the edges of the image with her fingertips, a silent communion with the past. She had her mother's thick, wavy hair, and her father's crystal blue eyes. Her mother's freckles faded with age, while Raine's remained a poignant reminder of her Irish heritage.

"I miss you, Mom."

As Raine prepared for the day, a quiet melancholy settled within her. She chose to wear her favorite corduroy pants and tattered sweatshirt, one large enough to hide her thin, yet maturing figure. While her friends had all blossomed head to toe with feminine curves, fifteen-year-old Raine had yet to develop, well, except for her breasts. The oversized shirts were to cover her chest, an effort to draw little attention to herself. No make-up, no lip gloss, and hair usually worn in a ponytail or braided bun. She did not want boys to notice her, so she went for the flat and frumpy look.

Raine added a delicate, silver crescent moon pendant that once belonged to her mother, a tangible connection to the woman who shaped her world. She tucked the necklace under her shirt, grabbed her backpack for school, and turned off the bedroom light. Each step on the old wooden floor echoed with the resilience of a young soul grappling with profound loss, yet she was determined to honor the memory of her mother today.

Descending the creaky stairs in her family's Kentucky antebellum home, Raine found solace in the familiar rituals of the morning—the smell of coffee wafting from the kitchen, the soft hum of her grandmother preparing breakfast, the warmth emitted from the oven. Their shared glances conveyed a silent understanding, an unspoken acknowledgment of the day's significance. In these moments, Raine glimpsed the strength inherited from her namesake, Lorraine Sommer, and a legacy of love that surpassed the boundaries of time.

"Blueberry pancakes okay with you?" Lorraine asked, then flipped one in a cast iron skillet before reaching for three plates in the cabinet. "Or chocolate chip?"

"Chocolate chip sounds good, thank you!" Raine poured herself a glass of orange juice and picked up the newspaper. The headline is about President Nixon visiting China. "Is he up yet?"

"Not yet." Lorraine turned to face the stove so Raine wouldn't see the concern in the lines of her face. David had had a few rough years, and she was at a loss on how to help him. More than that, she felt things were only getting worse.

"I'll go check on him."

In the darkness of the old house, the north wing living room, once refined in Southern charm, now lacked the polished elegance. Threadbare curtains hardly held back the feeble morning light, revealing worn, moth-eaten furniture and dirty Persian rugs. A nearly extinguished fire cast long shadows on the faded wallpaper, and a stale scent of beer and cigarettes whispered to the world a man's deep state of grief.

"Raine?" David moaned.

"Breakfast is ready," Raine said, frustration thick in her tone. "Will you join us this morning?"

A long sigh, followed by coughing, brought him to a sitting position. "Yeah, I'm coming."

David carried the weight of failure upon his shoulders. Each unfulfilled dream became a poignant reminder of what could have been, like a haunting cloud hovering over him. The residue of his time in Vietnam and death of his wife dulled the hues of his world. The once-vibrant colors of hope and ambition were now muted despair.

He took the seat across from Raine while his mother set a plate of pancakes in front of him. Raine, the only bright spot in his life, wore disappointment on her face as she scanned the morning paper. She passed the folded paper to him, pointing out an article on problems in the demilitarized zone of Vietnam.

"Not sure if this is something you'd be interested in," she said, waiting for a reaction of some kind. Any kind. Lately, her father's personality had been flat. No joy, no anger, no emotion of any kind was seen from the outside, yet she sensed the memories and feelings rumbled inside of him, on the verge of eruption.

As the sun ascended in the sky, Raine filled her backpack with books, grabbed the lunch box her grandmother packed, and stepped outside the side door of the dilapidated home, the world bathed in the golden hues of morning. While there was snow on the grass and barn roof, the driveway remained wet, too warm for the snow to stick on the pavers.

In the quietude of nature, aside from the ongoing rooster calls, she found a sanctuary for reflection walking the down to the path leading to school. With a heart both heavy and resilient, Raine carried her mother's spirit into the day, cherishing the beautiful memories etched into her soul.

***

At exactly 8 a.m. Wednesday morning, Ashlyne Morgan unlocked the doors to Hughes' Apothecary. Snow had fallen the night before, but Ashlyne smiled at the sun and was certain it would warm that day. She pulled a hooded sweater over her long, dark hair, to keep the melting snow above from dripping on her.

As one of the oldest businesses in town, she continued to open each morning despite the lack of foot traffic in the town square. She put out a sidewalk sign with an image of a steaming cup of tea to greet customers, twenty-five cents for a full pot. The bakery across the street sold a bottomless cup of coffee for the same price, but there wasn't competition in Cypress Grove, just neighbors doing business.

"Good morning, Paula!" Ashlyne waved to her friend.

"Good morning, Ashlyne!" Paula's short brown hair blew across her face with a gust of cold air, and she pulled her wool shawl around tight. The smell of fresh baked breads, Danish, pies, and cakes permeated the town square. "Is it ever going to warm up around here?"

"Yes, and today is the day." From behind the counter inside the apothecary, a German cuckoo clock chirped eight times. Ashlyne and her two siblings now owned the building and all its contents, including the antique clock, and not knowing what else to do, they reopened the nineteenth-century pharmacy, sans pharmacist.

The bakery had been in Paula's family for generations, just as the drug store had been in the Hughes' family. It wasn't much of a drug store anymore. Hughes Apothecary stopped filling prescriptions in 1968, when Ashlyne's grandfather passed away, although shelves still held bottles of aspirin and bandages, creams, and concoctions, remedies her family had made for generations.

"Are you planning to keep that stupid clock?" asked the oldest Morgan, Michael, dressed in navy slacks, a crisp button up shirt, and a white lab coat. It was the unofficial uniform of the town's newest and only physician. "That thing must be a hundred years old."

"Our great-great grandfather brought it from Europe and hung it behind the counter when the store opened, so I'd say it's a hundred-fifty years old, maybe older." Opened when Cypress Grove was nothing more than a livery stable, a mill, and two bars, Graham Hughes built the three-story building and opened the apothecary. Then, a hundred years later, a dam was built, creating Lake Barkley and Kentucky Lake, and everything changed. "I think it's charming."

"Well, I think it's annoying." Michael started a pot of coffee and prepared a large mug with cream and sugar. "Care for a cup?"

"No, thank you. I'll get some tea."

"I heard a new resort is opening by Cedar Cove. A big fancy one, with a restaurant, private docks, and bait shop." Leaning against the counter with his coffee in hand, he smiled. "You're doing a great job on the store, Ashlyne. It will be a hit with the tourists."

"I hope so." Southwestern Kentucky had changed drastically with the Land Between the Lakes. Many new hotels, cabins, campgrounds, and subdivisions soon followed to support the increased tourism. Eventually, a new Taylor Drug Store opened near the highway. While the small town of Cypress Grove grew, Hughes Apothecary became a relic of the past. "We needed a change."

The death of their grandparents brought the three Morgan siblings back to their Kentucky roots one at a time. Each left England for college in the States and eventually returned to the place they were born, to help their grandparents. Some practices had been passed down for centuries, which was how Saoirse Cromwell, their great-grandmother, met Samuel Hughes. Their daughter, Claire, married a young pharmacist named Rowan Frazier, who ran the Hughes' Apothecary until he became ill. Their mother, Erin, broke with tradition and married a Professor Morgan, who later took a position at the University of Bristol, and their mother, well, she worked as a healer, like her mother and all the women before them.

Ashlyne was the last to move back to Cypress Grove. When she visited after her grandfather's death, she knew it was time to return to her hometown to help her aging grandmother. Now, after a thorough cleaning and cleansing, the shelves were stocked with basic supplies, plus ice cream, chips, magazines... anything that might bring in customers. Besides tea and coffee, she served pastries from Paula's bakery, but business hadn't picked up. In fact, she hadn't had a single customer all week.

The front door rang a bell when it opened, and Ashlyne signed for six boxes of gift items. Basics, really. Candles, journals, charms, and jewelry. She stocked the counter with gift boxes bearing the new name of the store and unwrapped the new sign. Michael would hang it before the store had its official grand reopening on the new moon. She ran her fingers over the letters of the sign, with a blessing for good fortune of the store.

**

Starting out early so she wouldn't run into her friends, Raine walked to school alone. She heard them calling from behind, but by then, she'd crossed the street at the corner of their farm and the church lot. She met up with Lucy and Eva at the lockers.

"Raine! Why didn't you wait for us?" Lucy asked, stuffing her oversized coat into a locker. She wore braids, her blonde hair pulled so tight that her scalp was pink in the perfectly straight part down the back. "Like my new shirt?"

"Another horse shirt. Really, Lucy?" Eva was the unsanctioned fashion critic, even if she wasn't wrong about Lucy having too many farm-animal shirts. Turning to the side, she modeled her new outfit, a corduroy jumper dress and her favorite black go-go boots. "Mom made this."

"Another dress. Really, Eva?" Lucy's voice oozed with sarcasm.

"I think you both look nice." Raine was comfortable in her baggy sweatshirt and worn tennis shoes. Dressing like that meant no one would notice her. Hopefully.

"Come on, we'd better get to class."

Of all her friends, Lucy was the bossiest. She was competitive, smart, and the best cousin anyone could ask for. Lucy was more like a sister to Raine. Eva was also like a sister, but completely opposite, with a keen sense of style, flirtatious, and dramatic. She was a performer, taking the lead in the school play every year and practicing dance three days a week after school. She was also a loyal friend with a heart of gold.

Raine stared out the window in tenth grade math class. Two squirrels chasing each other in a tree were more interesting than algebra, which she clearly would have no use for on the farm. Maybe she should just quit school and help with the fields. Besides, it was expected that she would run the farm after her father, and lately, he wasn't doing such a great job managing things at Cypress Hill. The farming part he did—taking eggs to market, keeping corn and tobacco in the fields, maintaining the equipment. It was the home repairs that were neglected, and the smaller fields hadn't been planted in three years. She was only fifteen but already felt she should take on more responsibility at home.

"Raine," Ms. Tipton called, "can you find x in this problem?"

Put on the spot, Raine felt heat rise in her freckled cheeks. Heads turned to watch her squirm in her seat, and she flipped pages in the book to find where the answers were. She licked her dry lips and swallowed hard.

"It's on the board," Ms. Tipton said. "Pay attention to the class, not what's happening outside the window. Okay?"

"Yes, ma'am." There were a few giggles from the front of the class. She pulled her uncombed auburn hair down her left shoulder, running her fingers through the curls and nervously twisting to see how tight she could twist before it hurt her scalp.

"Lucy? Do you know the answer?"

"Um… I think x equals six." There was no guessing. She knew it equaled six because math was easy for her.

"Correct."

"Raine," Eva whispered from across the aisle. "You okay?"

"Yeah, I'm fine." Eva was her best friend, so, of course, she and her cousin Lucy knew what was going on. They both know why she was daydreaming today.

Sam, the boy who sat in front of Eva, turned around and gave a half-smile. That was all it took to get the butterflies in Raine's stomach fluttering and her face to flush a light shade of pink. Instantly, the gloom coating Raine's existence faded, and a warm sensation spread from head to toe.

Sam was new to the school. His family moved to Cypress Grove over winter break, from Michigan. She knew little about him other than they lived in a nice home recently built by the park, his father taught at Murray, and his dark eyes made her melt inside. Eva caught the glance between the two. It wasn't exactly subtle.

"You know I'm here for you, Raine."

"Thanks, Eva."

***

Sitting on a small table next to a rocking chair, a transistor radio spontaneously turned on and played Neil Diamond's *Sweet Caroline*. David stirred, blinked his eyes to the haze filtering through the curtains and pulled a pillow over his head. After breakfast, he fell asleep on the couch again, still surrounded by empty beer cans and cigarette butts.

"Stop it, Raymond," he said, grabbing the radio and, with one swift yank, unplugging it from the wall. Raymond was his grandfather, and he liked to play tricks with the electrical gadgets around the house. David's father always said he had an odd sense of humor, and it had apparently followed him into the afterlife. David sat up and ran his fingers through his too-long brown waves, stood to stretch, then used the tiny bathroom under the stairs, the one where he had to stoop to go through the door. Coming out, he hit his head. "Damn it!"

No one else was home, besides Raymond, who seemed to be hanging around all the time lately. He pulled the curtains back and saw dust floating in the air above the living room and into the kitchen. With a paper bag in hand, he emptied the ashtray and picked up the cans. He noticed the trash was overflowing, and that meant he needed to start a burn outside. Another job to add to his long list of things to do around this place.

In farm life of 1972, daily routine was filled with mundane yet essential tasks that defined the rhythm of agricultural existence. Ensuring a steady supply of warmth for the evening, David stacked seasoned wood by the fireplace and near the buck stove in his mother's room. The bucket under the sink was carried out to the compost by the barn, and the paper bags of combustibles were stacked in a large, stone-rimmed circle on the side field, far enough away from other structures so that embers would not spark fire elsewhere. He used a small amount of gasoline and a match to start the burn, then went on to feed the chickens, who had become accustomed to breakfast at almost noon. He gathered more than four dozen eggs, adding to what he'd collected the day before, and loaded the boxes in the back of his pick-up truck.

Early spring meant mending fences and repairing farm equipment was a perpetual endeavor, as the creaks and groans of aging machinery echoed across the fields, but not today. The broken screen door and leak in the kitchen sink wouldn't be touched today, either.

Cypress Hill dated to the days of the Lewis and Clark expedition, when Magnus Sommer arrived in Cypress Grove. Much of the home was built before the Civil War and maintenance had not been done for at least thirty years, some areas much longer. Paint was peeling and shutters drooping, not to mention the broken glass in the solarium. It was too much for David to manage, and then there was the matter of funding the repairs. It was all too much. The Sommer family lived in a two-story addition on the north wing, and the rest of the home was closed off, left to rot. While from afar, the main house appeared to have rustic charm, up close, it was an abandoned mansion from a time long gone.

After a shower and some lunch, and with a handful of daffodils and forsythia sprigs from the front yard, David drove his 1953 Chevy pick-up—the same truck his father drove until his death years ago—into Murray. He purchased a washer hose from the hardware store and headed back to Cypress Grove to drop off the eggs at Wendell's Feed Store. Finally, he stopped for a beer at Mack's.

Belly up to the bar, Mack tossed a white towel over his broad shoulder and nodded. "Pint?"

"Yeah, just one today." As David moved, his arms dangled almost listlessly; the pallor of his complexion betrayed the toll taken by his brewed indulgences, with dark circles beneath his eyes and a certain vulnerability radiating from the man.

"Guess who stopped by the other day?" Mack's deep voice was soft, yet still reverberated in David's throbbing head.

David gave a blank stare. David, his hair tousled and disheveled, seemed to mirror the aftermath of a night of revelry, evident in the fatigue etched across his face.

"Our buddy, Liam Baker."

David scoffed.

"His band is playing in Paducah this weekend, and I booked them here at the end of the month."

"Great…"

"I gotta book the local bands, David. They always pack a crowd." Known by everyone as Mack, his true name was William MacKenzie. Towering at six-feet-four inches and nearly three-hundred pounds, he held the title of the Strongest Man in Cypress Grove, earned in a monthly arm-wrestling competition in the pub. Despite his imposing size, Mack was a true gentle giant and one of David's closest friends. The bond between David and Mack formed during their high school years when they both played on the football team. However, it was their shared experiences in Vietnam that solidified their connection. They understood each other.

"Liam is an ass. Glad he moved to Nashville."

Mack said nothing. He knew better than to say too much or ask too many questions of his patrons, especially his friend David. He flattened his red and gray beard with a downward pull, taking longer than usual. Tilting a chilled glass, he skillfully poured brew from the tap and placed it on the counter. Without uttering a word, Mack conveyed a sense of understanding, offering the drink as a gesture of camaraderie. "This one's on me," he said.

"Thanks, man." David squinted at the light streaming in the window, and across the street, he saw a dark-haired woman and a small child leaving the apothecary. He mumbled to himself, "How about that? Another Morgan has returned to Cypress Grove. With a kid, no less."

"Yeah, they're all back. Fixin' up the place, making it a hippie gift shop of some kind, from what I hear." Cream was playing on the radio behind the bar, *Strange Brew*.

"I didn't know hippies bought gifts." It shouldn't catch him off guard that the girls he remembered from the past were old enough to be mothers. The last encounter he had with the Morgan sisters was right after high school, when they were roughly the same age his daughter was today, or younger. Time possessed a peculiar ability to warp, creating the semblance that certain memories are from yesterday while others belong to a distant past. The moment he departed for the army felt like an eternity ago and, paradoxically, as if it happened yesterday.

"Your niece will be there. Nothin' but trouble, that one." Mack held half a cigar between his teeth and chuckled, his rounded belly bouncing under a white shirt. "She'll the first one in that group to turn hippie."

"Lucy? Nah…" His words said no, but he knew it to be true. Lucy was smart and curious, a dangerous combination that could lead to no good. Her rebellious nature was obvious, constantly pushing boundaries and challenging authority, with a total disregard for rules, yet she was a bright girl, effortlessly excelling in school. Nothing like his shy daughter, always on good behavior, caring, and helpful. Yes, Lucy would be the hippie in the group.

"Well, we'll see." Mack continued washing dishes, picking up a glass and wiping it dry with a clean towel.

David watched the woman and child across the street. They sat on a bench in front of Michael Morgan's new doctor's office, the woman showing the little girl how to blow bubbles. They laughed, and the woman tossed her long hair back. It was in that moment he realized it was Ashlyne Morgan, his childhood crush.

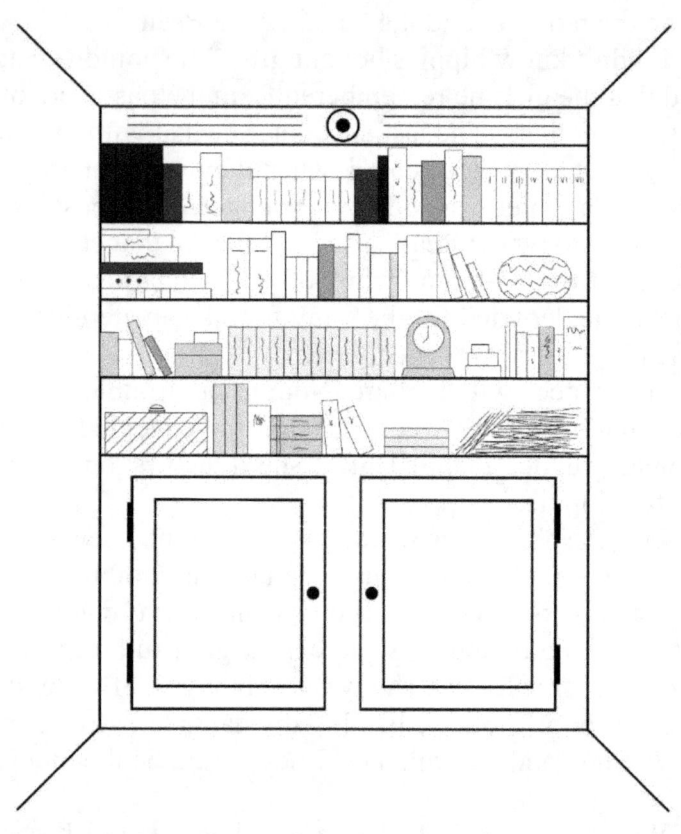

Chapter Two

"Come on, we're going to be late to class!" Lucy took the steps two at a time, with Eva and Raine close behind. Every day was like this for Lucy, always worried about being late for class. "Mrs. Weismann will close the door."

Everyone knew Mrs. Weismann was a stickler for promptness, and tardy students would be locked out of class until she decided to open the door again. This often meant missing the important announcements or assignments—her way of making a point to the late students.

They ran down the hall to room 242 and took their seats as the bell rang. Mrs. Weismann peered at the three girls over her horn-rimmed glasses adorned with a pearled lanyard that coordinated with the buttons on her blouse. She sported bright pink lipstick on her thin, pensive lips as she elegantly rose and wandered around the desks, hands clasped behind her back.

"History is written by the victors, a global phenomenon reflected in the recording and teaching of historical events." The teacher strolled past Raine's desk, leaving the scent of moth balls and stale perfume in her wake. They'd read about the Civil War for a week, and Raine was convinced Mrs. Weismann's tweed jacket might well belong to that era. "History can also change over time. It is dynamic, subject to transformation, as concealed facts come to light and truths are exposed."

"So, the Union decided what is in our history books, not the Confederates?" Lucy asked, her straight spine and blonde braids perfectly in place. Lucy was the teacher's favorite in every class, partially because she was so smart, but also because she knew how to play the teachers. "History is literally written by the victors."

"That is correct, Lucy. And what do you think, Raine?" She stopped at the front of the room, turned, and glared at Raine. *Why, Raine wondered, do the teachers love to call on me?* "Do you believe victors, not just of war, but of any dominating group in society, write history?"

"Um." She squirmed in her seat and noticed everyone was looking at her. She looked at her notes and hoped the answer would be there. The sound of nylon stockings swished as Mrs. Weismann meandered between the rows of desk to stand next to her. "Yes, I do."

"And why is that?"

"Um… because the victors have more money and power than the losers."

"Yes, that is true. The victors usually have more money, but more important than money, they have control." Her sensible low-heeled shoes clicked down the aisle to the back of the class. "What we find printed in textbooks is often biased, opting to present facts to glorify the victor and demonize the losers."

"Because the victors are usually the ones printing the books?" Eva asked. "We rarely hear about the Civil War through the slave's perspective."

"Exactly." Mrs. Weismann sounded excited and focused on Eva now, likely because she was the only possible direct descendent of slaves in her history class. "The war was about slavery, after all. Why do you suppose we are not reading textbooks written by slaves?"

"Slaves didn't win the war," Eva said, more like a question than answer.

"Slaves were ignorant, too," commented Priscilla. "Their owners didn't want them educated, else they'd run away. They couldn't read or write."

"Very interesting point, Priscilla, although many slaves could read and write." Mrs. Weismann didn't care for Priscilla's condescending remark. "Slave owners, for the most part, were doing what they could to run their farm, and at the time, slaves were part of the ownership of that farm. They wanted their slaves healthy and happy. Some landowners, however, were severely abusive to slaves, something we don't often read about in history books."

"Some slaves were educated," Eva added.

"Frederick Douglas wasn't an educated man," Sam said. "He was an escaped slave who taught himself to read and write. He became very successful."

"Yes, some slaves learned to read and write, even when there were laws prohibiting education of slaves." Reaching for her planner, Mrs. Weismann's hedonistic expression brought a collective moan from the class. "I think you all will enjoy this assignment. You will work in teams of three or four. The full instructions will be on the class board by morning, but here are the main points."

She wrote the numbers one through four on the chalk board, then explained each step. Lucy copied, scribbling as fast as she could, which Eva and Raine noticed. Eva raised one eyebrow, smiled, and put her head on her arm across her desk. Raine thought it was a waste of time and ink because it would be pinned to the board—Mrs. Weismann just said it would be posted. They were to choose a site of interest somewhere in Kentucky, research the historical significance in relation to slavery or the Civil War, do a trifold presentation board, and write a three-thousand-word essay. The group would then present their projects to the class.

"Each location can be used only once, so check the sign-up list on the board before you begin your research. You are only allowed to use the textbook as a reference once. The other five references must be from newspapers, historical documents, city archives. Does everyone understand?"

Lucy nodded, Eva looked up and rolled her eyes, and Raine stared blankly ahead. It seemed like busy work, a way to force students to work together outside of class. Nothing about the Civil War seemed appealing. It was a horrible period of American history.

"Well?"

A unified mumble, "Yes, Mrs. Weismann," rolled across the class.

"Wonderful! Everyone, be sure to read the details of the assignment. Ask questions—you have my phone number and I see you every day at 1:35." Mrs. Weismann was still grinning at the agony this assignment was causing her students. "This project is thirty percent of your grade, and you have six weeks to complete, so I don't want any grumbling about how much work it is."

The bell rang at 2:23 and twenty seven teenagers tried to squeeze around the group assignment at once. Lucy, Eva, and Raine looked at each other.

"There are three of us. How are we going to do this?" Lucy asked. "What's our location going to be?"

"How about the old mill?" Eva suggested. "It was built by slaves."

"Or the old livery?" Lucy said, "It was one of the first buildings in town, where the feed and seed is now."

"How about Cypress Hill?" Sam joined the girls, a half-smile on his face.

"Ha ha, very funny," Lucy said, then her eyes widened. "Yes, Cypress Hill is the perfect place!"

"No, I don't think so." Raine shook her head.

"That haunted place?" They all gawked at Eva. "Although, I don't believe in ghosts."

"We have to get it on the board before someone else does."

"Too late," Sam said. "I already wrote it on the board."

"You did? Why did you do that?" Raine asked in a high-pitched voice.

"It's an old plantation. I would assume slaves were there at some point, right?" Sam shrugged one shoulder. Truth was he just wanted to be in Raine's group, and writing Cypress Hill down on the board was the best way in.

"Everyone knows it was used as a hospital during the Civil War," Eva noted. "That could be something to work with."

"Everyone talks about it being a hospital, Eva. We need documentation—photos, articles, something concrete." Lucy stood taller than anyone in the group, and standing straight and tall, she made herself the project leader. "We need proof."

"If only we knew someone who lived there…" Sam nudged Raine, causing her to blush. Surely, he wasn't flirting with her. Raine wasn't smart like Lucy, or beautiful like Eva. She was plain old Raine, in dingy clothes with wild hair. "There is probably something at your house to prove it was used as a hospital."

"He's right, Raine." Eva smiled, seeing an opportunity to set-up her best friend with the new cute boy in class. "And since Sam signed up for Cypress Hill, looks like Sam is in our group."

"Then Cypress Hill it is," Lucy said. "Each team must turn in a one-page report by Friday, naming the site and how each will participate in the group project. We should start right away."

"Raine, your house is like two-hundred years old. It's perfect." Eva beamed. "A spooky, haunted house that was once a Civil War hospital."

Raine, Sam, and Lucy looked at Eva. "What? I said I don't believe in ghosts. That doesn't mean they wouldn't make for a very interesting project."

"I've never seen a ghost in my house." Raine walked away. "And it's not two-hundred years old."

"How old is it?" Sam asked. "It would be great if it really was a military hospital."

"I don't know if that is true. I mean, I've heard rumors, but how will we prove it? Part of the house was built before the Civil War, so at least that's something, right?"

"Yes, it is."

"And there are no ghosts."

"Yeah, but y'all only live in one part of the house. Maybe that's why Grandpa closed off the main part." Lucy watched the ground as she stepped, careful to avoid the cracks in the sidewalk. "And there is a ghost—Raymond. Grandma sees him all the time."

"She doesn't see him. She just blames Raymond when a light flickers, or the wind catches a door and it slams. There are no *real* ghosts at Cypress Hill."

"Whoa, that sounds so cool!" Sam grinned.

Eva was right, it did look like a haunted house. It had been years since Raine was in the old section of the home, and it was dirty and smelled funny then. There wasn't much furniture, and what was there had been covered with white sheets. The outside looked old and spooky, with paint peeling, shutters loose, and overgrown shrubs. It was just a big old farmhouse to Raine, nothing special. Nothing worth writing a history report about.

Raine admitted to herself there could be ghosts. She heard things, sometimes she saw things in the shadows, like a memory she never had of them. Them, as in more than one ghost. It's not like they were in physical form. Raine saw them with her mind, not her eyes. She felt them when they were in the house, and she heard their whispers. While she had always known they were there, she'd told no one about it.

"I've never been in the main part of the house," Eva said, noticing Sam eyeing Raine. "What's in there?"

"Oh, Eva, you would love it! When you walk in the front, wide stairs curve around the front room. Downstairs, there's a big ballroom on the right side, just beyond a music room in the front, and next, there's the sunroom made completely of windows. And the library on the left—so many books." Lucy smiled at the memory. "Raine, let's go in after school if it's okay with Grandma. Maybe we could find something for our report."

"Hey," Sam said. "Can I come?"

"You kind of need to come, since you signed up for Cypress Hill on the board. You're in our group," Eva said.

"So, we're doing our project on Cypress Hill?" Raine asked with trepidation.

"Hell, yeah!" Lucy shouted, one fist in the air. "Can we go this afternoon?"

"I have dance at four o'clock, so can't do it today," Eva said. "Tomorrow is good."

"Tomorrow is better for me, too," Sam said. "I am helping my grandfather this afternoon."

"Okay, then tomorrow after school. Everyone good with that?"

Everyone nodded in agreement, but Raine had other things on her mind. Today, was not a good day for her to have friends over, or to start on a school project. Thirty percent of her grade would mean the difference of passing or failing history. Repeating tenth grade was not something she wanted to do.

After school, Raine went by her Great Aunt Petra's flower shop, to buy carnations and daisies. Nestled in the quaint town square, the shop exuded rustic charm, with its weathered wooden facade and a colorful array of blooms spilling out onto the sidewalk. As the gentle chime of a bell announced each visitor, the shop became a haven where the fragrance of blossoms mingled with the wisdom of a seasoned florist. The shop owner was her grandmother's sister, and her weathered hands tended to delicate petals with care.

"Hi, Aunt Petra!"

"Hello, Raine! I was expecting you today." Petra wrapped her chubby arms around Raine in a warm embrace as she gave her a gentle lift. "I know this is a tough day for you, sweetheart."

Raine nodded, maintaining silence to prevent the tears that threatened to escape her eyes. Petra had been there through every phase. Raine regarded her not only as a great aunt, but also as another grandmother, believing that one can never have too many grandmothers in their life.

"Is that Raine?" Uncle Ed was tall and thin and was always making jokes, "Ain't you supposed to be in school? I'd better call the teacher and tell them you skipped class today."

"I get out at 2:30 now." Raine smiled and remembered what her father said about Uncle Ed's mind starting to go. "I'm in high school."

"Oh, the big school. Or is it the school for big kids?" When he laughed, she noticed his back teeth were missing. "High school."

"How is school going?" Aunt Petra pushed Raine's hair to her back, patting down the top of her head, "Have you had Mr. Roth yet for English class?"

"No, not until next year. He teaches upperclassmen." Raine pulled a bouquet of daisies from a large vase in the center of the store and looked around for carnations.

"He's my neighbor, you know. Very nice man." Petra looked around the store, searching for something. "Raine, I saved some carnations for you in the back. Let me grab them."

"Yes, that's what she likes," Raine said, then froze when she realized what she'd said. She likes… these are for her. She took a deep breath, noticing the raggedness of it and blew out hard. This was a technique she'd learned in counseling—a breathing technique to help with anxiety and stress.

"Wanna hear a joke?" Uncle Ed grinned. "Why was the bicycle lying down?"

"Uh, I don't know."

"It was two-tired. Get it?" He laughed at his own joke. "Too tired, so it lay down."

"Oh, that's funny." Raine forced a chuckle. Aunt Petra returned with carnations, handing them to her. Raine set two wrinkled one-dollar bills on the counter, but Petra pushed them back.

"No, dear, keep your money. These are on us."

"Thank you, Aunt Petra."

***

"How's business?" Sorcha asked, dressed in loose-fitting terry cloth pants and a Lake Tahoe sweatshirt. Her hair hung straight to her waist, like a copper waterfall, glistening on top from the fluorescent bulbs overhead. She'd tried napping with Kayleigh today, hoping to catch up from the lack of sleep the night before.

"Very quiet." Ashlyne stared across the store. It was mostly bare at this point, with boxes of new items stacked in the corner and the shelves pushed to the side so the linoleum flooring could be removed. Refinishing the wooden planks was a tedious job, but therapeutic, repetitive, and meditative, and that was what Ashlyne needed. Besides, there wasn't anything else for her to do at this point.

At 29 years old, Ashlyne received a BA in anthropology with a minor in archaeology from Vanderbilt, followed by a master's in history from UC Berkely. Still, job opportunities were slim. She'd applied for positions in museums and schools as far as Paducah, and every county around the lakes, but openings remained posted after her interview.

She tried not to take it personally, but her family's reputation eclipsed her qualifications. She spoke English, French, and Spanish. Considered well-accomplished in parts of the world, but the people of Cypress Grove thought Ashlyne an eccentric enchantress. She was barely able to find a job as a substitute teacher in the town she lived.

When their grandmama died, the sisters decided to reopen the store. Michael had already opened a small medical practice in the back room, now remodeled to accommodate patients. They needed each other—Michael, with a new medical practice and no patients to treat, Sorcha, with a toddler to manage and no time for a job, and Ashlyne, with two degrees and nowhere to work.

"I like how you've displayed the teas behind the counter. Each jar is labeled so people can read it from where they stand." The sisters preferred tea to coffee, so the pharmacy counter was stocked with a variety of tea blends, along with healing herbs. They were carefully presented as 'flavors' instead of 'remedies', especially after rumors spread of her grandmother's so-called magic. "Remember how Grandmama treated bronchitis with lemon teas and hot mustard packs to the chest, and she could reduce symptoms of heart failure with dandelion root and foxglove tea?"

"I do, and although poisonous, it worked. It was the best medicine at the time."

"It's still good medicine." Sorcha ran her hands over the shelves, picking up on the lingering spirit of her grandmother and her mother before. "I may be a nurse, but I never want to forget how nature cures."

"We will never forget the old ways."

The knowledge of earth medicine from her grandmama carried power and risk in a time when most Americans were convinced cures must be in pill form. A century before, this type of healer, midwife, and herbalist was sought for most all ailments the locals experienced, but now, a physician like Michael was desired, and prescription pills were used to treat illnesses. In the Appalachian hills where her great-grandmother, Saoirse Cromwell, was raised, where her mother before her was a midwife, practicing folk medicine from the old country was the way of life for many. 'Simple remedies often work the best,' she'd say, and Ashlyne found truth in those old ways.

Ashlyne and her sister Sorcha were at the rear of the store inspecting the delivered boxes, when the front doorbell chimed. "That's likely the mailman," Sorcha remarked.

"Hello?" A man's voice, but not the mailman. Ashlyne peeped through the shelves and recognized him from years ago, and it was not a man who frequented the apothecary. "Are you open?"

"Sorcha, you're a bit off. That is not the mailman," Ashlyne whispered. "Are you feeling okay?"

"I was up with Kayleigh last night, I guess lack of sleep is making everything seem unbalanced." Sorcha might be a modern witch, but she was no match for a restless toddler. Even with her sister and brother's help, being a single parent had its challenges. Sorcha naturally radiated an enchanting aura, seamlessly blending the mystique of ancient traditions with a contemporary allure to effortlessly navigate in this world. Today, however, she was an exhausted mother of a fifteen-month-old daughter who got less than two hours sleep the night before.

Ashlyne was convinced that this man hadn't taken the time to comb his hair or shave in days. His baggy jeans, torn shirt, and eyes concealed behind dark sunglasses suggested he put little effort into his outward appearance. His walk carried a subtle unsteadiness, reminiscent of someone with a sprained ankle, or perhaps someone who had indulged in a few too many drinks. Then, it occurred to her—this was David Sommer.

"I've got this," she whispered to her sister. Sorcha gave Ashlyne a sideways glance. He has a reputation for trouble. Ashlyne knew this, but that only meant he would be a challenge to read. Ashlyne appeared from the back room and smiled, extending a hand, directing him to a stool at the counter. "Yes, we're open. Come in."

***

David watched her emerge from an opening between the back wall and a bookcase, a beautiful woman who exuded an enchanting aura around her long, dark hair and ivory skin. Her eyes, pools of mysterious depth, held a wisdom that transcended time. Dressed in flowing fabrics and wearing long, celestial pendants around her neck, she seemed to float towards him. He cleared his throat and whispered her name, "Ashlyne Morgan."

"What can I help you find today?"

David looked around the store. The old soda fountain counter looked the same, but plants hanging in the front window were new. Shelves were mostly empty, but he noticed a display of hand carved bowls and boxes, recognized them as old man Whitmer's work. Jars lined the wall behind the counter, filled with what looked like dead plants and dried flowers. It was mostly the same store he remembered as a child, with plaster walls and florescent lights. The old floorboards even creaked in the same spots they did thirty years ago. "Is this still a drug store?"

"It's in transition. In time, a new type of store will emerge."

"So, you're selling, what? Herbs?"

"Endless possibilities." Ashlyne smiled, tilting her chin up slightly. She turned down the volume of the radio behind the counter where a Jefferson Airplane song played *Somebody to Love*.

"No pharmacy?"

"No pharmacist to run the pharmacy. Besides, I believe in treating medical conditions in a more… organic way." The sisters had worked diligently to rebuild the apothecary as a source for organic, rather than synthetic remedies, for a natural path to healing, rather than surgical or pharmaceutical.

"I'll have some aspirin if you have some." David was taken back by Ashlyne's amber eyes—not dark brown like her siblings, but more of a reddish-gold. With her jet-black hair and heart-shaped face, she has a worldly beauty. Trouble, without a doubt. The last thing David wanted was another complication in his life, and with the Hughes women, things were never as simple as they seemed. Their family had been in Cypress Grove almost as long the Sommer family, and he knew their story. "I could use some coffee too."

"My brother just made a fresh pot of Kona." Ashlyne sat a mug in front of him and poured steaming coffee. "Cream?"

"No, just black."

"We have aspirin, and we also have tablets of willow bark and magnesium for your headache."

"Just aspirin and caffeine will do." He kept his sunglasses on, watched her reach for aspirin on a shelf near the front of the store. This couldn't be Mike Morgan's little skinny sister, not with those curves and long legs. She was the odd one, and that was saying a lot, considering her two siblings. Everyone knew the story. Everyone knew why they moved away. "What makes you think I have a headache?"

"You're wearing sunglasses indoors and asking for aspirin." She opened the bottle and took out two tablets, setting the bottle on the counter for him. "It's a logical assumption."

"Oh, yeah." David sipped the coffee, something he should have had before the beer at Mack's. "You are Ashlyne, right?"

"Yes, that is me. Hold out your hand." With a deep concentration and skills as an empath, she read him. She took a deep breath and focused on his chest—the heart chakra, then to the spot just above his eyes, in the center of his forehead. When he extended his hand, she placed two aspirin in the palm, taking time to connect her fingertips to his skin. She sensed sadness, sorrow, with a little fear, yet strength and goodness ran through his veins. It was electrifying, and that moment of contact told her everything she needed to know about David Sommer.

"You might remember my sister, Maggie. When she was a kid, she would ride her pony up here and sell rides for a nickel so she could buy candy here. Sometimes our mother made me come with her."

"Oh, yes, I remember her well. That is the only time I've ridden a horse."

"You're kiddin'." It was a statement, not a question. Everyone rode—this was horse country. Even the odd kids, or at least he thought they rode.

"No. I have ridden elephants as an adult, but not a horse."

"Elephants?"

"In India, yes." Ashlyne turned towards an unopened cardboard box, a needed distraction from the man at the counter. She unwrapped a blue and yellow tea pot and set it on the shelf above the various teas. "I traveled a bit after high school."

"Yeah, me too. If you consider a tour in Vietnam 'traveling'."

"You were there?"

"Yeah," he let out the word as more of a moan.

"I am glad you made it back safely." The next teapot she unwrapped was white, with pink roses and gold trim. She said nothing more of Vietnam. It was clear the memories David carried were not pleasant. She watched in the mirror as he stared into his coffee cup, probably thinking of the men he served with who didn't return. She understood more than he knew. "Can I offer you a cookie? I made them myself."

"No, thank you." David put a cigarette in his mouth and fumbled in his pockets for a match. Ashlyne opened the drawer under the counter and found a pack of matches. Her heart skipped a beat when she saw they were from the Little Shamrock, one of the places she and her sister frequented in San Francisco. The place she met Brandon. The place where Sorcha later met Lee. She smiled and ran her finger over the name, taking it as a sign he was still watching over them.

What are the odds, she thought, *that those matches would turn up here at the apothecary, and that I found them when David, another man sent to Vietnam, needed a light?* Did she bring them, or did Michael have them from when he visited them at Berkeley? Maybe it was Sorcha who kept the matches. One of the oldest bars in the city, the bar with the ghost in the apartment upstairs. The place where Sorcha met Kayleigh's father.

He nodded, sipped his coffee, then lit his cigarette. David said nothing for a while, just smoked, drank, and ran fingers through his unkept hair, then popped two aspirin. "Sorry about your grandma. She was really nice."

"Thank you." Ashlyne sensed he knew loss as well, and that his headache was from the way he coped with loss. She also intuitively knew this was not a subject he would want to discuss. Sometimes it came to her like that—the feelings someone else was feeling. She couldn't prevent it. "You are our first customer since we opened this morning."

"Is that right?" David looked around. "It's almost three o'clock."

"Business really dropped off when Grandmama was ill, and we're updating things. Changing it around. There will be a grand re-opening next month. You're welcome to stop by, have another cup of coffee."

"And aspirin."

"Yes, and aspirin if you need."

"What, exactly, will you sell, besides possibility?"

"We have a large selection of teas, herbs, and trinkets from local vendors and from around the world. We'll also have convenience items, like the store always had, but no pharmacy. It didn't make sense because Taylor Drugs is nearby."

"Huh." David looked around at the empty shelves, the tools and ladders. He noticed part of the linoleum taken up and asked, "Are you doing repairs yourself?"

"We are trying," Ashlyne replied. "More coffee?"

David nodded. "I'll bet a lot has changed around here since you were last here. The Parkway was finished a few years back, and they have a new A&P in Murray. Opened one of those big shopping malls down in Nashville."

"Oh, yes, I've been to Harding Mall. I went to Vanderbilt and visit friends in the area now and then. Last time, we met up at the food court."

"That's nice…" David started to feel fuzzy, not like he'd drank the beer at Mack's too fast, but a feeling that his skin was warm and soft. Lightheaded, and his limbs heavy. He looked into his cup, wondered if there was more in there than just coffee, considering the reputation of the Hughes women. "The lake's been open for a while. Guess you've seen it."

"Actually, I haven't."

"Well, it's sight to see." He cautiously stood, holding on to the stool as he did, to gain balance. "I should get going. Pleasure to meet you, again, Ashlyne."

"You as well, David."

He held his breath for a second, then let out a raspy noise he doesn't recognize. "I didn't tell you my name."

"I'm pretty sure you did."

By the time he got to the truck, he was in a dream-like state. His headache got the best of him, and he sat behind the wheel for a few minutes. From where he parked, he saw Raine coming out of the florists. She had pink carnations and daisies in her hand and walked with her head down. He started the truck and pulled onto the road.

Chapter Three

Raine walked from the town square, past the church lawn, towards the north side of the farm. Crossing the street before the church took her to a field gate where she could cut through to get home, cross the bridge over Cypress Creek. Mitchell Farm, Lucy's house, was farther down, on the right. Walking behind the church led to a small area surrounded by a wood rail fence and was part of the original Cypress Hill farm. Now, it was Sommer Cemetery.

Within the community cemetery, the original Sommer family lot had a low limestone fence around it, as if keeping their souls safe. Colonel Sommer and his wife, Anne, were laid to rest years ago, but today, the church managed the cemetery and church members could purchase lots. The proceeds were in a trust to care for the cemetery another thousand years, or at least that's what Pastor Tim said.

Raine saw her father's truck before he saw her. She should have known he would be here today. He stood next to the tallest headstone in the cemetery.

"Hey, Dad."

"Hey, Pumpkin. Nice flowers."

"Yeah, Petra wouldn't let me pay for them."

David nodded and shoved his hands in his front pockets. They both looked down at the stone, Caroline Adele Sommer, died March 15, 1969. "I can't believe it's been three years."

"Me either." Raine pulled the vase from the ground and turned it over, placing the fresh flowers in it. She opened her backpack and pulled out a jar of water she'd brought to fill the vase. "These were her favorites."

"Yeah, they were." David sniffed and looked around. They were the only ones within sight. He added the daffodils and forsythia he'd brought. "Hey, wanna give me a hand with something?"

"Sure," Raine said.

David opened the tailgate on the truck and pulled on a wooden bench in the back, with a plaque that read, *Say a prayer for the lost souls.*

"Wow, Dad! Is this what you've been working on in the garage?"

"Yep."

"Groovy."

"Come on, let's get it down."

They set the bench under the dogwood tree not far from Caroline's headstone and sat down on it. "Sturdy."

"I figured I had to make it sturdy if Aunt Melinda is going to sit on it."

"Dad!" Raine pushed his arm and he pretentiously fell over. "That isn't nice to say,"

"Yeah, well, it's true. Her butt is bigger than both of ours put together." David laughed, then they sat in silence for several minutes.

"I miss her so much." Raine sniffed and let the tears fall without blinking.

"Me too, pumpkin. Me too."

"Do you think she can hear us when we talk to her? Or see us, like now?"

David scratched his beard before replying, "I don't know. I like to think so."

"I wish I could hear her answer me."

"Yeah…" David nodded. He sniffed and blinked away a tear before taking a deep breath. "If there is a way for her to do that, she would."

***

By late afternoon, Ashlyne and Sorcha had removed most of the linoleum from the floor. The rest of the day was spent scraping glue and using a hand sander, and the next morning the shelves would be moved so they could work on the rest of the floor. They took a break in lush chairs in the back of the store by a warm fire, each holding a cup of tea.

"What are we going to use for displays besides the old shelves? There are some things that would be nice in baskets, or large bins." Sorcha added, "And more importantly, what are we going to put on the shelves to sell?"

"I'm still working on that," Ashlyne said. "Did you see the earring stand that came with our order? It was a surprise! They sent it free."

"That's super cool, Ashlyne. Should we put it on the counter, out of reach of little hands?" Kayleigh had been with them all afternoon, and Sorcha was exhausted. Sometimes she wondered how her mother managed with three small children, each no more than two years apart.

"You're right. How about the top of the cabinet near the front?"

"Yes, she couldn't reach up there." Kayleigh stood in front of the fireplace, then reached for the poker. Sorcha was at her side in seconds, took her hand off the fireplace poker and showed her a doll she'd been playing with earlier, but Kayleigh wasn't interested in the doll and threw it to the ground. She waddled over to the stools at the counter, spinning one, then another, then she eyed boxes stacked by empty bookcases and trotted over. She opened one of the boxes and squatted next to it to explore its contents.

"Your daughter is certainly curious about everything going on, isn't she?"

"It's constant." Sorcha scooped Kayleigh up to sit on her lap. The toddler arched backwards and let out a loud, exasperated whine, making her displeasure known. She pulled away from her mother and climbed onto Ashlyne's lap, put her thumb in her mouth, and snuggled against her chest. "Well, how about that?"

"She's tired. Maybe she'll doze off."

The sisters chatted about the store, the changes to make now, and what else they needed before the re-opening. Without the pharmacy, the space on the right side of the store was open. They'd talked about removing the wall between the compounding area, leaving three walls of small shelves, ideal for display.

"What about Grandmama's concoctions? She made things in small batches, but we could produce in larger quantities."

"You could develop your own line of natural skin care products. Being a nurse, they could be promoted as homeopathic cosmetics."

"The pharmacy days are over, but you know who still comes in here? Grandmama's clients."

"Exactly. People trust her remedies, even if it involves a bean and dishrag to get rid of a wart." Ashlyne smiled with the memory.

"I remember when she did that to Michael years ago. It worked, just not because of the bean, like she tells everyone."

"Or the dishrag. It was the garlic and oregano oil on the beans that worked, but for most, it doesn't matter how it works, only that it worked."

"And people paid ten times what an oily bean is worth. What's the saying? 'Any sufficiently advanced technology is indistinguishable from magic.'"

"Arthur C. Clarke." Ashlyne smiled remembering the night Lee quoted him after Sorcha treated his upset stomach with peppermint and ginger tea. "Well, I don't want to sell snake oil, but I do think some of Grandmama's remedies would be a hit if we presented them in a more… conventional way. And I'm hoping to pull in some of the college crowd from Murray, selling incense, maybe hemp clothing, and locally made jewelry."

"Her face cream with egg whites, honey and coconut oil was delicious."

"Sorcha!"

"You know it was."

"Yes, it was." Ashlyne looked around the bare store. It was nearly seven at night and only one customer came in for aspirin. "We could serve coffee and breakfast, but we'd be competing with Paula's Bakery. A full lunch menu would compete with Mack's Pub. But no one around here sells local crafts, like Mr. Whitmer's woodworking."

"Do you think people around here would buy her herbal remedies?"

"They would if we teach them about the herbs. If they knew why Grandmama's remedies worked so well, instead of believing it's magic."

"I can work with that." Sorcha nodded. "Besides, I need to work where I can watch Kayleigh. There aren't many nursing jobs like that."

"You can always work with Michael once his business grows. Until then, we'll figure it out here at the store. We can do this together, Sorcha."

"I miss him," Sorcha said, melancholy in her voice. "I never thought I'd be raising her without him."

"I know you didn't. Grandmama always said your first love would be short-lived, but I never thought she meant it literally." They sat in silence for a moment, thinking about their grandmother's dooming prediction. It felt there was more to her premonition. "What did she say, Sorcha? I can't recall her exact words."

"She said my true love would depart by no doing of his own, but he would always be around."

"In Kayleigh, I presume. She thought he would live through Kayleigh."

"I don't think I understood the risk when I met Lee. For someone who can see the future, I was blindsided."

"Even more so, to learn he'd been killed his first week over there."

Lee, whom Sorcha dated before he enlisted, was killed the first week in Vietnam. Brandon, whom Ashlyne dated off and on for years, was part of the Enterprise flight crew. He moved around quite a bit, but Alameda was frequently one of his docking points. He was killed near Oahu, Hawaii.

"I never had the chance to tell him about her." She'd heard about Lee's death through a friend of a friend; a couple of weeks later, she'd realized she was pregnant. They'd never married, so she was not informed of the event. She'd tried to contact his parents, but they didn't respond to phone calls or letters. From what he'd told her about them, it was a blessing.

"He knows." Ashlyne looked up. "They can see us here, now."

Silence fell over them, with Kayleigh almost asleep on Ashlyne's chest, the fire nearly burned out. The old cuckoo clock chirped once at quarter after the hour.

"What will we call the store?"

Ashlyne smiled, proud of what she'd come up with. "Sage Sisters."

***

Morning light filtered into David's childhood bedroom, a place he slept often in the past few years. He couldn't sleep in the room he shared with Caroline. Too many memories there. Reflecting on what he lost when she passed away became a source of physical anguish at times. Caroline's spirit seemed to be embedded in the walls of the room, in the fibers of the bed they shared. The door to that room has been closed for three years.

"Dad? Breakfast is ready," Raine announced from the hallway. He knew she was waiting for an answer—he could hear the floor squeak outside his door. "Dad?"

"I'm awake. I'll be down in a minute."

He could smell sausage cooking, grateful his mother lived under the same roof as him and his daughter. She took care of almost everything inside the house, including Raine, and did quite a bit outside as well. His mother seemed to have endless energy, while in contrast, David considered it an effort to sit on the side of the bed, apply his prosthesis, and dress in a tattered sweatshirt under the overalls for the barn.

Today, for the first time, he felt something other than sorrow when he walked past the closed door to the room he and Caroline shared. He felt at peace.

Once downstairs, he picked up the newspaper and sat down. He opened the sports section to the back page, then folded over to read the comics.

"Raine, are your friends coming over today?" Lorraine poured a cup of coffee for David and topped hers off. She added cream and sugar, stirring as she took a seat at the table. Lorraine felt the pain in her knees and landed hard in her seat with a muffled, "Umph".

"Yes, I hope it's okay. I know the library hasn't been used in quite a while."

"If there's anything about the history of this place, that is where it would be. Isn't that right, David?"

"Yeah, probably so," he mumbled from behind the paper.

"Maybe your father will open the doors to air it out today," Lorraine added. She gave David a look, but only Raine saw the disappointment in her grandmother's eyes. David was disconnected, trapped in his own world of misery and grief, and it never seemed to change.

Raine grabbed a couple of carrots from the kitchen and waited outside for her grandmother. In the early morning frost over the bare fields, she noticed the horses and hens hadn't been let out yet, and she walked over to open the coop doors. Nearly sixty hens flooded out into a small, fenced area; the roosters were kept in another area and she opened the hatch to let them out as well. The horses enjoyed the carrots, and she opened the stall gates to the paddock. She hoped her father would let them out to pasture later.

A dream came to her, one she'd had the night before but just then remembered. She was standing in the same place by the barn, looking at an area filled with pumpkins growing on vines. In the dream, she'd walked through the pumpkin patch, but they were all green, and she worried they wouldn't turn orange before October. Her mother was there and told her the pumpkins always turn in August or September and not to worry. Then she woke up.

It was the first time she'd dreamed of her mother since she died. She'd had dreams about her mother dying, but not one where she saw her mother, and her mother spoke. It felt so real, her dream, as if it were really her. She tried to pull fragments from that feeling she had in the dream, the feeling that she really was able to hear her mother's voice again, talk to her, see her as she was before she became ill. Her heart literally ached thinking of her mother, so she closed her eyes and practiced her breathing, just as the therapist had instructed her.

While Lorraine drove Raine, Lucy, and Eva to school, David opened the doors to the library. It has been closed off for years. His father was the only one to use the room since David joined the army. It smelled of musty books, dust, and mildew reeking in from the main house. It was literally rotting, the plaster cracked above the desk, the pocket doors into the main house swollen with moisture and difficult to open. He opened the front doors in the foyer and turned on a fan blowing in from the kitchen, hoping some of the lingering sausage smell would replace the current stench.

Outside, facing the antebellum home, David audibly sighed at the raised stone foundation, crumbling and in desperate need of repair. The two-story porch was constructed with wooden planks and tall columns that were rotting, loose, or missing. Perplexed by the immense size of the house, he questioned the rationale behind building such a grand structure.

The north wing, where they lived, was larger than most homes in Cypress Grove, while the south wing was designated solely for balls and overnight guests. The central section boasted two intricate staircases leading to second-floor rooms, a total of ten bedrooms, four full bathrooms, three powder rooms, and eight fireplaces. Over the years, the original kitchen was joined to the main house with a breezeway, some plumbing and electrical updates were made, and a south-facing solarium was added before the turn of the century. She was once a true beauty, a plantation home with thousands of acres, but now she was worn out, crumbling, and a burden to manage.

Faced with the daunting task of figuring out what to do with this expansive home, David contemplated its future, and for that matter, his future as well. Should he sell it all, make a fresh start for his family, or try to save what was left of the Sommer legacy? Would selling some of the land provide enough money to restore the home so they could rent rooms, or was there some other way to generate income from the home? Should he do this, would Raine want to carry on the family farm if he made the updates?

"Caroline? Help me out here, babe. What do I do?" He looked up at a cloudy sky, hoping she would appear and provide him with the answers. Instead, it started to rain. With a heavy sigh, he climbed the steps to the veranda and back to the library.

Sitting at the large mahogany desk, he began sorting papers, stacking them in piles divided by date. He used furniture polish to clean the desk, then dusted the shelves, picture frames, lamps, and chairs. If Raine and her friends are going to be in the library, at least it would be clean, or at least, cleaner. It was cluttered with stacks of books, ledgers, papers, and boxes of who-knows-what. He did what he could, and after sweeping, he went out to take care of the animals.

***

"Want a reading?" Sorcha asked. She wore loose print pants and a white top, feeling fairly rested after a good night's sleep. She looked more like a hippie than a nurse, and to her, that felt natural. She waved a hand to the small room next to the back stairs—the same room where their grandmother and her mother before read palms and told fortunes. She'd cleaned and updated the room, hoping to follow in their grandmama's footsteps and provide readings.

"I can go in now?" Sorcha nodded, and Ashlyne moved the dark velvet curtain back and stepped in the small room.

The walls were painted a fresh plum color, a shade lighter than the curtain and ceiling, and three candles burned in front of mirrors. One large crystal ball sitting on a brass frame was displayed in the corner. It was best to read without electricity, so this was the perfect place. Talismans and charms, potions and tarot cards lined narrow shelves. There were several books on the ancient arts, casting, scrying, and incantations.

"Wow, this is wonderful. Grandmama would be so proud of you."

"I'm feeling the cards today, is that all right?"

"Absolutely. Whatever draws you."

Ashlyne watched Sorcha while she shuffled the cards, and when they were pushed toward her, she cut the deck in three. Sorcha began turning cards one after another, until thirteen cards lay in a circle.

"Hmm," she said.

"What's that mean?"

"The three of cups and magician are together, meaning a creative and powerful energy that brings abundance and joy. The hierophant could mean you are the mentor for new friendships, while your mentor… we know who that is. She helps in the shadows. The ace of cups could mean new love coming, and then the symbol to let go, be true to yourself."

"You're just saying that."

"No, I'm not the one who shuffled the cards. Look where the hanged man showed up. You know how these cards work, Ashlyne. I'm merely the interpreter. There is more happening than opening the store—this is a turning point in your life."

"I've had enough of those."

"Yeah, well, haven't we all." Sorcha turned three more cards. "Ace of swords. The business will do well."

"And… tell me about those two."

"The knight of pentacles with the five of pentacles means…" Sorcha looked up. "Ashlyne, these may not be good cards."

"All cards are good if they give me an awareness of what may be."

"That's true, so be aware of a dangerous man, someone who feeds on others like a vampire."

"Vampires aren't real."

"People say witches aren't real."

"Your point?"

"We are real, and some people call us witches. Maybe vampires are real in the same sense. Society has this false image of what a witch may be, same as vampires. Basically, vampires are those who feed off others—they take advantage of others. The real ones don't literally suck blood from the neck, but rather drain one of energy or resources."

"Do you think the people of this town will think we are witches, just because of what Grandmama did all those years ago?"

"Yes, I do. It wasn't that long ago that she practiced." Sorcha shook her head. "It wasn't her doing, I know it. Coincidence."

"It's why our father took us to England." Ashlyne sighed. "We need to be careful what we do, Sorcha. We know what is real. Others do not. They believe Grandmama caused the—"

"I know what they believe. They're wrong."

"I'd hoped we'd have a fresh start here."

***

Michael lingered outside the room under the stairs long enough to overhear his sisters, taking a moment to sip a fresh cup of coffee. He understood what he'd face returning to Cypress Grove and opening a medical practice. Being a man, and being a doctor, he did come back with an advantage. He befriended the pastor, attended church socials, attended service each Sunday. He had found a community within the church, unlike Sorcha, who had her own set of beliefs. She was a true healer as was Michael, but her path went in a different direction.

Ashlyne had experienced many religious traditions, occasionally accompanying Michael to Sunday services. However, she viewed organized religion primarily as a communal gathering, rather than a deeply spiritual experience. Nevertheless, she continued to participate, acknowledging the presence of forces greater than herself.

"Ashlyne, the tools of our ancestors have been passed to us. If the tarot does not suit you, we'll find another way."

"It isn't the tarot I'm concerned about. Michael has worked hard for his degree. A physician should be respected, not suspected of black magic."

"No one in our family has practiced the black arts." Sorcha and Ashlyne locked eyes and, for a moment, communicated everything each was thinking. They both wanted the same things—

to make Cypress Grove their home. Michael did, too, and for that reason, Sorcha nodded. "I will be careful."

"I appreciate that."

"Times are different now, Ashlyne. Women practice openly, the Church of Wicca is recognized by the federal government."

"We are not Wiccan."

"My point is the practice is more accepted today than it was two or three decades ago. We are healers, not evil witches who steal children."

"Or drown them in rivers?" Ashlyne and Sorcha stared at each other, exchanging an unspoken dialogue. Michael remained quiet, but shifting the weight to his right foot caused the floor to creak, confirming what Ashlyne already knew – he was listening. "I know what you are saying, but let's keep this room private. Okay?"

"Absolutely. Only for when Grandmama's regular clients ask, okay?"

Ashlyne nodded. "Tell me more about these pentacles." Sorcha continued reading the cards. It was something she'd learned long ago, and Ashlyne knew she was very good with the interpretation, magic or not.

"Then I will protect myself." Ashlyne fingered the crystal necklace her great grandmother gave to her years ago, before she left Kentucky for England. It was made to protect her then and she believed it still had that power. "Besides, I have you and Michael to look out for me."

"Overall, these cards are good. The store will do well, you'll make new friends, and help others through the offerings of the apothecary. Stay true to yourself. Love will find you, but beware of the vampires."

"I'll be fine." Ashlyne grinned, "Did you hear that, Michael? I'll be fine!"

Michael smiled, heading back to his office for the next patient. "I heard nothing."

Chapter Four

Lucy and Eva walked ahead of Raine and Sam, following the sidewalk from school. They crossed the street and went through the lower gate, over the bridge to the narrow stone path leading to Cypress Hill.

"It's pretty cool that you live here, Raine." Sam looked up towards the house, and from a distance, it looked nice. It wasn't until they were closer that he could see the torn screens and peeling paint.

"I've never thought about it much. It's just home to me."

"My Uncle Ned talks about a buried treasure here. Is that real?"

"The rumors are real, but I don't know if the treasure is real. My dad and my grandpa searched for years and never found it."

"Did your grandfather talk about the treasure? How did the rumors about a hidden treasure start?"

"Grandpa said his grandpa told him about it, but that's all I know. My grandpa died when I was nine, and we didn't talk much about hidden treasure." Raine looked at Sam, who seemed excited to see Cypress Hill. His dark hair was shoulder length and straight, not a style most Kentucky boys their age were allowed to keep, and he wore tight-legged jeans, not the bell bottoms that were in style. "Where do you live, Sam?"

"We're in Millstone, on the other side of the apartments. Dad thought living here would be close enough to his work, but not so close that he would run into his students everywhere we went. Said he needed space."

Sam glanced at Raine, whom he found attractive due to her uniqueness. She wasn't prissy or overdressed, like Eva, wearing a mini skirt and shiny black boots, and she wasn't in an awkward stage like Lucy, with lanky limbs and pants a couple inches too short. Raine was a natural beauty, even wearing worn jeans and oversized sweatshirts, she had grace, a beautiful smile, and eyes so blue that Sam thought they were the color of the sky at dusk.

David was unloading bags of feed from his truck when they reached the house. He smiled and followed them inside. Lucy led the way to the library, dropping her backpack on the floor by the desk. She led Eva into the foyer for a tour.

"Hello, Mr. Sommer, I'm Sam Hudson. Thank you for letting us work on our project at your home." Sam extended his hand.

"Absolutely, anytime," David responded, shaking the boy's hand, noting his surprising display of manners and maturity. "I unlocked the doors to the library, but the power is off and it's a bit musty in the old house."

"I brought a flashlight," Sam said, then, realizing that seemed strange, he added, "Lucy mentioned the power was off."

"How… efficient. Ya know, let me see if I can find a lamp and extension cord so you all will have better light." He disappeared for a few minutes then returned with a bright lamp. "Well, I've got some work to do out in the barn, so, y'all have at it."

"Thanks, Dad."

"Nice to meet you, Mr. Sommer."

"Yes, same. Good luck on the project."

Raine and Sam stepped into the library, a dimly lit space bereft of windows. Sam started by looking at books while Raine sat behind the large desk. Thinking about her grandfather and his father before him who sat at this desk, she wondered where on the farm a treasure would be buried. The old cemetery, possibly. No one really went there since the new one was built.

It's interesting, she thought, *that the entire town is aware of the legend of buried treasure at Cypress Hill, yet the Sommer family doesn't speak of it anymore. Dad has given up looking for treasure, and why should he bother to look in the first place? If it were real, it would have been found by now.*

The numerous stacks of books and scattered papers on desks and shelves presented a daunting task, requiring weeks to organize, and the uncertainty of finding useful materials for their project loomed. With a one-page paper due the next day, they quickly found themselves with little hope of finding anything significant by tomorrow.

Cabinet doors behind the large desk squeaked open slowly, without Raine or Sam touching them. Sam's eyes grew wide, having heard the stories of Cypress Hill hauntings. They exchanged a glance, and Raine shrugged. The room went completely silent, until, that is, the radio in the living room spontaneously turned on. The Temptations, *Just My Imagination*, began to play.

"Hey, can I see the rest of the house?" Sam gestured towards the old section.

Why anyone would want to see the house was beyond Raine, but she knew Sam was spooked by Raymond's tactics of opening doors, and she believed he was truly excited about an old house. This made her smile, and she nodded.

"Cool." He grinned, and for a moment, she thought he winked at her too.

"Why is an old house so fascinating?"

"The history, man. Look at this place!" He ran his hand over the hand-carved doors, and his eyes looked up at a large chandelier hanging in the foyer. "Is that a gas chandelier?"

"I have no idea."

"Can you imagine what it would have been like to visit this place a hundred years ago?"

"I've never really thought about it."

"That's because you grew up here. It's always been part of your life, so let's try something." He took Raine's hand and led her to the front door, opened it and, together, they stepped onto the front porch. He pulled the door closed, and they stood on the porch looking over the hill towards the road below. "Now, imagine this is the first time you've ever been here, and take it all in."

He opened the front doors, still holding her hand, and turned her to face the foyer. She stepped on the white marble floors and looked up at the crystal chandelier. Staircases on each side of the foyer led to a landing, another six steps to the second floor, while a wide hallway under the landing led to the dining area. The carpet was worn in the center of the steps but still a deep red color. The gas chandelier—which she'd never noticed before—was breathtaking. She imagined it glowing during a time before electricity, and then she understood. This was a magnificent home.

"Wow, I see it now."

"Do you? Raine, this home needs some repairs, but it is a historic masterpiece of architecture. Look at the banisters, all hand carved. And the paintings on the walls, the tapestry." Sam grinned like a kid in a toy shop. "I can't wait to see the rest."

They walked through a music room to the right and to the ballroom. Lucy and Eva had wandered into the solarium, and a wave of shame swept over Raine as the four of them looked over the once beautiful space. The pride she'd felt a moment before vanished at the wreck they looked upon now. There was no amount of imagination that could unsee the solarium.

The scene was a catastrophe, with lifeless plants, shattered glass, and toppled ceramic pots. Timeworn rattan furniture lay scattered haphazardly across the cold, terracotta tile floor. The solarium exuded a discomforting ambiance, shrouded in a perpetual gloom despite the abundant sunlight outside. Dilapidated vines clung to the decaying walls, casting skeletal shadows on the cracked, fogged windows. The air hung heavy with an unsettling stillness, broken only by the occasional creaking of the unlatched screen doors beyond the double French doors on either end of the area. Frozen in time, an unsettling blend of faded elegance and spectral neglect that sent a shiver down the spine of anyone who dared to step inside.

"This place is amazing!" Sam said.

"Really? You think this is cool?" Eva replied. "Gives me the creeps."

"I can see what it once was and the potential it could be again, with a little TLC." Sam gazed at the glass ceiling, the steel beams strong and ready for a second life. Most of the glass was intact but opaque, with years of dust and mildew. "When was this room last used?"

"I remember my great-grandma Adeline sitting out here, and it was an overgrown jungle back then, maybe eight or ten years ago."

"I vaguely remember her, Raine. We were so little."

"I'm ready to get out of here. I've seen enough." With arms tightly crossed, a scowl etched on her face, Eva stood defensively, hugging herself as though warding off the eerie atmosphere from seeping into her soul. "Let's get what we need from the library and leave this place to the ghosts of Cypress Hill."

"There are no ghosts," Raine declared, but as if in response, a sudden loud noise startled her, a sound resembling a slow squeak of a door hinge coming from somewhere inside. "That might be the front door. We left it open."

"That's Raymond," Lucy sang the words to Eva, then led the way from the solarium back into the gilded ballroom.

"Who is Raymond?" Sam asked Raine, holding the door to the solarium and gesturing for her to walk through before him.

"My great-grandfather."

"Is he—"

"He died before I was born." Raine sighed, realizing she should explain. "Anything unusual that happens in the house, Raymond is the reason. Unexplained creaks and moans, flickering lights, you name it."

"Those things can be explained, just being in an old house."

"Exactly what I say, but everyone blames Raymond."

The ballroom extended the entire length of the south wing, a vast space supported by poles in the center to uphold the second floor, each surrounded by cushioned mahogany benches. The walls were covered with baby blue and gold cherub toile fabric above chair railing, while below, rich mahogany panels added a touch of elegance. Heavy blue curtains adorned the windows and doors, and embossed gold tin tiles covered the ceiling, complemented by four crystal chandeliers.

Eva's foul mood quickly changed when she looked around the ballroom. She strolled counterclockwise through the room like the belle of the ball, imagining the lively parties and romantic escapades that must have unfolded in this century-old home. Thoughts of the parties that must have been held filled her head—the dancing, the lovers sneaking off into one of the many alcoves or private rooms upstairs. The house had seen so much, and the carefree spirit of festivity was felt in this room. "All right, this is pretty cool."

Raine pulled a sheet off one of the chairs, noticing a matching cherub pattern. "Yeah, it is," she commented, coughing from the dust stirred.

"Why did your family close off this section of the house?" Sam inquired, his gaze drifting across the architecture and decor. While Eva viewed the room through a lens of romance, Sam perceived the history embedded in its structure.

"I think it was just too big for our family. Grandma once talked about turning it into an inn, but then—"

"That's when our grandpa passed away. He was working on the kitchen, which used to be a standalone building, like a lot of these old homes had, in case of a fire, you know," Lucy rambled. "He added the breezeway connecting the dining room and the kitchen, planning to open an inn at some point."

Raine followed Lucy as she guided the group from the ballroom into the expansive dining room featuring a table accommodating at least twelve people. A large mahogany cabinet held delicate China and crystal bowls, and a liquor cabinet in the corner still held a few dusty bottles of bourbon. Double doors revealed a room with an outdated couch and a small television, eventually leading to a kitchen that reeked of a rather unpleasant odor. "Oh my God, what is that smell?"

"No way. I ain't going in there," Eva said, pivoting on her heels and heading back towards the library.

"Yeah, me either. We need to find something for our paper anyhow."

Undeterred by the pungent odor, Sam descended two steps into the large kitchen. On the left, a cast iron stove rested on a stone floor, while at the far end, a spacious open fireplace seemed to be a forgotten element from the original log cabin. The walls and ceiling consisted of hand-cut wooden beams, likely crafted and arranged by Sommer settlers long before the Civil War. "Maybe this could be our project... if we can't find anything on a military hospital," he pondered.

***

The group met before school and organized the information gathered the day before, shaping it in a presentable format to turn in. They'd worked through dinner at Cypress Hill, with Lorraine serving grilled cheese sandwiches. While the girls sifted through notes in the library, Sam took notes and composed a preliminary report, and Lucy, being the perfectionist she was, rewrote it the next morning at school. However, the sheer abundance of books, folders, envelopes, and scattered sheets of paper surrounding the desk meant they made only a minor dent in the overall organization, and creating a one-page overview was challenging.

"The drawings you made are a nice touch, Raine."

"Thanks, Lucy. I've not drawn the house in a long time."

"Your mother used to sketch the house, with us in her drawings. Do you still have any of those?"

"I do, in my room. Someday, I'll have them framed and hang them up."

Sam placed the project summary into the wire basket on Mrs. Weismann's desk. Lucy observed from nearby, attempting to sneak a peek at the titles chosen by other students for their project. Randal's team opted for the old mill, given his family once owned it and it was the largest business in town during the Civil War. Priscilla Hopkins' group picked the Confederate Memorial in Mayfield, attained by the United Daughters of Confederacy—no surprise there. Faith's team, on the other hand, was delving into the predominantly African American town of Birmingham, a place destroyed by flooding during the construction of Land Between the Lakes.

The summary was presented as a research project, because currently, they didn't know the true history of Cypress Hill. It was old, they knew this, but they found no evidence of a medical unit where injured and ill soldiers came for treatment. Many questions need answering, such as, how long this went on, who the physician was treating the injured, and if they were confederate or union soldiers. Gil Sommer claimed Colonel Sommer was a Union soldier, but most of the area was sympathetic to the Confederacy There were photos, but none were found as far back as the 1860s. The Civil War was recognized for being one of the first wars to be widely documented through photography, and they were optimistic that photos would eventually be located.

"Glad that's done," Eva commented, slipping into her seat behind Sam.

"All you did was read the Jane Austen book you found yesterday." Lucy laughed, as did Eva, because she knew it was true. She loved Austen, and the book had the most beautiful embossed blue cover with colored illustrations, printed in 1921. There was so much more in the library for them to review. "You need to help us on this project, Eva."

"I helped... some."

The rain started as school let out, continuing all weekend. Raine focused on the algebra homework, which always seems to take so much longer than it should. She sketched another picture of the house to possibly use for the project. Lucy watched her younger siblings overnight on Saturday because her parents were shoeing horses near Lexington. Eva had a dance recital, and Sam was helping his grandfather at his office. Monday came around fast, and so did Mrs. Weismann's lecture about the project.

"I hope everyone put the rainy days to good use this weekend, working on your reports. I want you all to think about it—the more you work on it now, the less you will have to do in April, and heaven forbid anyone wait until the first week of May when it's due. I'll bet for those of you who started, you will have a better report."

Lucy smiled. "We need to get together again. I've got chores all week because Dad's working in Lexington, but how about Friday? We can have a sleep over, Raine."

"That's good with me," Eva said. "We should go right after school."

"You seem awfully enthusiastic, Eva. Why so eager?"

"My mom," she rolled her eyes, "she's having what's his face over for dinner on Friday. I'd rather not be there."

Marilyn Hadley was a single mother and had dated regularly since Eva's father left them, a new beau every few weeks, but never the right one. This guy—Joe something—tried too hard to get involved with Eva, and she found that odd. Suspicious, even. He made her uncomfortable.

"Can I come over too? I mean, not for the sleepover part…" Sam looked away and grinned, thinking about what it would be like at the girls' slumber party. What happens at a sleepover, anyway? Would there be a pillow fight? Would they gossip about him?

"You'd better come help us go through all that crap in the library!" Lucy scowled.

"You're welcome to join us, Sam," Raine said, giving Lucy a sideways look. "And you're welcome to stay for dinner if you want."

"Sure, sounds great."

Mrs. Weismann used the class time to read a little from each group's project—all seven of them. Lucy listened intently, comparing the Cypress Hill topic to the others, including the Battle of Paducah, a courthouse in a nearby town built by slaves, a confederate cemetery, but nothing like a Civil War hospital. Lucy smiled when the teacher read their project plans.

"We have the best subject," Lucy whispered to Eva.

"It's not a competition, Lucy."

"No, but we're still the best."

Raine listened silently. Her emotions were conflicted regarding the intense emphasis on her home, and her anxiety grew as Mrs. Weismann read about Cypress Hill in front of the entire class. While a sense of pride filled her for being connected to a family with ties tracing back to the earliest settlers in Kentucky, the declining condition of Cypress Hill left her uneasy.

Then there was the family history. There was more than a good chance that Colonel Sommer was a Confederate soldier and supported slavery. Things that her grandparents had said in passing when she was a child echoed in her mind, about the workers, about labor costs, about the changes that came with the end of the war.

There was certainly a gilded age at Cypress Hill and the ballroom was evidence of that, but it seemed the two World Wars each had a negative effect on the profits of the farm, and with that, cutbacks were made. Gilbert, her grandfather, served in World War II, and this was when the family business suffered the most. Raymond died just after Gil returned, and much like her father returning from Vietnam, it was all too much. Cypress Hill was no longer the center of Cypress Grove's social life and was in a spiraling decline.

Chapter Five

David's discomfort was growing, the scar tissue and phantom pain of his left leg and the arthritis on the right, both which caused his back to seize while mucking stalls. He knew he was fortunate to be alive. He was a couple feet from the grenade when it blew, knocking him unconscious. The next memory was his commander shouting, the sound of the helicopter, then he blacked out again until after surgery.

The pain in his body was a constant reminder of his time in Vietnam. It never went away, never left him. He did the best he could to push forward when he returned. Therapy helped some, pain medications were numbing and dangerous. He had to be present for his wife and his daughter. He had to take care of them. He felt alcohol was the better option.

So much to think about, so much to do, but he was a changed man when he returned. Caroline was sick, and he did the best he could to hold it together for her sake, but all motivation disappeared after Caroline died. He knew he drank too much. He knew he didn't put in the work to care for the farm the way it should be done, yet all he could do was think about his first drink of the day.

The air around him seemed thick with missed opportunities and unrealized dreams. In those moments, he wrestled with the internal turmoil of inadequacy, feeling he had failed his family, his comrades, his country, and the people of Vietnam. Some returning vets had taken the easy way out, but he couldn't do that to Raine, or to his mother. They both depended on him so much.

He recalled what Raine asked him at the cemetery, if her mother could hear them talking to her, and if she could, then why didn't she answer. "Caroline? If you can hear me, what am I going to do? How am I supposed to do this without you?"

At the same time David was asking Caroline for help, his daughter was at the cemetery doing the same. Looking at her mother's headstone, she sighed and pulled the wilted carnations and daffodils from the vase. She'd make a point to bring fresh flowers during the week, and it was Friday. "I can't believe it's been more than a week since Dad and I were here. I sure do wish you were here too, Mom."

Raine was walking up the hill to the farm when she spotted Lorraine pulling into the driveway, stopping to collect the mail at the gate. The recent rain and lingering mist left her gray curls limp, stringy, and she appeared pale, with dark circles under her eyes. Having completed her fifth shift at the nursing home this week, one more than her usual four-day workweek, she looked exhausted.

***

Lorraine felt the pain in her back after a long day in the kitchen, mostly standing on hard, concrete floors in her old shoes. Although she should be thinking of retirement, the constant stream of bills meant she had to work. Her feet hurt, her back hurt, and she had a headache, but she put on a smile seeing her son. David met her at the screened porch door, and while still sober at this time in the afternoon, his appearance reflected the immense amount of pressure on him.

"Hey, Ma," he said, pulling a pack of Marlboros from his front pocket, popping one between his lips with one hand and flicking a Zippo with the other. "How was work?"

"It's fine, just busy like always. There's never enough help." She tossed the mail on the kitchen table, and without stopping to rest, she immediately pulled out the cutting board to prepare dinner. "The girls are sleeping over tonight, and that boy... he's coming to work on the project."

"Good, I like him."

"Well, I'm not so sure. That boy—"

"Sam, Ma," David said, "his name is Sam."

Lorraine exhaled sharply, eyeing David with one hand on her hip and another on a butcher knife pointed his direction. "Sam—"

"What about him?"

"He's Ned Baker's nephew, you know."

"I know that. His great-nephew. Sam's mother, Colleen, is Ned's niece."

"And that doesn't bother you, even a little bit?"

"Why should it?"

Lorraine gave a flat-lipped frown, then waved the knife at a letter on the table. "Read that."

David unfolded the letter from the Lakes Trust Bank, slowly sinking into a wooden chair at the kitchen table. "Ma, how long have you known about this?"

"About the loan?"

"Yes, Ma, the loan. Why haven't you told me about this? We already have two loans, why did Pa take out a third?"

***

Voices wafted through the open windows and screened porch. Raine caught snippets of her grandmother talking, but the exact words remained unclear. In contrast, her father's voice carried more, with a deeper pitch. She hesitated at the door, and instead of going in, she slipped between the forsythias next to the screened porch. She squatted between the bushes, waiting to hear more.

"I wanted to apply for the loan, but the bank wouldn't allow me to without your father. Shoot, they won't even allow a woman to cash a check without her husband's approval."

"So, Pa approved?"

"Of course he did. I was with him when he signed the papers at the bank, five or six years ago, just before he died." Lorraine chopped onions, a great cover for the tears pooling in her eyes. She knew this was bad news for the family. "Ned's been in touch a few times about the late payments, and now he's calling me at work."

"He called today?"

"Yes, he wants to meet with us. We're a little behind."

"Behind on loan payments?"

"Yes, but don't you worry about—"

"Ma, don't tell me not to worry about this." David ran his rough hand through his hair, then leaned back in the chair, allowing his emotions to cool before he responded to his mother. His calm nature and respect of his mother was one of his best qualities, and Raine could hear it play out in their conversation. "This letter says foreclosure."

"Let me talk to him, David. He's a reasonable man."

"Not according to this letter." David's voice became softer, his tone less accusatory. "Ma, he wants the farm."

"No, that's not it. It can't be. He knows we took out the loan because of—"

"Because of Caroline. This is how Pa came up with the money. I always wondered how he did it."

"We'd do it again, too. She had to try those treatments."

"This is mine, Ma. The loan is mine to pay." David leaned back with his fingers locked behind his head. "He knows that, and that's why he's coming after me—not us—but me."

"Why would he do that, David? What does Ned Baker have against you?"

"It's not Ned."

"Then who? Tell me right now!" Lorraine shouted. David might have the cool head of his father, of a Sommer, but Lorraine had the red-headed temper for which the McGill family was known in the area. She shook her head and threw the cutting board in the sink.

"It's Liam."

"Liam? What does he have to do with this?"

"He never got over his high school crush—the girl I happened to marry." Liam Baker and David had had it out on many occasions, and Ned resented David for stealing Caroline away from his son.

"That doesn't mean Ned would collect on a loan that we are behind on, David. It's his job! He's the bank manager."

"Yes, it is his job."

"Ned has been very generous with us, allowed us to refinance when Caroline needed those infusions down in Nashville, and waived the late fees up until two years ago. It's time we paid up."

"He knows you don't have the money. He knows I don't have the money. The only option is to foreclose, and the property is his."

"We have a couple weeks. He said we have until April to pay the balance owed, and he'll let us keep the loan."

"So, we have two weeks to come up with nearly a thousand dollars."

"Yes. I'll make the appointment and we'll go together." Lorraine's voice calmed and quieted. She rested her hands over David's shoulders and hugged him from behind. "You are a good son, David, and you were a good husband. Caroline was fortunate to have you take care of her."

"Yeah, well, I would take her place in a heartbeat."

"That isn't how it works." Lorraine's heart ached for her son, wishing there was more she could do for him, something she could say to take his pain away. "We'll come up with the money, David, we always do, and we don't have to pay it off right away."

"Yes, we do. I need to do something, Ma."

The house was silent, and Raine leaned back against the peeling paint amidst the overgrown bushes. Her eyes burned and cheeks scorched. The peanut butter sandwich she ate at lunch rose in her throat, and her breaths came in small gasps. The finances were far more dire than she suspected—they could lose their home.

She'd lost so much already, now her home could go away too. They would be homeless, forced to live with her cousin at Mitchell Farms, or worse, with Aunt Melinda in their larger home. Raine shook her head, trying to get that image out of her mind. She couldn't imagine a world without Cypress Hill. She took a long, deep breath.

While aware there were always money problems, at least during her life, she now realized that a significant portion of this loan was spent on treatments for her mother. Grandpa tried to help, and the treatments she received must have been very costly, something Raine had never considered before. Three years later, her father was still burdened with the medical bills. She took another slow, deep breath.

When her mother first became ill, David was in Vietnam and didn't know of Caroline's diagnosis. Everything fell apart at once for Raine. In the years following her mother's passing, Raine struggled with her emotions. She saw a therapist in Murray, went to group sessions to talk about the loss. She still remembered what the therapist taught her about breathing—she never knew breathing could change your mood or how you felt about something. It worked. Whenever she felt overwhelmed, she focused on her breathing. Just breathing.

For a while, she worried she would lose both parents. First, her mother's cancer diagnosis, then her grandfather died suddenly. David came home for the funeral but was sent back to Vietnam after a short visit. A few weeks later, he suffered a near-death injury in Vietnam, was sent to Walter Reed, then transferred to a local rehab facility. A few months after David came home, Caroline died.

Physical therapy didn't do much to help David, so he stopped his outpatient therapy to care for Caroline. He did the best he could, but there was nothing that could save her. After her death, David shut down emotionally and physically. The fields went unworked, animals went unfed. Maggie and her husband, Bryce, helped when they could, but it was a challenging time for everyone. David's work had become sporadic, and a substantial portion of money was spent at the bar or liquor store.

Lorraine, witnessing the pain and loss experienced by those she held dear, empathized deeply with David and Raine. David, having lost the love of his life and high school sweetheart, struggled with the void left by her absence. For Raine, the loss of her mother felt like the theft of a part of her childhood, and this loss would shape her for the rest of her life. Lorraine did what she did best—kept them well fed and connected to family, making sure each milestone was a huge celebration.

Raine understood the varied nature of grief and its unique impact on each individually. It wasn't just a parent she'd lost, but also a friend, along with the missed opportunities for all the typical mother-daughter experiences. Despite the presence of her father,

her grandmother, and the aunts—Maggie, Petra, and Melinda—it was never quite the same. Tears stung her eyes, thinking about the loss she'd experienced. The loss she still experienced daily. With pursed lips, she slowly exhaled. *Breathe.*

Raine recalled a few days before, when she and her father were at the cemetery, and David's playful joke about Aunt Melinda sitting on the bench had made her laugh so hard that her face hurt. In that moment, she found solace, taking a deep breath as a new memory formed. They needed more new memories like that—not to replace old memories, but to provide balance. That's how things are—the then, and the now. Her life seemed to exist in two realms—the one she had before, with her mother alive and well, and the one she currently navigated.

On top of reeling in grief, the family's financial situation seemed to have escalated from challenging to catastrophic. Perhaps this was how things would always be for the family—poor, barely enough money for the things they needed. There had been a time in her family, long ago, when money wasn't always a problem, a time when they managed the home well, entertained dignitaries, held glamorous balls, and not held debt. The ballroom and solarium were evidence of this time at Cypress Hill.

"Mom... if you are there, send me a sign. Let me know it is going to be okay. Let me know if there's hope." Raine sniffed, wiping the tears from her eyes. "Please, Mom. I need you."

Raine waited in anticipation for her mother to appear before her, but of course, that didn't happen. Instead, rain pinged on the metal porch roof. She squatted down between the bushes, looking out towards the back of the house at the barns. Gray, dreary, run down. She closed her eyes, wanting to feel something, hear her mother's voice, sense something. When she opened her eyes, the sun was out, shining down from behind the clouds, a bright ray of light on the large barn. A rainbow appeared against the dark clouds. Hope.

Raine stood, shaking out the needle pricks from squatting for so long, and walked to the fence by the barn. She turned her gaze to behold Cypress Hill. The clouds parted, the home basking in the warm embrace of magical sunlight. Everything looked greener, bolder, fresher as the light spread across the lawn. The daffodils were in full bloom and bright yellow, and small butterflies fluttered above them. The dogwoods, locust, and cherry trees were starting to bud. Even the dead trees somehow seemed beautiful, natural. And the house—it was beautiful. Even with its peeling paint and weathered facade, there was an undeniable allure to the structure. It stood as a testament to years gone by, each crack and faded hue telling a story of the Sommer family's enduring legacy. This was not just a house—it was the memories, it was life, love, family. This was her home. She wasn't going to let some bank take it.

She smiled at the sun, wondering if that was her mother's answer, that it meant there was hope in this situation, or was it only a coincidence? There was one thing she could do to help. She was only fifteen and there wasn't much she could do, but if she got a job, it meant she would contribute a little. She had to do something.

The warm sun in late March always brought joy. While she felt better facing the sun, after overhearing her grandmother and her father talk about the money, she recognized that her family needed more than just hope. They needed a miracle. Raine shook off the mini-pity party and went into the kitchen. Lorraine stood at the counter cutting vegetables—onions, celery, carrots, and potatoes. A whole chicken was in a roasting pan, and she tossed the veggies in the pan with it, adding sage and rosemary, salt, and pepper, covered it, and shoved in a hot oven.

"Hi, Grandma."

"Hi, Sweetie! How was school today?"

"Good. Ms. Tipton says I need tutoring."

"Tutoring? In math?" Lorraine avoided eye contact, immediately wondered how much a tutor cost. "I'm not sure we have any tutors around town."

"Yeah, she gave me a letter for Dad. I think there are some tutors from high school who could help."

"Students," she said, relieved. "That sounds wonderful."

"Need any help with dinner?"

"Sure, could you set the table?" Lorraine checked the timer on the stove. "Set it with six plates—don't forget Sam is joining us."

The radio played a Carole King song from the other room, where David sorted through papers on the library desk. She listened to words that might be a message from her mother. Raine set the table, careful to have the knives facing towards the plates with the spoon on one side, fork on the left by itself, just like her mother taught her.

You just call out my name
And you know, wherever I am
I'll come runnin'
To see you again
Winter, spring, summer or fall
All you have to do is call
And I'll be there
You've got a friend...

"Grandma," Raine says. "Is it possible to, um, do you believe it's possible for someone to communicate with someone who has died?"

"Oh, sure! I talk to your Grandpa Gil all the time."

"Can you, I mean," Raine searched for better words, "does he respond? Not talking, like I am now, but in your head?"

"Oh, he most certainly does. He sends me little messages all the time." Grandma stopped and wiped her hands on her apron, then pulled Raine in for a big grandma hug. "I know what this is about. You miss your mom. That's perfectly normal, and you want to have a conversation with her."

Raine nodded. The overhead light flickered, making a popping sound. Lorraine's upper torso giggled as she laughed. "Well, I know for a fact that our loved ones above watch over us. Your grandpa talks to me all the time, and you know his father is still in this house. Raymond likes to flicker lights, just like that, and he messes with the T.V. reception."

"That might just be old electrical wiring," Raine smirked. Anytime strange things happened in the house, Grandma said it was Raymond.

"I'm pretty sure it's Raymond." Both looked up at the ceiling and it flickered once more. "He's been messin' with us since he died."

Raine had seen the TV reception change and the radio turn on without anyone touching a knob, but that wasn't proof enough for her to believe it was really her great-grandfather doing it, and if it was, flickering lights weren't the same as having a conversation with a ghost. If there was a way to communicate from the other side, her mother would find it and would talk to Raine. She just knew it.

David was studying ledgers when Raine walked into the library. He looked up at her and smiled. "Hey, sweetheart."

"Hi, Dad. Find anything we can use in our project?"

"Nothing about a military hospital if that's what you mean. I found some old letters in a box, some back as far as 1880s."

"Really? What kind of letters?"

"I didn't read them, but some were from France. That's where Adalbert Sommer went for a while."

"Adalbert?"

"The colonel." David thought about it, squeezing one eye shut and looking up to the ceiling for the answer. "Um, he would be your great-great-great-grandfather.

"Then there was Franz, also in the same war?"

"Yes, I'd heard Adalbert was a Confederate soldier, and his son, Franz, ran away at fifteen, to join the Union. I'll bet that was quite the family squabble."

"Hey, what's going on?" Lucy, Eva, and Sam joined them in the library.

"Dad just said our great-great-great-grandfather, Colonel Sommer, was with the Confederate Army, and his son, Franz Sommer, ran away with the Union soldiers."

"At fifteen—y'all's age," David added. "And don't go getting any smart ideas, Lucy."

"Very funny. I thought they were both Union soldiers," Lucy said.

"That's what Pa used to say, but my grandpa told me otherwise. Maybe y'all can uncover the truth with your project."

"Have you found anything interesting, Mr. Sommer?"

"Not really, Sam. I'm looking for maps, surveys of the farm. If you see any, will you set them aside for me to look through?"

"Yes, sir," Sam replied. Raine listened, wondering if Sam is nervous or if he was always this polite, because her father was impressed, she could tell. "I'll put them in the top desk drawer."

"Thank you." David grabbed his notebook and got up from the desk. "I'm going to wash up before dinner. You guys okay in here?"

"Yes, thank you, Dad."

"You're welcome, sweetheart." David kissed his daughter on top her head, leaving them to the stacks of papers, books, and dust in the library.

They spent more than an hour looking at old photographs, reading ledgers, mail from long ago, and found nothing about the Civil War hospital. The letters from France were from a friend of Adalbert's, inviting him to visit, telling him how therapeutic it had been for him following the war. There was no mention of Franz, nothing of the hospital, and absolutely nothing about a buried treasure at Cypress Hill.

They ate delicious roasted chicken and vegetables with homemade biscuits and jam. Lorraine reported what she knew about the history of Cypress Hill. She'd heard about the treasure, telling Sam that she knew Gil believed it was under a tree somewhere on the farm, maybe the cypress trees in the swamp, but she couldn't remember for certain. "It was all so long ago," she said.

"Why would they bury treasure in the swamp?" Lucy asked. "It doesn't make sense—it would sink, and a treasure chest could migrate in the swamp. No one would ever find it, even if they knew where it was buried."

After dinner, they started going through papers again in the library. Lucy was looking in the lower cabinets behind the desk, Sam had a stack of random papers on the desk in front of him, while Eva and Raine were going through books on the shelves. Sam showed Raine surveys of the farm and placed them in the top desk drawer for her father, just as he'd promised.

"Hey, look what I found," Lucy said like she was purring. "I know what we can do tonight."

"What is that?" A game?" Eva asked.

"Better than a game—it's a Ouija board."

"A what?

"A Ouija board, so we can talk to the ghosts."

"There are no ghosts here," Raine said, and right on schedule, the floor above them creaked. Eva's eyes grew, Lucy huffed a laugh.

"Wha-what was that?" Eva asked.

"That's Dad's room above us. Come on…" Raine shook her head.

"This will be fun, Raine. If we can't talk to the civil war nurses, maybe we can talk with the colonel. Or maybe your mother."

"If Mom was going to say something, she wouldn't use a board game to say it."

"Well, then let's hope for some ghostly help with this project."

Looking around the library, Raine closed her eyes and silently asked for help from her mother, or God, or any spiritual being willing to help. Well, maybe not any spirit, only the good ones. There were so many books all the way up to the ceiling, a couple of old paintings—one of horses in the field and another of trees—and an old oval photograph of a beautiful woman in a light-colored dress, wearing pearls. She pulled a box from the bottom shelf and set it on the desk.

"Find any more maps?" she asked Sam.

"No, most of the papers in the desk drawers are receipts and invoices from the 1950s." He removed the lid from the box. "What's in here?"

"I have no idea."

Raine sat in the chair across from Sam and started with the papers on the top of the box. She was not sure what to say to him, and the longer she waited to speak, the more awkward it became for her to say anything. She wasn't sure how she felt about Sam or how he felt about her. She had never had a boyfriend before. If he liked her, maybe she'd like him. But if he didn't like her, then she never liked him. That was her plan for now, anyhow.

"Hey, your father's room is above the living room," he said, gesturing towards the north wing room leading back to the kitchen. The room where David often slept on the couch, surrounded by beer cans and cigarette butts.

"How do you know where my dad's room is?"

"Here—a floorplan drawn in 1892. This must be when the north wing was added, and the second floor of the north wing does not open to the rest of the upstairs."

"Really? That's odd. I always thought Grandpa built the wall at the top of the steps when he shut off the main part of the house."

"No, it was built this way. I'll bet the north side was built for employees, like a housekeeper or farmhands."

"Oh, that's interesting. I know it's a newer part of the house, but you think it could have been built for employees? I wonder if that could fit into our research somehow."

"It was decades after the Civil War, so not something we could use for the project, but it is interesting." They continued working together until after seven, when it was starting to get dark. Sam walked home, Lucy grabbed the Ouija board, and the girls headed upstairs for the night.

Chapter Six

"Are you sure about this?"

"Absolutely." Raine kept steady eye contact with Lucy.

"This isn't a game. It's real. You okay with that?" Lucy covered her head with a black scarf, leaving wispy blonde bangs peeking out above eyes painted in heavy black eyeliner. She placed five purple candles on the floor outside the circle.

"Yes." Raine nodded, biting the inside of her lip, and pulling the tangled mess of hair to one side, she twisted in front of her chest. This type of thing might bring up not-so-happy spirits, the kind who were angry when they were living and in full rage being awakened from dead. The source of unexplained knocks on the wall, doors slamming shut, and sounds coming from nowhere in her home were benevolent to this point, but summoning the spirits might prompt some sort of retribution. Then again, maybe nothing at all would happen, especially with three teenage amateurs performing a séance. Still, it was worth a try if it meant communicating with her mother.

"Come on, girls, let's do this!" Eva was far more excited than Lucy, and Raine suspected this was how she coped with her fear of ghosts. She grinned like a kid in the front car of a roller coaster before it took off. To her, this was like theater class with the stage set and Lucy in costume. "This will be fun!"

"We are not having fun, Eva. This is serious, okay?" Lucy turned off the bedroom lamp and lit one more candle, a white one. She stepped in the circle of salt poured on the wooden floor in Raine's room and took a seat.

"Okay." Eva made her eyes big and stuck out her tongue.

"Okay, good." Lucy inhaled deeply through her nose and blew out through pursed lips. She placed the white candle in the center and turned the Ouija board toward Raine. "Okay," she repeated to herself, so jittery, she shook her hands in the air to release the tension, consciously remembering to take another breath. "We'll start by joining hands and asking the white light of goodness to pour over us in this circle and protect us from any negative energies that might try to come through."

"Definitely don't want negative energy," Eva echoed. Her green eyeshadow sparkled in the light, and while all three agreed to dress in black for the séance, Eva chose a more fashionable black and green sequined shawl she found in Caroline's old clothes, and she wore her shiny black patent-leather boots.

Lucy glanced at her with narrowed eyes, a warning to let her focus on the task as they joined hands. The witch-like persona was who she would like to become—someone other than teacher's pet. She watched *Bewitched* on television. She'd seen *Bell, Book and Candle*. She had read many books, fiction and non-fiction, about witchcraft and supernatural happenings, so this sort of made her the expert in the group.

"Go on, Lucy." Raine squeezed both their hands and nodded, anxious to get this started. Candlelight reflected across their faces, masking trepidation. "We're ready."

"No matter what happens, we must stay in this circle of salt. It's our protection." Lucy looked at them both and motioned to lift their hands together. "Repeat three times with me—circle of salt, veil of white, keep us safe, in this rite."

Eva lifted one brow to throw a "whatever" her way, then followed Lucy's instructions.

"Circle of salt, veil of white, keep us safe, in this rite." Nothing happened.

"Circle of salt, veil of white, keep us safe, in this rite." The white light flickered a little, then shot out two sparks. Eva gasped.

"Circle of salt, veil of white, keep us safe, in this rite."

Lucy focused on the candle. "We ask our heavenly angels to watch over us and help guide the spirits of our ancestors to this Earthly plane and to allow communication with us. We invite the kind spirits of Cypress Hill to this Earthly plane and seek resolution of Earthly matters so they may peacefully pass on to the next plane of existence." Lucy closed her eyes and took a deep breath. "We ask for protection in the white light of the divine energy as we ask the Ouija specific questions." Lucy let go of their hands. "Okay, now we all put our fingers on the planchette and, Raine, you ask a question."

"Me?" Her fingers trembled above the heart-shaped piece of wood. "Like what?"

"Anything you'd like. Ask if Grandpa Gil is present, or Colonel Adalbert, see if they're doing strange stuff around in the house, or if they have any wisdom from the other side."

"Like where we can find the treasure," Eva added, "if it exists."

"Okay." Eva, Lucy and Raine touched the planchette. Raine closed her eyes. "Grandpa, are you here?" The planchette shook but did not move.

"Ask again," Lucy instructed.

"Grandpa? Are you listening?" The piece slowly moved to the "Yes" answer on the board.

"Raine, he's here!" Eva said, more worried than surprised. "But I don't believe in ghosts. Remember that."

They looked at each other, because it was more likely one of them moved the pointer that direction just to mess with the others.

"Is Momma here? Is Momma with you?" Under their fingers, the heart-shaped piece slowly moved to the letters "C" and "S".

"C.S., that's Caroline Sommer," Eva said.

"Mom? It's really you? Are you okay?" and the pointer moved to "O", then "K". "She's okay!"

"You're Momma is here, Raine!" Eva grinned, half-believing this game and half-worried it might be real.

"Shhh!" Lucy scolded. All three felt the piece move again, this time to a "B", then it slowly moved to the "E", and "W". They watched while it continued to spell out a word, letter by letter. Lucy called each one, then said it aloud, "Beware."

Raine pulled her hands back and instinctively wiped them on her pants to get rid of whatever caused that to happen. "I'm not sure if I like this." She rubbed her arms, noticing they ached in a weird way, either from holding them out or from nervousness, but it didn't feel good. She moved to get up when Lucy grabbed her wrist.

"Don't leave the circle. You're protected in here," Lucy said, and trusting her cousin, Raine sat back down. The circle was glowing in a white luminosity coming from beyond the ceiling, and the rest of the bedroom was pitch black. She sat on folded legs, grabbed her hair over the left shoulder and twisted it down the front again, a habit she developed when her mother was ill. She found a hair tie on her wrist and wrapped it around the end of a bushy ponytail.

"Raine, ask another question!" Eva urged. "Let's see what he has to say about the treasure."

Lucy felt a surge of adrenaline in her veins and swallowed hard. She'd researched séances and has heard of Ouija board before but never imagined it would work so well. "Keep calm, y'all. Let's go on. Ask Grandpa a question, Raine."

Raine licked her dry lips and inhaled, slowly blowing out. "Okay." She rubbed her hands on her legs before putting fingers back on the planchette. Looking at Lucy, she followed her lead and closed her eyes, later regretting the exact moment when she trusted Lucy to summon the dead. "Grandpa, is there a treasure at Cypress Hill?"

The board shook and shifted, and all six hands lift from the device. The planchette quickly moved itself over the word "Yes".

"So, there really is a treasure…" Eva whispered, mostly to herself.

"That thing moved on its own, Eva! And you think the treasure is what's important?"

"Come on you two, fingers back on," Lucy said. They glanced at each other and settled fingertips back on the wooden piece as it moved under their fingers. Lucy read the letters out M - U - R - D - E…

"That's not funny, Eva!" Raine shouted, pulling her hands away. "I don't like this game."

"It wasn't me! I swear!" Eva held her hands to her chest, fingers spread to reveal long green acrylic nails she'd bought at K-Mart.

"Look… there's more. Get your hands back on, Raine," Lucy urged. "No more messing around, Eva."

"I'm tellin' you, that wasn't me. Had to be one of you." Eva smiled at Lucy and nodded, "Nice one."

Lucy sighed. This was not going like she'd hoped. Not at all.

"Grandpa, is there a treasure on the farm?" Raine asked. "Where is it?"

With fingers back on the planchette, first to the word "Yes", then the letters T - R - E—E—S…"

"No way…" Now, Eva was wide-eyed with mouth gaping. Everyone knew the rumors of a treasure lost somewhere on the farm—Grandma said so. The family has dug for decades, under the oak trees, under the sycamores and cypress and cedars. It was supposed to be somewhere under the trees. Somewhere.

The board shook, moving the planchette to "L", then "O", and on to spell out the word LOVE. They lifted their fingers and it continued to move on its own, pointing to the letter "T" then to "R", to the "E", circled the board, again to the "E", and "S". The air became cool, and a soft voice whispered, "Rain-eee…. Rain-eee."

She recognized the voice, and she immediately called out, "Momma? Is that you?"

The voice sounded like she was far away, in a tunnel or in a hole. "Careful… Raine…" The planchette moved to "R", then "S", and repeated those initials several times.

"R.S., is that me? Raine Sommer, or Raymond?"

It was calm and light inside the circle, but outside the circle of salt, the air began to stir, moving in small gusts at first, then it picked up. It blew stronger, moving up loose papers and hair ribbons, and then it got stronger, turning pencils into projectiles and necklaces into metal whips. A cyclone spun around the room, around the protected circle. The purple candles blew out, leaving just one white candle burning calmly in the center of the circle with no more than an occasional flicker. The gusts did not cross the line of salt where the veil of white light spread to the circumference and up to the ceiling in a cone shape. The air became so cold, the girls saw their breaths.

Grabbing onto each other, the girls held tight. They all felt a strong pressure and an electrical impulse in their spines and immediately jumped, but Lucy pulled them back and yelled, "Don't move! We must stay in the circle!"

"What's happening?" Raine shouted. The wind in the room roared around them so loudly, they could barely hear each other shouting, screaming. Bits of gum wrappers, hair ties, and art sketches spun outside the circle of salt. It thickened, and it became a cloud of metallic gray swirling around the room, bantering against the walls and ceiling. A deep, vibrating moan sent tingling impulses up Raine's spine until the swarm let out a slow, long groan, "AAAAWWWWWWGGG."

"I don't like this…" Eva cried. Her long nails dug into Lucy and Raine's forearms.

"Hang on," Lucy instructed them. She grabbed the Ouija board and tossed it outside the circle, then tossed the planchette too. "Repeat after me… circle of salt, light aglow, make it stop, make it go."

"Circle of salt, light aglow, make it stop, make it go." They repeated until the window opened hard, slamming the frame at the top, and the swarm-thing bounced a couple more times on the wall and ceiling before it flew out the window. The wind stopped, dropping the projectiles to the ground in a shower of confetti. The Ouija board landed in front of Raine and the planchette pointed to "Good Bye". One at a time, the five purple candles relit. The girls gasped with each spontaneous combustion. Their forearms locked, and eyes squeezed tight. Gradually, Raine opened one eye, then the other. They looked around at the debris left behind.

"What the heck was that?" Eva asked.

"I don't know," Lucy said, "but it's pissed."

Chapter Seven

Raine was first to awake the next morning. Golden beams cast shadows across her room, the scattered debris a harsh reminder that the sleepover went a little off track. Whatever happened, no one else in the house must have heard it. The girls cleaned up the mess, sweeping the debris into a pile that now sat on Raine's desk by the window. The Ouija board was put outside the room the night before.

Eva was asleep in the one of the twin beds and Lucy on the chaise by the window where swarm-thing escaped, now closed tight with no sign of it inside or out. There didn't seem to be any other ghost, or spirits, or dead folks lingering. Raine didn't believe swarm-thing was her grandfather. Grandpa Gil was so nice, at least what she remembered of him, and everyone talked about how kind and generous he was. The initials R.S., could be Raymond Sommer, but could also be Raine Sommer, even though her name was Lorraine—she went by Raine for short.

She dressed in her brown and green striped pants with a green turtleneck sweater, then added a brown vest, fringed and frumpy, just like she preferred. Outside the bedroom door, where they'd left the Ouija board, was the painting of trees from the library. The Ouija board was gone. "How odd," Raine whispered to herself.

Raine tiptoed to the bathroom, careful to not wake the others. The smell of bacon and the sound of coffee gurgling were signs that Grandma was up. She washed her face and pulled the mass of curly hair up to a tight bun, secured with wide pins, tucking loose strands behind her ears. Speckles in the cloudy mirror made it difficult to see, but the reflection was so much like her mother's, with reddish hair, unlike her father's sandy hair. In the mirror, she saw a young woman, not a child, and for once, she thought herself pretty, like her mother.

It was eerie to think this mirror had hung in this house for more than a hundred years, and so many women before had gazed at their reflection in the same way. She wondered if they worried about their shape like she did, then she was thankful for the baggy clothes to cover her womanly development. She knew she'd eventually wear a form-fitting blouse like Lucy or a miniskirt like Eva, but for today, an oversized turtleneck and vest would do the trick.

"What if I wore one of Mom's shirts instead?" she mumbled. Goosebumps started on her right leg, moved all the way up the side of her body, into her neck and right arm. Strange, she thought, considering it wasn't too chilly upstairs. There was something lurking that she just couldn't put her finger on, something—or someone—leftover from last night.

She carried the painting down the creaking steps to the library and returned it as quietly as possible. The Ouija board was on the shelf where Lucy found it. Raine shook her head, unable to make sense of how these things moved around. Her father was in the kitchen, which surprised her. She usually needed to wake him.

"There's my girl. Good morning!" David beamed a wide grin her way while buttering toast. Dressed in pajama bottoms and a white tank top, it was clear he hadn't shaved or put a comb through his shaggy hair. The table was covered with plates of bacon, potatoes, biscuits, jelly and more, set for five people. "I'm a little surprised to see you up this early."

"With all the noise they made last night, it's a miracle," Lorraine grumbled. So, Raine mused, they did hear something, but doubtful it was the freight train noise that the girls heard. Lorraine carried a pan of scrambled eggs to the table and grabbed the ketchup from the refrigerator. "You'd better get the girls up. Breakfast will get cold."

"We're up." Eva and Lucy were close behind, still wiping the sleep out of their eyes. Lucy helped herself to a cup of coffee and sat down. "Smells delicious!"

Eva and Raine looked at each other and shrugged, both impressed by how calm Lucy was after poking a stick at poltergeists the night before. They didn't speak much after the indoor tornado flew out the window. Lucy had closed the window and picked up the candles while Raine cleared the floor. Eva put her hair in sponge rollers, apparently in what appeared to be a state of shock that continued this morning. Raine followed Lucy's lead and grabbed a cup of coffee, something she had never done, but today seemed like the perfect day to start drinking coffee.

"And what no-good are you girls up to today?" David flipped through the newspaper without looking up, finally folding it in half, and half again, to the job postings and clicking a pen to circle one of the ads. "Starting the weekend off with any exciting adventures?"

"Not really," Lucy replied. "I thought we'd go into town, maybe go by the apothecary and see if it's open. Mrs. Weismann said they might have some town archives stored in their attic."

"I hear they're remodeling. Planning a grand re-opening in a couple of weeks. I saw an ad in the paper." Lorraine was the last to sit at the table. She spooned jam on a biscuit and poured ketchup on her scrambled eggs. "I remember the Morgan girls when they were little. They'd spend summers with their grandparents."

"A pharmacy," Raine asked, "why are there city archives in a pharmacy?"

"Cypress Grove didn't have a courthouse until the 1920s, so the Hughes' kept records for the town." Lorraine chuckled, every part of her upper torso jiggling as she did. "The counter along the wall on the right was the only place to buy a soda when I was a kid. The Morgan girls are turning it into a gift shop of sorts."

"More than that," Lucy said. "They're going to sell herbal teas and crystals—cool stuff. You'll love it."

"Yeah, they had a lot of different stuff last time I went in," Eva added. "But I have dance class at eleven o'clock and need to babysit this afternoon, so not much adventure for me today."

"How do you know so much about what they're going to do, Lucy?" David folded the paper, recalling what Mack had told him about Lucy. "You've been there?"

"I stopped by a couple weeks ago. I wanted a soda, but ironically, that's the one thing they no longer sell."

"Their grandmother did some of that hocus pocus stuff, you know. Fortune telling and whatnot." Lorraine was finished eating before anyone else got started. She traded her plate for a basket of strawberries and began cutting the stems off with a paring knife, tossing the berries in large pot. "Eva, are you going to the dance camp this summer?"

"Oh, yes." Eva sat straight up. "It's a *Summer Dance Intensive*, and I go for two weeks to New York and study at Juilliard. That's where I want to go to college, you know. It's the best school in the world for dance."

"That sounds like a wonderful experience, Eva." Lorraine knew nothing about dance but seemed happy that Eva was happy.

"I will stay in the dorms and everything, just like real college will be!"

"That's exciting, Eva. How about you, Lucy? Any plans for the summer?"

"Dad wants me to lead riding groups this year. It's good income for the farm, and money is good, so, yeah, I'll probably do that." Lucy shook her head and reached for the jelly. "Go back to the grandmother's hocus pocus, Grandma. What do you mean by that?"

"Oh, it's some things they do for extra money. It's not real, you know, but they'll sell you a rock to protect you while you travel, or they tie a bunch of herbs together to hang on the door and protect the home." Lorraine laughed. "One time, Melinda asked them for something to help her fall in love. They gave her a mirror."

"That's, well, kind of smart, and rather profound," Raine said. "If you can't love who you see in the mirror, you'll never fall in love with someone else."

"Wow, Raine. That's so… insightful," Eva said.

"So, did y'all hear the wind last night?" Lorraine asked. "On a clear night. So strange."

"Um, Grandma," Raine asked, "have you ever… I mean, this house is really old. Have you seen a ghost? Like a real one, not Raymond flickering lights?"

"Like an angry ghost?" Lucy blurted.

"Well, the whole place is strange." Lorraine nodded and sighed, looking up to the right to pull memories from the past. "And it's run down. Looks a lot like a haunted house, but I've not encountered angry ghosts."

"Well, there's a lot of history here." Raine carefully chose her next words. "Have you ever, or do you think it's possible, that a ghost might be here?" Raine watched as Lorraine's shoulders shook, a cackle coming from her throat. "I mean, it's possible. Right?"

Lorraine set the spoon down and turned to Raine, hand on hip and big grin on her face. "Have you seen a ghost, Raine?"

"Why are you laughing? Grandma, I'm serious."

"Oh, I know." Lorraine kept cutting strawberries like this was a normal conversation. "When we lived in the main house, things happened all the time. Doors opened and closed, creaky steps, things moved around. Once, I went to the kitchen and all the cabinet doors were opened and the dishes stacked on countertops. It's one of the reasons we moved in here."

"That's just my grandpa, Raymond," David said. "He's harmless."

"The Hughes' grandmother tried to get him to move on, you know. He's still around, but Adeline felt better. She worried he wasn't at peace."

"Are y'all serious?" Eva's mouth hung open in shock.

Raine thought for a moment. She was sure she'd heard her mother's voice, but maybe it wasn't Caroline. "Who's the woman?"

"A female ghost? I'm not sure." Lorraine thought. "Maybe Adeline? That's Raymond's wife, Eva."

"Wow, so the ghosts are real?" Eva mumbled, letting it all sink in.

After the girls cleared the table and helped wash the dishes, they headed upstairs to gather their things before going into town. Raine was the last up the stairs and stopped when she heard her father and grandmother talking in the kitchen.

"I know it's not ideal, but it's better than nothing, Ma."

"I just don't think you leaving town is going to help anything. It's more important for you to be here, with Raine." Lorraine spoke in a low quiver, barely getting the words out. "We'll get by—I'll pick up shifts at the nursing home, and I'll have at least thirty-six pints of preserves to sell next week."

"Don't worry, Ma. Things always work out, you know that." David's voice was soft and low. "I'll go talk to them at Bridge Cross, maybe pick up some work with them, and we'll figure things out when I get back."

The old oak steps let out a long, creaky moan, and the door to the kitchen quickly closed. Raine was more concerned about the family needing money than she was about the ghosts last night. If they lost the house, ghosts wouldn't matter.

Lucy and Eva dressed, had their backpacks over one shoulder, and were ready to go in five minutes. Raine threw herself across her bed, face down. This was one of those times when she wondered if there was an alternate reality, one where her mother hadn't died, one her dad hadn't been injured fighting for our country, one where her great-great-grandpa hadn't buried treasure but invested in something instead, like the automobile industry or television. She tried so hard to remember what her mother even looked like, then thought about her reflection in the mirror.

"Raine, what's the matter?" Eva asked.

"Nothing," she muttered into the covers. "I'm not feeling so well."

"Yeah, that swarm thing last night kind of makes me nervous being in your room now."

"We need to go talk to the ladies at the apothecary, Raine," said Lucy. "And not for a soda, but we need to tell them what we did last night. I'm sure they'll know how to make sure the swarm-thing is cleared."

"Why would we tell them about our séance?" Eva shook her head. "That's none of their business."

"It's exactly their business. The grandmother there was a spiritualist," Lucy said. Raine and Eva gave blank stares. "She was a fortune teller. A witch."

"No way," Eva said. "I don't believe that."

"Like you don't believe in ghosts?" Lucy crossed her arms. "Well, I don't know anyone in town who might know how to explain what happened last night, and if the old lady's grandkids are running the place now, maybe they can."

"I know." Raine sat up and took a deep breath. She wasn't worried about Raymond—and she knew it wasn't him last night. She felt like swarm-man was family, and although he was a ghost and reckless, it might be that he was finally free. Maybe he'd been locked up like a genie in a bottle and finally someone uncorked him. But he wasn't a genie. He was a lost soul.

"Do you have cramps?"

"No, that's not for another two weeks."

"Do you need some Pepto-Bismo?" Lucy asked.

"No, I'll be fine."

The girls were heading out when Raine saw her grandmother standing at the stove stirring a large pot. Lorraine wasn't very tall and had to crane her neck to see what she was cooking. Dressed in baggy, cropped pants and a short-sleeved top, Raine could see wrinkles, sagging skin, and sunspots from years of farm life. She looked older than her sixty-plus years, probably from garden work and too much sun. Raine told Lucy she'd catch up with them and she went over and put her arm around Lorraine.

"Thank you for fixing us breakfast. It was over-the-top delicious!" She peeked at the brewing concoction and asked, "What's that?"

"Strawberry jam." Lorraine added sugar to the pot and turned to Raine. "And you're welcome."

"I'll be home after we find enough information for the report," Raine said with effort, to make it sound casual.

"Do you need shopping money?"

"No, thank you." Raine had money hidden in a box under her bed, but she didn't want to spend any money. There was nothing that she needed.

"It's no fun to shop without money." Lorraine smiled. She dried her hands and reached for a jar behind the cereal in the pantry. She pulled out a five-dollar bill and pushed it into Raine's hand, folding her fingers around it. "Take it. If you don't spend it on yourself, buy something for your dad. His birthday is coming up, you know."

"I almost forgot it was his birthday soon. Thank you." Raine shoved it in her pocket with premature regret. She eyed dozens of jars on the kitchen counter, ready for the jam. "Where will you sell those?"

"The jam? Well, I sell them at the church's market. Gives us a little extra cash around here."

"That's nice." Raine had never paid much attention how jelly or jam was made, but she knew her grandmother made it every year. She supposed she just didn't care before now—before knowing how badly they needed cash. "Hey, Grandma?"

"Yes, sweetie?"

Raine was going to ask her how she could help, if she could earn some money with Aunt Petra at the florists', or babysitting for the Wickham family, but she heard Eva call from outside. So instead of offering to help, instead of letting her grandmother know she knew about the money problems, Raine said, "I'd better go. Thanks again, Grandma."

Giant elm trees arched over the long drive and oaks stood along the street. Looking back, Raine saw the dilapidated plantation. She easily imagined what this place was like a hundred years ago after the war, maybe two hundred years ago, when it was built as a homestead cabin. Now, the overgrown bushes hid the shutters, hung askew with missing louvers and peeling blue paint. Raine inhaled deeply and noticed a faint floral scent of lilac coming into bloom.

The house has really been neglected over the years. Cypress Hill was too large and too much for Lorraine and Gilbert Sommer to maintain. David had joined the military the year before Gil had his first heart attack, and that was when Gil decided to close the main section of the house, moving himself and Lorraine into the north wing.

"Ah, what is that? Love that smell," said Eva.

"Serviceberry trees," said Lucy. "Maybe the lilac too."

They cut across the front yard, through an archway and down a few stone steps. Tall evergreens formed a fence around three sides, with rose bushes growing up a trellis on the gazebo, also in need of repairs. Behind another row of tall evergreens, down two more stone steps, and past two large oak trees was the cemetery, surrounded by a limestone fence and an iron gate.

"Look, Colonel Adalbert Sommer was the first Sommer buried here, 1910," said Lucy. "Raymond, our great-grandfather, and his brother, Henry, are buried over there next to their wives and, aw, a baby just three months old…"

"Grandpa is over here." Raine stood near the newer headstones along the fence. Gilbert Ulysses Sommer, and Caroline Adele Sommer. "No Franz Sommer inside the stone fence?"

"No, he isn't here. Huh, I'd never noticed that before."

Raine looked back towards the house before they headed down the hill. It was barely visible through the trees.

"Hey, we should go riding today, Raine. Eva, you too."

"Ride horses? Oh, not today. I'm busy." Eva was not comfortable around horses. It wasn't that she was afraid of them, but she just didn't have much experience riding. Lucy's mother, Maggie, and her husband, Bryce, ran a stable near the front of the park. Lucy grew up around horses. Her father was a farrier, as was his father before him, and David had been learning the trade as well. They know horses. Eva did not.

"We have the perfect horse for you to ride." Lucy bounced, her pigtails catching the wind. "She's a seventeen-year-old mare, a retired police horse, and such a gentle creature. Her name… is Diamond."

"Aww, I love Diamond!" Raine smiled so wide that her face hurt, although she wasn't sure why mentioning a horse she'd known for years would make her smile so much. "Eva, you'll love Diamond."

"Okay, I do love diamonds. That sounds like a horse I might ride, but not today. I have dance, then I babysit.

Remember?" Eva looked at her watch and said, "Oh no, we gotta go."

There was a path from the rose garden to a wooden bridge crossing Cypress Creek, and from there, they crossed Cypress Road. Then there was a sidewalk to a subdivision where Eva lived, Millstone Place. Eva waved to her mother standing outside a white two-story with pale green shutters and a perfectly manicured lawn. It was like the bridge took them from the eighteenth century to present day.

"Think about how this used to be part of Cypress Hill," Lucy said, and she put her finger to her chin as she thought about it.

"Yeah, the farm was a lot bigger when it was a working plantation."

"It was huge, like back in the day when Adalbert Sommer lived here, but every generation has sold off pieces of the farm. And the spring, where it comes up, I think there were cottages along the creek for slaves."

"I don't think there were slaves here," Raine said, almost defensively.

"I hope we find out, one way or the other."

"Yeah, me too," Eva said. "They could have been my relatives."

"Ironic that the place where slaves lived is now a fancy subdivision."

"We don't know if slaves lived here, guys. We don't know if this was part of the underground railroad, and we don't even know for certain it was used as a military hospital." Raine wasn't sure she wanted to know the truth. How would she feel if her family, the colonel, was one of the abusive slave owners, or what if he kept his slaves in shackles? Yes, it was long ago, but it was her bloodline.

"The stories of the military hospital had to come from somewhere. Most likely, there is at least some truth to it." Although Lucy had the same ancestors, the possibility of the colonel being a Confederate soldier with slaves didn't seem to faze her.

"I hope they can sell more of the farm." Based on the conversation this morning, her dad and grandma would be selling more land. It was how they'd gotten by for years, because farming wasn't a very lucrative business. Not anymore. The more land they had, the more work there was for her dad to do. "It's not like I'm going to be a farmer. Who else would want it?"

"Not my parents. Mom and Dad got all they need—just enough to keep horses and grow hay and corn for them." Lucy rolled her eyes. "I'm hoping they don't expect me to take over someday."

"You still want to be a mad scientist, Lucy?" Eva asked.

"Yeah, something like that." Lucy's eyes widened. Maybe, just maybe. "Raine, do you remember seeing a map in the library? An old one of the farms?"

"I think Sam found some maps. He left them in the desk drawer, but let's first see what's at the apothecary first."

"Then let's go!"

Chapter Eight

"Ready for tea?" Sorcha's voice, warm and inviting, carried a gentle melody as she gracefully placed a tray on the table. Positioned between two sumptuously cushioned chairs near the crackling fireplace, the area at the back of the apothecary was one of comfort and intimacy. The clink of porcelain resonated as Sorcha arranged a teapot, flanked by two delicate cups, each with tiny, pink rose patterns. A matching plate held freshly baked scones from Paula's bakery, the scent of butter wafting through the air, promising a delightful pairing with the tea. Sorcha's thoughtful gesture conveyed a sense of exclusivity that this morning was reserved for sisters.

"Tea just like Grandmama made," Ashlyne sighed. "I miss her."

"I do too." Sorcha poured steaming tea, both inhaling the fragrance. "Orange, cardamom, and black tea."

"Perfect for today. Sweet and spicy."

The girls talked of changes to the apothecary. The constant flow of deliveries now on shelves, the new sign hanging out front, and the fresh coat of paint Michael put on the front had transformed the space from a bare-shelved pharmacy to an interesting shopping adventure. Grandmama's remedies were packaged like upscale cosmetics, each branded with the Sage Sister's logo, the history of the treatment printed on the label. Ashlyne hoped this would avoid any suggestion it was a potion or magical cure, but rather a natural remedy with ancient roots.

"Shall I read your leaves?"

"Of course." Ashlyne couldn't read leaves like Sorcha, and at times, she wondered if Sorcha knew how to read them, or if she improvised. Grandmama, however, always seemed to get it right.

"A bird, long neck, maybe goose? Near the rim, I'd say a good encounter is approaching."

The bell rang and three young girls came in, standing shoulder to shoulder, wide-eyed and awkward. One, quite pale with hair so blonde, it was almost white, one, covered in freckles with reddish-brown braids, and one, dark-skinned with short, curly hair.

"Well, that was fast." Sometimes Sorcha impressed herself, but she knew her grandmother was always guiding her when reading leaves.

"Hi." Ashlyne walked towards them. She wore a simple long skirt today, with a belled-sleeve paisley shirt that fluttered as she walked. "How can I help you ladies?"

The three girls looked at each other, then the freckled girl elbowed the blonde.

"Um, hi." Lucy straightened her spine with courage. "We need help with a ghost at home. We want to banish him."

"I'm not sure how I could help with a ghost," Ashlyne replied, her tone cool and nonchalant.

"Well, I've heard the lady who used to run this place would know how to help and that you are her granddaughters."

"Many thought my grandmama could help with any concern, but my sister and I are not like her." Ashlyne focused on each young girl, picked up on their vibe, and understood what was happening. Maybe she was a little more like her dear grandmama than she admitted. "Are you certain there's a ghost in your house?"

"Oh yes, he's a relative," Raine replied matter-of-factly. "He flickers the lights and opens cabinet doors, and well…"

"We summoned him." Lucy smiled.

"You summoned him? But you said you wanted to get rid of him."

"We weren't expecting him to be… so… physical."

"Physical?" Sorcha set her teacup down and joined Ashlyne, arms crossed.

"Yeah, like blowing around, knocking stuff over."

"He made a mess out of my room," Raine said. "My dad and grandma have encountered him before, and we were thinking we'd ask him a few questions with the Ouija board, and—"

"You used a Ouija board?" Sorcha and Ashlyne said in unison.

"Where did you get a Ouija board?" Ashlyne asked.

"We found it in the library when we were researching for our school project," Lucy said. "I think it might have been used before, maybe by our grandmother. Do you know Lorraine Sommer?"

"No, I don't believe I've met her," Ashlyne said. Yes, she knew who Lorraine Sommer was—David's mother. She looked at Sorcha, who was shaking her head. Ashlyne turned to Raine, and then she saw it—she saw him. "You must be David Sommer's daughter."

"Yes," Raine said, not sure if this would be a good thing or not, considering her father's reputation around town. He hadn't always been a drunk, and Raine hoped this woman knew the man he was before their world fell apart. "I'm Raine."

"And this ghost is at Cypress Hill?"

"Yes." Raine pleaded, "Can you help?"

"Are you witches?" Eva finally spoke.

"Do we look like witches?" Sorcha smiled when Eva nervously shook her head. "And who are you?"

"I'm Eva. No… you don't look like a witch, but can you do stuff?" She giggled. "Like your grandmother?"

"Eva, I don't think we're supposed to ask that," Lucy whispered.

"Maybe what you mean to ask is will we help you, like a mentor of sorts." Sorcha nudged Ashlyne, recalling the reading earlier where she saw Ashlyne as a mentor. "Why did you summon a ghost in the first place?"

"We have a class project on the civil war and so we thought talking to the… people who were there would be easiest way to get accurate information," Lucy said, chin high. "Our great-great-great-grandfather was a colonel."

"But instead, we got Raymond. And Raine's mom." Eva nudged Raine.

"Your mother is a ghost?" Sorcha asked.

Ashlyne tilted her head, pondering that statement. David was a widower, which explained so much to her, and Raine, all of them, had more than one reason to want to communicate with the deceased relatives. Lucy seemed to want information. Raine, to speak with her departed mother, and Eva, Ashlyne couldn't get a read on her. She had built a wall around her heart, a wall of glitter and showmanship.

"Yes, she died a few years ago."

"Is the necklace you're wearing something of hers?" Ashlyne grasped her own necklace, the one from her grandmother. The chains they wore were different, but the crescent moon pendants were identical.

"Yes." Raine grabbed her own crescent moon necklace, not realizing it was outside her shirt.

"It's beautiful." Ashlyne didn't intend to, but her empath abilities kicked in, picking up on what Raine was feeling now. Grief. Sadness. Loss. "This project you're working on, it's about the Civil War?"

"If we can prove Cypress Hill was used as a hospital during the Civil War, or if it was part of the underground railroad, if we can find proof of that," Lucy added, "we'd have the best project ever. But strange things happen in the house."

"It's haunted," Eva said. "I don't want to go in there, especially to the old sections. Even though the ballroom is amazing."

"I think if it's really haunted, and the ghost is our great-grandfather, then he could help with our project."

"So, you need our help with the project, not the ghost?" Ashlyne said, turning to her sister. "Sorcha, do you still have those old newspapers and boxes to go through upstairs? The ones to take to city hall?"

"Oh, sure." Sorcha didn't confirm or deny she was a witch but didn't want to use magic to help the girls. They needed to do this on their own. "We can't help with the ghost, but you can look around upstairs for papers and documents."

"Yes, we could help with the project," Ashlyne added. "I recall seeing some of the original township records. This is one of the oldest buildings in town and they were stored here years ago, before the courthouse was built."

"Okay, I thought that talking to ghosts was part of the fortune telling thing you do." Lucy was sure they could help with ghosts but didn't want to ask again.

"I entertain some of the women with tarot cards, you know, but that is something anyone can do," Sorcha said bluntly, waving her hands in the air. "Buy a deck of cards and read a book, then you're in business."

Sorcha and Ashlyne knew that wasn't true. Sorcha also knew Ashlyne and Michael did not want their grandmama's reputation as an occultist to follow him into his medical practice or Ashlyne's teaching career, but what could she do? They were who they were. Due to the spiritual movement at the turn of the century, reading cards and fortune telling was like being a magician. Someone you could hire for entertainment. Sure, there were some regulars who depended on her turning cards, but Sorcha saw them more as her patients, and the cards were part of a therapy they needed to deal with life situations.

"So, you're not witches?"

"We're just wise women." Sorcha shifted her eyes and whispered, "But don't tell anyone it isn't real, okay? I must earn a living somehow."

"Would you girls like to look through the boxes upstairs?" Ashlyne asked, redirecting them from the question about witches.

"Yes, please," Raine said, then, getting back on topic, "what do you recommend we do about the ghosts?"

"Ghosts, as in more than one? Have you seen them?"

"No, not really. Just the one time, like we saw the wind swirling in my room."

"And the noises. They stopped once it flew out the window." Lucy bit her bottom lip, Raine sighed, and Eva was distracted by something shiny hanging near the window. This kind of blew a hole in Lucy's plan, because finding out the truth about Cypress Hill might be more difficult than she anticipated. "Things happen in the old section of the house. We hear doors close, and Raine's heard things, right, Raine?"

"That could have been wind in my room, a weird indoor wind. And the noises I hear, just a creaky old house," said Raine.

"Wind inside the house?" Lucy asked. "What about when the window opened and closed on its own?"

Raine shrugged, not sure how to explain that. Or the noises she heard at night, like squeaky hinges and floorboards. Laughing. The smell of cigars and a flowery perfume. "So, if we did have a ghost, what would you recommend?"

"Depends on the type of ghost." Ashlyne thought carefully, knowing whatever she told them would come back around. It always did. If she said anything the slightest bit off from the small-town mindset, the girls tell their parents, the parents tell one of the teachers, and from then on, Ashlyne would be the last substitute the school called. "If it's a friendly ghost, I would talk to them like I would anyone else. Like an angel, or how you ask St. Anthony to help when you've lost something."

"We just talk to them. Like no incantation or spell to use?" Lucy felt a little disappointed. Surely, there was more to it than talking.

Ashlyne remained tight-lipped and shook her head. Sorcha smiled.

"What's an incantation, anyway." Sorcha wasn't asking as a question. She walked towards the stairs, hands flittering in the air, long hair waving, and loose top flowing behind her. "Doesn't the priest at church repeat the same phrases every Sunday? And don't his words change bread and wine into the body and blood of Christ?"

"Yeah…" Eva thought carefully. "But not literally. It's still just cracker and grape juice."

"Exactly, but the words the priest says are like an abra-cadabra for everyone at church."

Lucy rolled her eyes at Eva. "The church is just a reinvention of pagan rituals."

"That's right," Sorcha added. "Isn't that right, Ashlyne? You teach history."

"I do teach history, but I'm not an expert on Catholicism." Everyone, even Sorcha, waited for Ashlyne to continue. With a deep breath, she added, "If you're going to talk to a ghost, I suppose you should say something beforehand. Like a prayer, asking for good spirits, and for angels to protect you."

"We don't even know if Cypress Hill is haunted," said Raine.

"It's haunted," Eva and Lucy chimed.

Raine suspected it was too, but this was her home. It was bad enough the place looked like a haunted house, but she didn't want to be known as the weird girl who lived in the big, haunted house on the hill—or worse, a big, haunted house on the hill that once had slaves. "What if it isn't a friendly ghost? What if they're angry?"

"If I were you, I would leave them alone." Ashlyne spoke the truth. These girls were not familiar with banishing ghosts, and it could be tricky. "How about we go upstairs and look around first, then talk to ghosts as a last resort."

"Aw, where's the fun in that?" Lucy smiled.

"Thank you for your help," Raine said as the girls headed up the narrow stairs in the back of the store.

They went through boxes of city records, newspapers, photos, and other things dating back to when the city was founded. Sam joined them after school, and every day that week, they searched, eventually gathering enough to begin putting together a report.

***

On Friday, the last day of March, Ashlyne walked with the group of high schoolers to the corner of the farm and Millstone subdivision at 6:00 when the shop closed, as had become the norm. Raine would go through the stone gate and up the hill while Sam, Eva and Lucy walked down the sidewalks, Eva and Sam to Millstone neighborhood and Lucy to her family farm.

Ashlyne walked back to the shop alone, careful to step into the grass along the road as a car passed. There were only two places open after six in this town—the pizza parlor and Mack's

Pub. She spotted two familiar forms coming out from the side of the apothecary and called out for Sorcha and Michael to wait for her.

"Pizza, or pub food tonight?"

"I vote for burgers. Manly food…" Michael beat his thin chest and coughed twice. He'd always been skinny, no matter how much he ate, and he ate a lot. He was in his thirties now and still waiting to fill-out, as their father called it.

Mack's not only served hearty pub foods but was the only place in town for locals to hang out, shoot pool, throw darts, and get drunk. It was smoky and dimly lit, reeked of cigarettes, beer and fried foods, and the juke box in the back was playing Guess Who's *These Eyes*. There was a family with kids sitting at the front booth, an older couple next to them, a few guys playing billiards, and a couple dancing next to an empty stage set up for the band to play later. One man sat at the bar, cigarette in one hand, beer in the other. David Sommer.

All eyes were on the girls at that moment. Cloaked in flowing, dark fabric that seemed to dance with unseen energies, they both defied convention with their eclectic wardrobe, jewelry adorned with symbols of the supernatural and cosmic motifs.

"Let's sit back here," Sorcha said and led her siblings to a table in the middle, close to the stage. "I wonder who the band is tonight."

"Noctis Kiss starts making noise in about an hour." A woman in jeans and tank top met them at the table. Her voice was raspy from years of smoking, skin was tan and leathery from sun exposure, and her smile genuine, but her eyes were tired in a way that said she never imagined being where she was today. "I'm Annie. What can I get ya to drink?"

"We'll get a pitcher of whatever you have on tap," Michael said. "And I already know what I want to eat."

"I haven't seen you here before, Annie," said Sorcha. "Are you new?"

"Yes, and no. I worked here a few years back, but I quit before I got married. Just moved back in with my mom, so now

I'm working here again." She rolled her eyes and looked away, holding back the tears. "Guess marriage isn't for me."

"That sounds like some adventure you've been on," Ashlyne said.

"That's one way to say it. I'm getting divorced, needed a place to stay, and Mom's getting older, so it works out. We're helping each other."

"How sweet," Sorcha said. "That's what family is for, right, guys?"

"Yes. We're siblings, Annie. Family is everything to us."

"Right now, dinner is everything, so can we order?" Michael said sternly, then laughed. "I'm starving!"

"Oh, you're always hungry," Sorcha mocked.

"Alrighty, what'll it be?" Annie rested a tray on her hip and wrote down the order, giving Michael a wink.

Michael ordered a cheeseburger and fries, Sorcha, a grilled cheese with a cup of vegetable soup, and Ashlyne, a fish sandwich on rye with slaw. While Annie gave the cook the order, Sorcha went to the juke box. Walking back, she brushed against Annie, now taking another order, as CCR played *I Put a Spell on You*. Her hand lingered across her shoulders, Sorcha briefly closing her eyes as she passed.

"I saw that," said Ashlyne.

"She needed it."

Ashlyne talked about the girls' history project while Michael talked about the cabin he recently purchased, currently turning soil for a small vegetable garden. "Y'all need to come up and see it. It's pretty rough but has potential."

"We should go up this weekend. Neither of us have seen the lakes."

"Yes, we have. Grandpa took us when we were little."

"He did? Why don't I remember this?"

"You were so little, Ashlyne, probably why you don't remember."

A group of five came in and started setting up the stage. The last man, carrying a guitar case, got Ashlyne's attention, and not in a good way. When he passed by, every hair on her body stood up. He was tall, clean-cut hair and freshly shaved, wearing jeans and a black t-shirt. His teeth were gleaming, and his eyes sparkled a pale blue. She couldn't hold back a grin, and he gave her a wink.

"Do you know him?" Sorcha asked.

"Not yet." She wasn't sure if it was attraction she felt, or something else. She suddenly lost her appetite, her mouth went dry, and she found it difficult to take a deep breath. Anxiety and excitement had the same feelings sometimes. "Not sure I want to know him."

"The band's name is Noctis Kiss." Sorcha's face pleaded for her sister to be careful. "That is a very vampirish name. Be careful, Ashlyne."

After their bellies were full, Michael and Sorcha played darts while Ashlyne watched from the table. Ashlyne hadn't been able to eat. The handsome guitarist approached her, sitting in the chair closest to her. He introduced himself as Liam Baker, and he was a charmer. It didn't take Ashlyne long to see that Liam was the most important and fabulous thing in Liam's life. It was a full ten minutes before he asked for her name. He belittled his fellow band members, bragged about his family's money, and then he took it to a new level.

"Man, do you see that bum sitting at the bar? He used to be the hotshot in town. Captain of the football team, married the prom queen, lived in the biggest house. He had it all, and somehow, he managed to throw it all away."

"How did he do that?" Ashlyne sipped a glass of water, more interested in the man at the bar than the band member at her table.

"He was set for college but joined the army instead. What a fool. Then he got roped into a marriage and it all fell apart—all he does now is drink."

"I'm sure there is more to the story."

"Nah, he's just a loser. A drunk." Liam moved closer and put his hand on Ashlyne's knee. Call it kinetics, instinct, or shock, but the contact caused her to jump and abruptly take refuge behind the chair. "Hey, calm down, missy."

"I'm perfectly calm. And my name is *not* Missy." She joined Sorcha and Michael, then Liam left the table and went back to set up mics on stage.

David watched as this played out. Liam glared at David, staring long enough for the burly bartender to step out from behind the counter and distract Liam, asking him questions about the stage set-up. David's aura turned a deep red, something Ashlyne noticed. There was history there. Whatever was between those two men, Ashlyne could feel it in her bones.

It was only 8:45, but she'd had enough of the bar side of Mack's. Besides, Paula was watching Kayleigh. While she never minded watching her while the Morgan siblings went out for dinner, it was getting late, and Paula started her days early at the bakery.

When the band began to play, Ashlyne noticed David was no longer at the bar. She scanned the pub, looking for him, and felt a pang of loss that he had left. With Liam on stage, Ashlyne put on her jacket and told her sister she was walking home. They started playing their rendition of *Help*, which sounded nothing like the Beatles' version.

> *Help me if you can, I'm feeling down,*
> *And I do appreciate you being 'round,*
> *Help me get my feet back on the ground,*
> *Won't you please, please help me...*

That's what David Sommer needs, she thought, *a little help.*

Stepping outdoors, she noticed the air carried a sharp coolness, tinged with the invigorating scent of fresh rain. A delicate mist descended, and she tilted her face skyward, relishing the first droplets. Crossing the quad, she reached the fountain, where she paused to toss in three pennies. Each coin bore a wish: one for David to recognize his significance, one for his family's fortune, and one for the girls to find the essentials for their project. With closed eyes, she uttered thanks to the sky for the anticipated assistance before making her way to the shop. She heard approaching footsteps from behind and turned around.

"Hey, where are you running off to?" Liam stood too close, causing Ashlyne to back up towards the fountain.

"I'm not running anywhere. I'm going home."

"I was just getting to know you." Liam grabbed her elbow and she pulled away. "Let's go back to the pub, find a private area to talk."

"No, you weren't getting to know me at all. You were telling me all about *you*, about how great you think you are."

"I thought we hit it off; come on, baby…" He moved in fast and had his arm around her waist, pulling her close.

"Back off, asshole!" She pushed, but he wrapped both arms around her and pressed his hips against her. Then, his eyes widened, and he quickly let go, stepping back. Someone else was at the fountain.

"Hey, no problem here, Stumpy. Just mind your business, go find a beer to suck on someplace else." The words rolled off Liam's tongue like acid, burning as they landed a verbal slap in the face. Liam grabbed Ashlyne by the arm and pulled her towards him. "Me and the lady are leaving."

"No, *you're* leaving." Ashlyne couldn't see who stood in the shadow of the fountain, but she suspected she knew. She felt safe and protected with his energy. When he stepped into the light, David looked like a different man than the one sitting at the bar minutes ago. He looked strong, confident, and above all, calm. She let out a gasp of relief and smiled at him.

"What, you think that drunk is going to protect you?" Liam huffed a laugh. "That lousy son-of-a—"

David's fist stopped him from finishing that thought. One punch, Liam was down, and David didn't say a word. He didn't move, other than a slight twist at the waist and the extension of his arm in a quick, precise movement. Ashlyne didn't know if he was so relaxed because of the beer he'd consumed, or if he was naturally well-composed, but in that moment, he reminded her of a highly trained martial artist she'd met in California. He motioned towards her shop, and he walked behind her, in silence.

While Liam's energy didn't show itself until he'd physically touched her knee in the bar, Ashlyne felt David's presence ten feet behind. She watched as he turned, making sure Liam was still down and that he didn't see where she was going. Knowing to avoid the front of the store, she led David around back, entering through the side door between the shop and the doctor's office. Fumbling with the key, she unlocked the deadbolt. David paused outside, looking toward the fountain, where Liam was sitting up, holding his head.

"Come in, please," she whispered.

He glanced at her, then turned back to the fountain where Liam was getting up. David stepped inside with Ashlyne. The shop was dark, other than a few dim lights around the wall of jars filled with teas and flowers. He slid on the end stool and watched as she lit a candle on the counter between them.

Chapter Nine

There aren't many days that David woke without a headache. On this Saturday, however, with the sun shining through his bedroom window and the smell of coffee from the kitchen, he felt better than he'd felt in years. His fist was a little sore, and the events of last night played back in a flash. He hadn't been in the mood to drink, so after one beer, he'd left to sit at the fountain and think. He heard Liam's slimy voice, then a woman saying to back off. One punch, that was it. That punch he'd waited nearly twenty years to give, since high school.

The biggest surprise was Ashlyne inviting him inside her shop and upstairs to her apartment, where they couldn't be seen from the store windows. He wasn't surprised that he accepted her invitation. Something about her, even as a child, was special. The way she smiled. The mystery that surrounded her and the family.

David made his way to the kitchen and poured himself a cup of coffee. Strong, black, and sturdy coffee, such contrast to the herbal tea last night with Ashlyne. She made it while he watched, a pinch of this tea, some of that flower, a splash of this and that from bottles. It was a fuzzy memory, in the dimly lit kitchen on the second floor with dark wood shelves filled with corked bottles and elixirs. He wasn't sure how it would taste, as she named each ingredient in sort of a rhythmic recipe, vowing that this tea would change his life. *Right,* he thought, *a life-changing tea.* It wasn't particularly flavorful, but he willingly drank every drop.

Morning chores were done before his mother had breakfast on the table, something that hadn't happened for a long, long time. Even the hens were confused, having the coop doors opened before nine in the morning. The horses had been set out, the stalls cleaned, and David opened the calf barn too. They hadn't had cows for a while, but he was considering getting a few to raise this year. That would be income for next year when they sold, he thought.

"You're up early," Lorraine said, turning the page of the newspaper.

"You're not working this weekend?" he asked.

"Nope, and I have a meeting with Ned on the Tuesday after next."

David knew what that meant—loan negotiation. "Want me to come along?"

"Ned said you needed to be there, in case there were papers to sign." She folded the paper and sighed. "When your father split the property into parcels, I think he knew it would come to this— selling off each piece as we needed to."

"Which part now?"

"The loan was originally $10,000, so to pay it off, we'd have to sell the field near the mill, and possibly a developer would buy it. Rather have another subdivision than more debt."

"People want cheap homes here, send their kids to our school, but shop and work in the larger towns nearby. We just can't do that to Cypress Grove." David looked down at the worn kitchen floor, hands on hips. He felt… good. His mind felt clear today. "How much do we need to catch up on payments?"

"More than we have, even counting the coffee tin in my closet."

"How much?"

"We need $800 to catch up, about $4000 to pay it off."

"Yeah, well, I'll see what I can do." He sipped his coffee and exhaled the breath he didn't know he was holding. "I will figure something out."

Lorraine looked at her son, not sure if he was serious. He'd been made executor of the estate, and on paper, he was the primary, but she'd always dealt with banks. He dealt with grief with a bottle, so she'd not expected him to want to participate. "So you're going to the bank with me? Maybe if you get cleaned up. Shave. Put on a clean shirt."

David held his hands up and looked down, then ran a hand across his chin. "Fine. A week from Tuesday. We'll go to the bank."

An hour later, David came down the steps, this time to see Raine and his mother staring at him, chins dropped. He'd shaved for the first time in months, leaving smooth cheeks and chin, and he'd combed his hair back. It was still wet, and it was long, with curls resting on a blue-collared shirt. Clean jeans and boots below. "What?"

"Wow, Dad…"

"You look nice, David." Lorraine smiled. "Is this April Fool's Day, or what?"

"It is! April Fools!" Raine had forgotten it was the first day of April.

"Whatever." He smiled, knowing it was a huge improvement. He felt good for the first time in quite a while, and within his veins, he felt a tinge of motivation to take care of things. To take care of business. "I'm going with you on Tuesday. Today, I have something to do."

David drove into town and parked by Mack's Pub. From where he sat, he saw the back of the apothecary. He saw the door he entered the night before with Ashlyne. It wasn't a hard decision to walk past Mack's, cross the street, and head over to see her. He needed to know she was okay.

He noticed Sorcha going in the front door of the apothecary with the little girl. Was that Sorcha's daughter, or Ashlyne's? He felt the urge to walk over, stop in, just to say hello. They'd changed the front, painted it green, and a new sign hung above the door, *Sage Sisters*. He didn't notice this last night. A hippie gift shop, like Mack told him they would do. The bell chimed when he entered.

"Hello," Sorcha said, holding a sleepy, red-headed little girl. "Can I help you?"

"Um…" David didn't know what to say. He wasn't sure why he was there, and looking around at the store, he realized it was completely different. The floors had been refinished, the wooden shelves restocked, and the lighting updated. No more noisy fluorescent bulbs. "Y'all've done a lot in here."

"We've made some changes. Is there something you are looking for?" *Or someone,* Sorcha thought, and the edges of her lips curled up, realizing why this man was standing in her store.

Kayleigh whimpered, right on cue. "I'm sorry, if you'll excuse me, I need to get my daughter down for her nap. My sister should be out in a moment."

David nodded, then removed his hat from his head, nervously feeling the edge of the brim. He could smell coffee and gravitated towards the counter. One of the shelving units he passed was full of candy—some made locally, like honey chews made in Mayfield, and caramels from Nashville, and some from farther away, like New Orleans pralines and Jersey saltwater taffy. He picked up the box of taffy and turned it over to look at where they were made, the ingredients, the price.

"There's no salt water in the saltwater taffy, if that's what you are wondering," Ashlyne said. She wore a tunic dress cut just above her knees, in dark-red crushed velvet, and black boots. Strands of long, lustrous hair framed her face, cascading like a waterfall of obsidian waves. David couldn't help but to stare and take it all in. She was truly stunning. "I was hoping to see you today."

"You were?"

"Yes, to properly thank you for coming to my rescue last night."

"Oh, yeah, that. It was nothing, really." The room started to spin, his body swaying to keep balance. Was that last night that he'd punched Liam? He squeezed his right hand and felt the soreness from the impact on Liam's face. It seemed like a dream—the bar, the fountain, the tea Ashlyne made him.

"The guy is an asshole. I don't want to think of what could have happened had you not been there."

"Yeah, he's an ass all right."

"I take it you two have history?" Of course, they did. Last night, before she made his tea, she intuitively connected to him. It was something she did for any customer requesting a custom tea blend because it helped her create a little magic in their tea, but in his case, she did it out of curiosity. There was an attraction, something she couldn't understand and couldn't describe. Something more than his looks, although he was extremely handsome, in a rugged, country boy kind of way. He was an old soul, and it was that part she connected with the most. It was like they'd known each other before.

"Unfortunately." David struggled to keep eye contact with the woman. It was like she could look right through him, that she could see how he felt. She could see the true David, and he didn't want anyone to see that part of him right now. Not the drunk, broke, loser that he had been lately. He hadn't always been that way, but he wasn't sure she would see that.

"Would you like some coffee?"

"Sure, thank you." David sat on a swivel stool, setting his hat on the one next to him. "I actually stopped by to check on you, to see how you are doing after last night."

"That's very sweet of you. I'm good. Hopefully, we won't see that man around here again. What is his name?"

"Liam Baker. I went to high school with him."

"I see." Ashlyne clearly saw the conflict between them. She set a cup of steaming coffee in front of him. He'd shaved and worn a dress shirt. It was like he was a different man today. She smiled, wondering if the tea would have such a dramatic effect on someone in such a short time, but she supposed if it was a change he truly needed, then it was meant to be.

Trying to think of something to say, something to talk about, he said, "There's an Easter egg hunt tomorrow after church. In case that little girl would want to go."

"Kayleigh? Yes, I'll let Sorcha know. It would be fun for her."

"Do you go, I mean, to church?"

"My brother does, and I usually go with him. I see your mother and daughter when I go, but I haven't seen you there that I can remember."

"It's been a while." He sipped the coffee, not sure how to explain his absence, or if he needed to explain anything. "There are always chores on the farm."

"I understand. What do you have on the farm? Horses? Cattle?"

"A couple mares. My wife used to ride, but lately, only Raine and Lucy take them out. Maggie sometimes borrows them if they have a large tour planned."

"Horseback tours in the park?"

"Yes, through part of our farm, mostly in the park, along the river. There's a view of the lake. City folk can't ride that long, so walking a horse on trails for an hour or two doesn't take you far."

"Some of the trails are quite rugged. Can you imagine how long it would take people here a hundred years ago to ride trails into Nashville, or Mayfield?" Ashlyne smiled. "Things have changed so much in such a short time."

"Things used to be so simple."

"I couldn't agree more," Ashlyne rested her elbows on the counter, leaning over closer to David. She locked her fingers under her chin, her eyes looking around the store. "When this place was built, they used hand-cut beams and wood milled a mile away. It was a time when I'd like to have lived."

"Me too. You would love Cypress Hill." David held her gaze for longer than he'd done before and was mesmerized. They talked about everything from the history of Cypress Hill, the city archives in the attic, and how the kids hadn't given up the search for a link to the Civil War in the records. David left feeling like he had a new friend, a beautiful one, but a friend with whom he had much in common. They'd connected.

***

Lorraine, Raine, and David dressed in their Easter best for Sunday morning services. Lorraine wore light blue slacks and a flowered top, Raine wore a lavender dress from Aunt Melinda's granddaughter, her second cousin, and for once, she didn't mind wearing a form-fitting dress. It had short sleeves with a square neckline, gathered under her breasts for a flattering A-line. She really liked what she saw in the mirror that morning.

David wore his father's dark blue suit and striped tie. He hadn't worn a suit since Caroline's funeral, and while the suit was not fashionable and slightly baggy, it was classic in style. He'd combed his hair back, shaved, and dabbed a little cologne on his neck. He paused at the top of the steps of church, turning to scan the crowd coming up from the parking lot. Mrs. Weismann looked at him and smiled, as did several others. He'd missed Christmas mass and his second cousin's wedding. In fact, he wasn't sure when he was last at church services. Smiling, he realized it took someone special to get him back.

"Are you looking for someone?" Lorraine asked.

"Uh, yes, Ma. I am."

"Come on, Gamma." Maggie's son, Ben, took Lorraine's hand and pulled. "We go to church. Now!"

David gave her a half smile, and Lorraine didn't need to know more. She was elated that her son had met someone. Although he hadn't talked about it, she knew the Morgans' youngest child had caught his eye. The way he cleaned up yesterday, the way he dressed today, and she hadn't seen him smoke a cigarette for several days now. It had to be Ashlyne.

"Okay. We'll save you a seat.

"Hey, hey, David." Uncle Ed slowly made his way up the steps, holding the center railing with both hands. "Why don't eggs tell jokes?"

"Hello, Uncle Ed." David extended his hand for a shake, helping the elderly man up the last of the steps. "I don't know. Why don't eggs tell jokes?"

"It would crack them up." Ed gave a robust chuckle. "Get it? They'd crack up."

David laughed, more at how delighted his uncle was to tell the joke than the joke itself. "Oh, that's a good one. I'll have to remember that one."

"See ya around, David. Happy Easter."

"Yeah, you too, Uncle Ed." David was surprised that he remembered his name. *It's funny,* he thought, *how memory works.* His uncle could forget what day it was, or how to button a shirt, but he could remember every joke he'd ever heard, and he remembered all his nieces and nephew's names.

When she appeared in the crowd at the bottom of the church steps, Ashlyne took his breath away. With Michael, Sorcha, and Kayleigh by her side, they joined the Sommer family in the second and third pews. Maggie showed Sorcha where the nursery was, and with Kayleigh and Ben being about the same age, they immediately hit it off. Ashlyne sat with Raine to the left and David to the right.

That's when David felt it. A warm sensation in his chest, tingling over his shoulders and into his head. Those feelings lifted his heart and brought an easy smile to his lips. He felt good. He felt complete. Whole. With Ashlyne next to him, the world was right again.

***

The next day, Raine, Lucy, Eva, and Sam got together to work on the project. It was spring break, and they needed to take advantage of the time they had to work on the project research. With Lucy and Eva in the living room organizing the report by subtopics, Sam and Raine looked around the library for more information.

"There is more upstairs, but I didn't see anything about Civil War times, the hospital, or slavery at Cypress Hill."

"We may be at a point to take what we do have and go with it." Sam furrowed his brows and added, "I may go with Dad to Murray and see what I can find at the library there. I don't know if anything would be specific to Cypress Hill, but having historical references of the time and area would meet Mrs. Weismann's criteria for the report."

"That's an excellent idea. Lucy will love references—what does she say? Credible, reliable, and—"

"Free of bias," Lucy shouted from the living room.

"Thanks, Lucy!" Raine rolled her eyes and quietly laughed with Sam. "She did say that history is written by the victors, and I think she was telling us to be careful where, or who, is the authority writing the articles."

Despite the absence of solid evidence supporting Cypress Hill's use as a hospital during the Civil War, the project was taking shape. Their search had yielded no proof regarding the colonel holding slaves, nor had it provided any indication of the absence of slaves or the existence of an underground railroad. What they did uncover were post-Civil War plans for manor renovations, including the addition of the north wing. Moreover, they stumbled upon letters addressed to Adalbert from a friend in France. These letters extended an invitation for Adalbert to join his friend for a visit in the South of France during the winter of 1889.

"We know more about the colonel after the Civil War than before or during the war." Lucy frowned. "This isn't going to help us at all."

"We found town maps from 1840 that show an area marked as Cypress Hill," Raine said. "It was huge—included the mill and land from the Clarks River all the way up to Jonathon Creek, where my aunt lives."

"Raine, you've learned more about Cypress Hill than any of us. Great work!"

"Thanks, Sam."

"We can assume, with a large tract of land, that slaves were used to farm if it was farmed."

Lucy said, "We can't assume anything for this project, Sam. We need evidence. We need to cite references, like Mrs. Weismann said." Lucy shook her head in frustration.

"We'll keep looking."

"Here's an obituary in the Cypress Grove Weekly Post. It says Adalbert Sommer, a Confederate Colonel during the Civil War, was no young recruit, his age being a contributing factor to his elevated position entering the war. Born in 1824 in the Netherlands, Adalbert migrated to the United States with his parents, taking residence on the land granted to his grandfather, Magnus Sommer, after the Revolutionary War."

"Where did you find that?" Raine moved to sit next to Sam, as did Lucy. He leaned so close to Raine, she felt his breath on her neck. She didn't mind at all. In fact, she rather enjoyed him being so close.

"It was in the desk drawer. I had put the maps in that drawer for your father, and today I noticed the inside of the drawer was too thin. Seems there was a secret compartment. I lifted the bottom of the drawer up and found this. There's more."

"This land was given to Magnus for serving in the Revolutionary War. I've never heard about this before, have you, Lucy?"

"No, never. I wonder if our parents know. And we thought he was a Confederate soldier. This confirms it."

The Sommer family history wasn't something often discussed, at least not in the younger generations. Not since Franz and Raymond sold off most of the land. Now, with Lorraine and David close to losing the farm, the legacy was something they'd rather not remember. Raine wondered if her friends had picked up on the fact the farm was about to be taken from them. If so, they hadn't mentioned anything to her about it.

Adalbert's grandfather had chosen a small clearing near water for settlement, but Adalbert's mother feared the creatures looming in the dark near the swamp. She had heard stories of the wilderness and dangerous animals of America and was reluctant to make the journey without a promise of a new homestead on high ground.

"Here's an article about Cypress Hill, dated 1860. It says when Magnus' son and his family joined him in the United States, they erected a new cabin atop a hill, christening it Cypress Hill, after the bald cypress trees flourishing in the swamp in the lowlands. It goes on to give the history of the home and the new ballroom. So, the ballroom was added around 1860. This was written before holding a ball in honor of John Bell."

"Who was John Bell?" Eva asked.

"I have no idea," Lucy said. "Don't we have an encyclopedia here?"

Raine found the Encyclopedia Britannica on a shelf and learned John Bell was a member of the Constitutional Union Party. "It says he ran against Lincoln, the Republican, Douglas, the

Democrat, and Breckenridge, a Southern Democrat. There were four parties in the 1860 election."

"Wonder if that is what caused the south to secede from the Union? Having a strongly divided political landscape."

"That's great, Sam, but maybe we stick to facts about Cypress Hill and if it was used as a military hospital." Lucy slammed the encyclopedia, writing down the name of John Bell as a guest in 1860. She was not always pleasant when stressed, and Lucy was very frustrated at the progress of the project. "I wonder, though, if the colonel hosted John Bell, does that mean he was for or against slavery?"

"Could be either, I suppose."

"Back to the cabin on the hill," Raine mused. "Do you suppose that's the old kitchen, with the log cabin look to it?"

"Very possible," Sam said. "Are there any other cabins on the land?"

"I remember some ruins by the spring; that's part of Mill Park now."

"There's another, down the access road. Remember?" Lucy nodded as she talked.

"In the swamp?" Raine looked puzzled. "I remember an old stone fireplace, but the cabin was pretty much gone. Why on earth would anyone want to live there? And it may not have been Magnus who lived there, you know."

"That's it. In the swamp, and Lord only knows why Magnus would build a cabin in the swamp when he had all this other land. Maybe it was for slaves."

Little did Magnus know, a portion of the land concealed a perilous swamp, teeming with snapping alligator turtles and venomous cottonmouth, copperhead, and water moccasin snakes. Despite the inherent dangers, the area boasted breathtaking beauty, with serene waters and a diverse array of flora and fauna unique to Kentucky. There were elk, bison, wolf, beaver, and plenty of deer. That was why Magnus chose to build his home there.

"The cabin is near Cypress Creek, close to the swamp. Not really in the swamp, like it's not built in the water."

"Yes, Raine. You know the one." Lucy let out an exacerbated sigh. "Let's go riding. Let's go see it."

"Aunt Maggie told me once, she took a group down the access road and a snapping turtle was in the middle of the path. They turned around—those things are mean."

"Before we go anywhere, let's review what we know about the history of Cypress Hill from the beginning, all the way back to Magnus receiving the land grant to when the colonel visited France in 1889," Sam said.

"We know the colonel was invited to France," Lucy corrected. "There's nothing so far to say he went to France. I mean, he's buried here."

"Yes, but in 1910. He could have gone anywhere during those years before he died." Raine sat next to Sam on the floor, surrounded by papers and books and maps. The single lamp on the desk provided little light to see the documents, but they were indeed documents that could help the project.

"Let's get what we know straight. Colonel Adalbert Sommer was most likely a Confederate soldier, and his son, Franz Sommer, was a Union soldier. Adalbert's grandfather, Magnus Sommer, fought in the Revolutionary War and was awarded a five-thousand-acre parcel, including the swamp." Sam studied the maps, a few papers he'd set aside, and a ledger from the city records. "If the colonel and his son left Cypress Hill to fight in the war, who was here taking care of things? Who could have run a hospital?"

"Would the military take over? I've heard they did that a lot. The soldiers would take over the plantations in the south, eat their food, set up tents and stay for weeks sometimes," Lucy added.

"What about the women?" Raine said. "Who was Franz Sommer's wife?"

"I don't know—there are no records of a wife," Lucy said, still looking at photos.

"We know they had children. Any birth records?"

"They didn't always have birth records during the nineteenth century," Sam said. He went to the shelves in the library, pacing back and forth. "Is there a family bible?"

"A bible?" Lucy gave a head tilt, unsure how a bible could help.

"Yes, that's where many families documented births and deaths. Our family has one from Michigan. Do you know of a Sommer's family bible?"

As if the spirits heard, the shelves behind the desk started to shake, and with a noise like what they heard in Raine's room a few weeks prior, a wind burst through the double pocket doors leading in from the main house. The swarm thing was back, hitting the shelves, causing books to tumble through the air and fly across the room. Sam grabbed Raine and pulled her down, ducking under the desk to avoid being hit in the head by books.

"What is that?" Sam shouted.

Then it was gone, leaving papers and books scattered on the floor and desk. The painting of the trees had fallen to the ground, papers scattered across the floor, and books fell from the shelves.

"That's our ghost," Lucy said. "He's a bit much, you know?"

"Oh my God, let's get out of here!" Sam's eyes were wide, looking around the disarray left behind. He moved quickly, then stopped suddenly next to the desk. Raine waited behind him, looking around the room. Sam picked up a thick book with worn pages.

"What is it?"

"The family bible," his words slower than usual; obviously he was in disbelief, "sitting right here, on the desk, turned to, of all things, a list of Sommer ancestors."

"Raymond found the bible." Lucy laughed. "Thanks, Raymond!"

"Your great-great-whatever grandfather needs to learn some manners," Sam said. "What a messy guy."

The second page of the family bible bore details concerning the Sommer men—birth and death dates, spouses, and the names of their children. Magnus Sommer's entry, however, included only the date of his passing in 1802. His son, Lars Sommer, born 1780 in Roosendaal, Netherlands, and Adalbert, born 1824 in Zundert. Everyone gathered around Sam as he read the list of names in the bible. "Adalbert married Anne Belle Wilson in 1852."

"When was this bible printed?" Lucy asked, then reached across to turn pages to the printer's mark. "The bible was printed in 1855, so it was likely Anne who started writing this down, you think?" Lucy mused.

"Maybe." Sam flipped the pages back to the family list and read on, "Anne and Adalbert had three children, Franz, Symon, and Grace. Franz married Margaret Kundsen, and they had Raymond, who married Adeline Lischka."

"I wonder what happened to Symon and Grace." Raine saw nothing on the page about them after their births were noted.

"It looks like Symon died the same year he was born." Sam shrugged his shoulders. "Sorry."

"That must be the baby in the cemetery," Raine said.

"Grace likely moved away when she married and started her own family."

"Margaret—that's my mother's name. Maggie is short for Margaret." Lucy smiled, wondering who she was named after. Raine was named after Lorraine, so surely, someone named Lucy was in the bible.

"Raymond and Adeline had Gilbert, who married our grandmother, Lorraine. I can't believe all this is written down in a bible," Raine said, looking at all the books they hadn't looked at yet, the portrait of the woman and painting of unusual looking trees on the wall. "Makes me wonder what else is in here."

"All this is interesting, but it won't help us be the best project in class," Lucy pouted.

"Do we need to be the best?"

"Yes!" Lucy raised her voice, "We need the highest grade!"

When Lucy began shouting, the house responded. The temperature dropped suddenly, and the lamp on the long extension cord flickered. Papers began to stir, and the pocket doors leading into the sitting room slammed shut.

"Come on—let's go!" Sam shouted, the roar of the swarm thing growing louder. Eva was first out the door, back into the safety of the north wing living room, followed by Lucy, Raine, and Sam, who pushed the doors closed and locked the library.

Raine stood holding the bible in her hands, visibly shaken by the return of the swarm thing. Something was different, however. This felt like a calmer spirit. It wasn't the same swarm thing, or at least he was more intentional. Less destructive, albeit still a messy ghost. This one was helpful, like he was trying to help them discover the Sommer family history.

"What the hell is that, really?" Sam asked, running a hand through his hair.

"Our great-grandpa. I told ya that already." Lucy shrugged, half a smile on her face, as if she was proud of her work the night of the seance. "I summoned him."

"You should know, Sam, we, uh, had a séance."

"A séance? When?" Sam shook his head in confusion. "Why?"

"We thought it would help with the project, and Lucy—"

"Oh no… did you all use the Ouija board?"

"Yes. It was Lucy's idea."

"Don't blame me. You and Eva were there too."

"Yes, the night of the sleepover. And swarm thing showed up. I think our grandpa, maybe my mother. They spelled out the words "beware" and "murder" on the board."

"And treasure," Lucy added. "Grandpa spelled out treasure."

"So, that was your grandfather?"

"We don't know exactly what, or who, but maybe Raymond Sommer? My grandma says he's haunted this place for years." Carefully choosing her words, Raine added, "I don't think it's Raymond. That is not how Raymond behaves."

"Murder? Who was murdered?"

"We don't know anyone who was murdered in our family."

"Might have been someone else?"

"So, you're saying there are ghosts?" Sam's sarcasm oozed, then he laughed.

"At least one ghost. Maybe more."

"I knew it all along," Eva snarked.

Chapter Ten

With a forceful pull, the garage door swung open, causing the lights to momentarily flicker as he toggled the switch. "Stop messing around, Raymond," David exclaimed. Navigating through the cinderblock garage, the latest addition to the property housing his most prized machinery, he headed towards the rear. In one corner, a tarp concealed a pile of metal, and as he unveiled it, there lay his most cherished possession—the potential savior of the farm.

They'd encountered this situation before. Finances had consistently been tight, and when there was a shortage, they somehow got through. This time, the impact was going to be significant. Creating a pathway in the garage, he maneuvered the 1942 Harley-Davidson XA onto the gravel drive. Clearing away spiderwebs, he inspected the gas tank, oil, tires, plugs, and the overall condition. Draining old fluids, he replaced them with new ones. An hour later, he mounted the bike and attempted to kick-start it on the left. It failed, and a sharp pain shot through the entire left side of David's body. After expressing some choice words and allowing ten minutes for the pain to subside, he positioned himself beside the bike, kicked three times with his right leg, and it began to purr.

There was another reason to sell it besides needing money. Since David's injury in Vietnam, he had not been able to ride the motorcycle. With an unusual left kick start and left foot shift, he physically could not do it anymore. He went inside, sat on the dusty couch, and removed his prosthesis. The pain radiated through the part of his leg that was missing. Phantom pain, they called it, where the severed nerves continued to send messages to his brain that his left leg was still attached. He applied ointment, then reattached his wooden lower leg.

Considering a drink to ease his pain, he instead opted for two aspirin. Holding the bottle in his hand, he thought of the mysterious woman who'd sold him the medicine. So beautiful, educated, and while he preferred to believe he rescued her the night by the fountain, it seemed to be she had saved him. She was his motivation; she made him want to be a better man.

"Caroline," David said to the space around him, "what's happening? Is it possible for me to love two women at once?"

He knew it was possible. Many men had been in affairs, where they love their wife, but also love someone new. David's situation was different, however, in that one of the women he loved was a ghost. He felt Caroline's presence in the home. He knew she was around, but not like Raymond, who messed with the lights, caused the floor to creak, and left a lingering cigar odor in the library. Caroline's spirit was soft and comforting.

They'd talked about David's future before she died. Caroline told him she wanted him to find love again, and he'd become upset. At the time, he thought it impossible to love anyone again, but since he'd met Ashlyne, he believed it possible.

There was a part of David that felt guilt. He'd felt survivor guilt since he returned from Vietnam where so many of his comrades perished. He felt guilt for the loans owed on the farm, some to pay for the tractor his father bought. They were needed, and the loans were justified at the time, but the home mortgage and second mortgage had been refinanced twice already. The other loan was to cover Caroline's treatment, and that was also needed. And now, he felt guilt for loving someone new, for moving on with his life when the past was so connected to the finance crisis in the family.

He'd adjusted by giving up cigarettes and alcohol, which had cost the family quite a bit of money lately. He was ready to give up the Harley. It was his responsibility to solve this bank problem, yet all he could think about was Ashlyne. She was kind, mysterious, intelligent, and he felt a connection to her that he never thought was possible. When he saw her with Raine, how she helped her with the project, and he saw Raine smile at her, laughing again, well, that warmed his heart. Loving Ashlyne felt right.

After services the day before, most everyone went out to the lawn for an Easter egg hunt. Kayleigh and Ben were inseparable, and, after filling their own baskets, Maggie's older children helped them fill theirs too. Lorraine invited the Morgans over for a meal, enticing them with a description of roast beef and potatoes simmering in the oven. Ashlyne and Michael joined the Sommer family, but Sorcha took a very tired and whiny Kayleigh home for a nap.

Bryce and Michael hadn't met before Easter but became fast friends. Michael described the cabin he'd bought up by the lake and got a few gardening tips from Bryce, particularly how to prevent wildlife from eating everything he grew.

Ashlyne looked at the research Lucy and Raine had compiled, giving them pointers on how to arrange information on the board for visual effects. Raine had been working on drawings for the project and showed Ashlyne the art she'd worked on— horses, flowers, the fountain in the town square. Ashlyne took an interest in her art, something that made Raine beam with pride.

David gave her the grand tour of the house. Like Raine, he felt a twinge of embarrassment about the condition of things, but it quickly passed as Ashlyne expressed true appreciation for the structure, the antiques, and the possibilities of the house. She marveled at the exquisite display of fine China in the dining room. She found an eighteenth-century butter churn in the old kitchen, likely left from the original Sommer family. David hadn't thought about it, but Ashlyne thought some of those pieces could be worth hundreds.

She was like no one he'd ever met. At times, he felt she was too good for him—too beautiful, too intelligent, too kind. Yet in the way she regarded him and spoke to him, he dared to entertain the notion that perhaps she found him appealing. That, or she made everyone feel like they were special. He was not ready to say he was in love with her, but there were possibilities.

The radio turned on, playing the Beatles song *Something*, and David shook his head. "Raymond!"

David picked up the phone and called Bryce, who answered on the second ring. He'd known Bryce since high school, and Bryce knew what this bike meant to David. Bryce immediately wanted to know more about Ashlyne, how they'd met, and if it was serious.

"I just met her, Bryce. Rather, just met her again."

"David, this could be a good thing. She seems like a very special lady."

"Yes, she certainly is. That's not why I called, however." David filled Bryce in on the bank loan situation and how he hoped to resolve the immediate issue of paying the overdue amount.

"You really doing it?"

"I gotta sell it, Bryce."

"I hear the disc wheels make this model extremely rare."

"Of the one-thousand made, only sixty were made with those wheels."

"All right, I'll give Tall Charlie a call. I'm sure he'll be interested."

Knowing the sale of his father's motorcycle would easily cover the overdue amount at the bank, David drove into town to see if he could come up with additional funds to pay off the loan. He was prepared to do whatever it took to keep the farm from Ned Baker. He'd checked with Bridge Cross, a nearby racing stable, but his mother was right—leaving town with the racers was not ideal. He needed work nearby, and he stopped by his friend Mack's to see what he knew.

"Hey, buddy. Why'd you get all fancied up?" Mack greeted David with a grin and a firm handshake. "I have a hunch it's because of a certain dark-haired woman."

"I'm not sure," he said, shaking his head. He really wasn't certain what possessed him to shave his beard, or put on his nice clothes, albeit still denim today, not a suit and tie. "Wonder if you might have some ideas for me."

Mack poured David a beer and listened to the dilemma he faced. He needed money, and soon. Besides selling the motorcycle, what else could David sell? "You need how much more?"

"A few thousand, by sometime in June. The sooner, the better."

"Well, my cousin goes to a flea market up in Paducah the second weekend of the month. He'll probably be up there this weekend. How about I give him a call, maybe you could drive up with a few things, see how it goes?"

"Every little bit helps. Yes, give him a call, please. I'll look around inside the house. If I find something interesting, I'll take it up for him to look at, at least give me an idea." David left payment and tip on the counter, leaving nearly a full beer.

"Sure thing." Mack looked puzzled, because he'd never known David to not finish at least one beer when he stopped by.

Heading back to the truck, he couldn't resist the urge to go to Sage Sisters, just to say hello. As he walked over, he thought of an excuse to go in. More aspirin… too soon. Maybe a gift? He really shouldn't spend the money, but maybe something for his mom for Mother's Day next month. Ashlyne greeted him at the counter.

"I'll bet you came in to see what your daughter and her friends have been doing here. Am I right?" Ashlyne knew that wasn't what brought him in. She'd wished for him today, and he showed up. Still, to know she was able to summon him with a mere thought was not something she was proud of, and he would likely feel manipulated if he understood her manifestation powers.

"Yes, the kids are here working on some kind of history project?" He didn't realize the kids had left the house, but this worked. The kids were the reason he stopped in.

"They've told me about the ghosts. Sounds like Raymond made a visit, so they packed up and came here. They're upstairs if you want to go check on them."

"No, I'm good." David didn't do well with stairs, and his left leg was still bothering him from the motorcycle's kick start earlier. He didn't want to risk going up two flights to the attic, much less coming down. The impact coming down steps always hurts more than going up.

"I'm happy to help them. I teach history from time to time, as a substitute teacher."

"Is that so?"

"Yes, although I have not taught Raine's class. Word is, Mrs. Weismann has not called in sick for over a decade, so I'm usually called to sub for the elementary school."

"How do you think they're doing on the project?"

"It looked like it was coming together. There are more boxes upstairs, and perhaps they will find what they need to prove Cypress Hill was a Civil War hospital."

"I'd heard it was, but my father never talked much about the history of the place. In fact, I don't recall us talking about much of anything except farming."

"Being a historian myself, I would imagine there is a great deal of history at your place. It must be fascinating to have grown up around it, in that house."

"I've never thought much about it."

"One of the reasons I became interested in history was because of the architecture, the designs, furniture, kitchenware, paintings of the time. I love antiques."

"That's interesting, you think, even if there are ghosts?" David tilted his head slightly. "What are you doing this weekend, Ashlyne?"

"I have no plans."

"Would you like to join me for a little adventure?"

"I'd love that."

***

Late night rain left a mist hugging Cypress Hill and down along the creek. It was cooler than the past few days, enough to send a chill if not dressed accordingly. David was pleased to see Ashlyne waiting by the side of the store, a thermos of hot coffee in her hand. She wore bell bottom jeans and a paisley top, a thick lavender sweater to keep her warm, with a matching lavender headband, carefully tied between bangs in the front, hair teased and slightly raised in the back, cascading long, loose onyx curls.

"I haven't been to Paducah since I was a child. Grandmama brought me to this flea market a few times when I was very little. She sold oils and soaps, and her sister sold hand woven baskets, bags, bowls," Ashlyne said. She watched out the window as if she was seeing Kentucky for the first time, the trees coming to bud, the freshly plowed fields, the horses, and the cattle in pastures along the highway. The last time she was on this road, she learned of her grandmother's powers, and those of her sister. "I can barely remember my grandmama's sister. We moved to England that summer."

"I remember your grandmother well, and there was another older woman who sometimes helped at the store. That was her sister?"

"Yes, she moved away after, um, you know. I think she moved up to Louisville to be near her son, but the incident at the lake had a lot to do with it."

"That was an unfortunate accident."

"That is my understanding." Attempting to change the subject, she asked about the items in the back of the truck. "That is a lovely sofa. You said Mack's cousin has an antique shop?"

"Yes, he does this for a living. This will be my first visit to a flea market. I guess I'm late in the game. Mack said this market has been running since the 1920s." David drove the pick-up loaded with a few things he'd found in the house that seemed valuable—a Victorian love seat settee covered in purple suede, a couple of Tiffany lamps, matching hurricane lamps, a set of dishes that Ashlyne chose from the old dining area, and a gold pocket watch he found upstairs in Raymond's room. He hoped to make a few hundred dollars from the items.

Ashlyne examined the watch, fascinated at the craftsmanship. "This is exquisite. I would think you could sell it for at least fifty dollars, maybe more."

"You think it's real gold?"

"Yes, the watch appears to be gold. The chain looks to be some type of brass, not original to the watch."

"Then I hope Mack's cousin is able to sell it for me, along with the other things."

Billy Wilson met them at the curb, near the vendor entrance. They unloaded the settee and carried it inside while

Ashlyne unloaded boxes from the back of the truck. David parked while Ashlyne and Billy waited by the door.

"You from Cypress Grove?"

"Yes, I'm Ashlyne Morgan. My grandparents ran Hughes' Apothecary."

"I remember the two older ladies who worked the soda fountain. When we were about eight or nine years old, my brother and I would go in with a dime each, and that bought us a two-scoop root beer float. It was years later, I realized it cost more than a dime, but they never said anything. Real nice women."

"Thank you. They were amazing, and that sounds like something my grandmama and my great-aunt Isabella would do."

"I was sorry to hear about y'all moving over the pond. Or, well, that your father felt he had to move his family."

"Thank you; that means a lot." Ashlyne searched the parking lot for David. This was not a conversation she wished to have today. Since she'd returned to Cypress Grove, no one had so much as mentioned what happened all those years ago. Until today.

"Who'd ever think a bunch of church ladies would come up with that craziness, right?" Billy wiped his nose with his hand, shaking his head.

Ashlyne was a child when it happened. A group of boys came into the shop, caused problems, stole candy and magazines, then ran out. Her grandmother ran out after them, but they were too fast.

"You little thief!" she shouted. "Don't ever come back in this store, else I'll make sure you get what's comin' to you!"

It wasn't a threat. Her grandmother wouldn't harm a hair on their heads. If they came back, she planned to detain them and call their parents. Tell the parents what their children had done to the store by knocking things over and stealing from them. She planned to teach them a lesson on being good citizens, not delinquents. Her grandmother had nothing to do with what happened to the boys after they left the shop.

"Do you sell elsewhere, besides this flea market?" Ashlyne redirected the conversation. Talking about what happened to make her parents move to England was not an easy thing to do.

"Yeah, we have a shop up in Hopkinsville. Once a month, I load the truck up and drive out here. There's another I do in Lexington, one in Elizabethtown sometimes. Depends on what the wife finds at the yard sales."

"I'll have to drive up to visit the shop. I love antiques."

"Gotta say I was surprised to hear David is sellin' off things in the house. It's about time, I suppose. Ain't doin' nothin' but gatherin' dust up on that hill. But what else can he do?"

"I'm not sure." David returned, and the three carried the remaining boxes to Billy's booth inside. She wondered what that meant—what else could he do? Logically, these were things a farmer wouldn't really need or use. Intuitively, she knew he needed money, and there was some anxiety around finances.

"David, you brought some nice items. I'm sure these will go fast." Billy held up the matching Tiffany lamps. "These will bring a pretty penny."

"Hopefully more than a penny." They discussed a price, and David looked to Ashlyne, "What do you think these are worth?"

"I think Billy has a good price in mind for them." She studied the older gentleman. Tall, heavyset, with a long beard like Mack's, but this man looked to be in his seventies. He wore bib overalls and worn brown boots, and the items in his booth were first class antiques. He had a wide range of items, from Rookwood pottery and very nice Wedgewood, to women's corsets and hand tools dating back to before the Civil War. There were many first edition books, political campaign buttons, and costume jewelry from the 1920s. She picked up a small, framed note, a prescription for whiskey, written during the prohibition years.

"How much for this?"

"How much you willing to pay?" He grinned. "Everything has a price, but you notice nothing has a price on it."

"I've noticed. Seems like an interesting way to do business."

"That's the thing about antiques. To me, that's just a piece of paper in a wooden frame. I'd not give more than fifty cents for it. To the right person, it may mean something more."

"I'll give you two dollars for it," Ashlyne said, reaching in her pocket.

"Sold!"

David caught the end of their conversation, curiously looking over Ashlyne's shoulder to see what she bought. "A prescription?"

"Yes, I thought it would be something interesting to hang in the store. Something to remind us it was once a pharmacy."

"Did doctors really do that? Write a prescription for whiskey?"

"They most certainly did," Billy said, a wide grin curling up his cheeks. "And there's your proof. Get it? Proof. Like whiskey."

"Yes, I get it, Billy." David felt fantastic today. He knew he was the same height, but somehow, he was standing taller, seeing things from a new vantage point, or maybe seeing things for the first time in a quite a while. He was on what could be considered a date with a beautiful woman, he hadn't finished a full beer in at least a week, and he had a strange feeling of... optimism. He felt there was hope, and the only thing he could think of that had changed that, was Ashlyne.

"Whiskey was classified as medication during prohibition. Strange concept for Kentucky, where there are so many distilleries." Ashlyne tucked the small frame into her oversized macrame bag. "David, would you like to walk around with me, see what else is here?"

David nodded, then looked towards Billy. "You okay taking these things for a while? If they sell, let me know. If not, I can pick them up later if you'd like."

"You kids run along. I have a feeling that couple eyeing the couch will make an offer. We still good on a seventy/thirty split?"

"Yes, sir, and I really appreciate this." David shook the man's hand, then turned his focus on Ashlyne. Her beauty was undeniable, a constant, but today, it seemed to shine even more. Perhaps it was her graceful manner, or the unique fashion sense, blending vintage styles with contemporary ones, or maybe it was the captivating contrast of golden eyes next to her dark hair, accompanied by the sparkling earrings gracefully dangling against her neck. Whatever the reason, David found himself drawn to her charm.

They caroused the aisles at the flea market, looking at bottles and fabrics and paintings, all marked to sell. David bought his mother a new apron made by the Amish, embroidered with *World's Best Mother.*

"I'm planning ahead for Mother's Day."

"She will love it. Lorraine certainly loves the kitchen."

"Absolutely. She cooks at home, then goes to the nursing home and cooks for sixty-something patients there, comes home and cooks again."

"I didn't realize she worked at the retirement home."

"Yes, she started working there after Maggie and Bryce married. I was stationed at Fort Bragg, and Caroline was with me. Raine was born in North Carolina, but when I deployed the first time in 1961, I sent them back to the farm."

"Where did you deploy?"

"South Vietnam." He looked away, not comfortable talking about his time in Vietnam. The 5th SFG was first deployed as a battlefield advisory group for the Army of the Republic of Vietnam, or the ARVN. He looked at some candy, his belly rumbling with hunger, then decided to wait for dinner.

"Was that your stomach?" She intentionally changed the subject, sensing Vietnam was something he'd rather not speak about. "Let's get something for lunch."

"I think they pump the smell of hot dogs through the air vents here, because I've been smelling it since we got here but haven't seen a vendor."

"I'm convinced Paula does that to get me to buy the cherry Danish she makes. I always know when she has them in the oven."

David bought two hotdogs and they ate them standing near a booth of fishing rods, lures, boxes, and a few survival tools.

"I'm not much of a fisherman, but I love collecting lures."

"That seems to be a big part of the fishing experience."

"Say, we should stop by the lake on the way home. You said you'd not seen it before."

"Actually, my brother told me we went with our grandfather. I was very young and don't remember going."

"Was he a fisherman?"

"Not in the slightest."

Ashlyne stopped at a booth of Amish women and asked them about selling their handmade sewing products at Sage Sisters. She scheduled a meeting with them to discuss her purchasing items in bulk, rather than selling on consignment. David waited until they were out of earshot to speak about it.

"That's a very good idea, for the store, I mean."

"What idea is that?"

"Selling things from locals. We've never seen a store anywhere around here that sells local products like you're doing. Well, other than eggs George sells for me at the feed store."

"It's how my grandmama always did things, but people have forgotten. The new consumer trend is to buy from big chain stores, manufactured items, not local." Ashlyne stopped at a booth selling fresh baked goods, buying a large oatmeal cookie from an elderly woman wearing a bonnet, most likely part of the Amish community north of the lakes. She broke it in half, handing the larger piece to David.

Taking the cookie, he wondered how she knew oatmeal was his favorite. "Thank you for sharing."

"You're welcome." They found a bench along the wall and sat together, sharing the cookie. "Think about how many ways there are to make oatmeal cookies. We can see the cookie, and it looks soft and tasty, but it may not be good at all."

"This must be one of the best I've had. Please don't tell my mother I said that…"

"Your secret is safe with me." Taking a bite, she looked at him, admiring how much a simple cookie could make him so happy. "It is delicious."

"Nothing like a packaged cookie from A&P."

"There is something called brand recognition, where psychology mingles with marketing to better understand why people buy what they buy. Branding would mean making the same cookie every time, having consistency in taste, texture, and packaging. For larger companies, like Nabisco, that is a very difficult thing to do."

"I've never thought about it before, but I get it. An Oreo is always the same, no matter where or when you buy it. That would have been difficult to do a hundred years ago," David said.

"Very difficult. In a way, having that type of consistency is why people keep buying them. But a homemade oatmeal cookie, well, the next batch this woman makes may be crispier, or have more honey."

"Is that honey I taste?"

"I can taste honey in this cookie."

"How about that…" David inspected the last bite closely, then popped it in his mouth. They brushed the crumbs from their fingers and headed down the next aisle. "I didn't know anyone put honey in cookies."

"It isn't common, I suppose." She looked at him, wondering if he'd ever made cookies. Ashlyne couldn't see Lorraine letting him in the kitchen to cook anything. "Did you know I purchased honey from your sister, Maggie? It's on a shelf next to prepackaged teas."

"You did? I wonder why I didn't hear about that. How did you end up with Maggie's honey in the store?"

"It happened yesterday. I wasn't aware she raised bees until her husband went in to see Michael for bee stings. Thankfully, he wasn't allergic, but his ear was swollen from the stings—and there were about six stingers on the left side of his face and ear."

"I'll have to give him a hard time about that." David laughed. "Bryce has always been a little bit clumsy, I suppose. Not really accident prone, but things tend to happen to him."

"I heard he and Maggie dated in high school and married the summer after."

"They did. He's been my best friend since I can remember. Then one day, he came over to the house to see Maggie instead of me. By then, I'd starting dating Caroline, and the four of us would go out together. Double dates."

"I'm so sorry to hear about your wife, David. Raine told me what happened."

He nodded, looking away. It was his automatic response to those who offered condolences—nod and look the other way, to avoid further conversation. It had been three years, and people still apologized for Caroline's death. "Raine talked to you about her mother?"

"Yes, quite a bit. Has she not spoken about it at home, to you?" Ashlyne wondered if David knew the girls used a Ouija board to communicate with the spirit world, or that a ghost in his house could physically move things.

"She asked me once if I thought Caroline could see her, could hear her when she talks to her."

"What did you say?"

"I said I like to think she can hear us. That if there was a way for her to answer, she would."

"That's a very good answer."

"Yeah, well, what else could I say?" David stopped and looked at hand-tooled chairs, like the bench he made for the cemetery. These were not antique, but new woodwork, something he loved to do himself. He checked the prices, wondering if the man sold many. Would it be worth it to load the truck and sit in a booth one weekend a month.

"Raine and Lucy seem very close, Eva too. They've found a lot of information about Cypress Hill."

"Yeah, they've spent a lot of time working on it."

Ashlyne studied David's face. "They tell me there is a ghost at Cypress Hill."

David smiled and shook his head. "There might be a couple."

Chapter Eleven

With her father gone, Raine stayed in her room drawing after church, each sketch of Cypress Hill looking better than the one before. She used the oil pastels that her mother had once used, and she pretended that her mother was guiding her hand as the brown lines turned into trees, and the blue marks took on the look of shutters. She could feel her mother with her at that moment.

The phone rang, and her grandmother called her down to answer. Probably Lucy, she thought, even though she had talked to her at church. She was being pushy about when the sketches of the house would be completed. They were mostly done, except the one of the ballroom.

Opening the bedroom door, the painting of the trees from the library fell towards her. It must have been leaning against the door outside her room, unusual that her grandmother would do that. Her father left before she closed the door, so it had to be her. "Grandma? Why did you bring this painting up here?"

"What painting?"

"The one from the library."

Lorraine stood at the bottom of the steps, and Raine held up the frame by the wire on the back. Lorraine gestured towards the library. "Wasn't that by the desk, in there? How did it get up there?"

"I thought you moved it. This is the second time I've found it outside my room."

Lorraine shook her head. "Maybe it was Raymond."

"So, you're saying a ghost moved the painting up the stairs? There's no way! Flickering lights, maybe, but this is a heavy frame."

"It is unusual, but some crazy things have happened here before."

Raine carried the painting down the stairs and returned it to the library, leaning it against the desk. The only phone was in the kitchen, and Lorraine had set the receiver on top of the wall-mounted phone for Raine to pick up. "Hello?"

"Hi, Raine, it's Sam."

"Oh, hello." Raine licked her lips, looking around to see where her grandmother went. A boy had never called the house for her before, and whatever he was calling for, she didn't want to be heard. She untangled the long, curly cord and stretched it into the pantry for some privacy. "How are you?"

"I'm good, thank you." Sam paused, not sure what to say himself. "I'm not sure what you have planned, or if you have plans today, but remember when we talked about the old cabin down by the creek?"

"The one in the swamp?"

"Yes, where there's a road going back."

"I know the place."

"Could we look? I mean, all of us, that is. For the project. Lucy, Eva, you know."

"Um, well, Lucy is watching her little brothers and sisters this afternoon, and I'm not sure what Eva is doing. I can call her."

"Yeah, you could, but she didn't seem very excited to go to the swamp." He took a deep breath.

"No, not at all." With Eva out and Lucy busy, that meant she would be alone with Sam should they get together. The thought of being alone with him made her stomach feel strange, her mouth dry, and her heart flutter.

"Well, are you up for an adventure?"

She laughed, maybe a bit more than was appropriate. "An adventure," she repeated.

"We could walk down there and see."

"Absolutely not. We can take the horses. Do you ride?"

"I've ridden before, but it's been a while. Can you show me?"

"Come on over. I'll get the horses saddled."

The access road was nothing but an overgrown dirt path with deep tractor ruts. Her Uncle Bryce used the road to get to the very back field, where he grew about five acres of corn. The rest of the area was heavily wooded, and the right side of the road drops off to the creek below.

Raine rode Star, a black mare with a white, star-shaped patch between her eyes. Sam rode Freckles, an appaloosa gelding. He seemed comfortable in the saddle, like he was meant to be on top of a horse.

"This is the swamp, on the right?"

"It's the edge of it. We need to ride down a path coming up, and then we'll know if we can get passed."

"If we can pass?"

"Yes, it's rained a lot in the past week, so the path may be covered with water. If it is, we can't take the horses down."

"It doesn't make sense why Magnus would build a cabin in a swamp, really."

"It may not have been as wet when he settled. I've heard that when they built the first dam at the lake, the water level went up. It caused some shifting of the terrain."

"But it has always been a swamp?"

"The bald cypress are hundreds of years old, maybe more than a thousand, so yeah. It's old. We've had groups from Murray come out to study them, take samples of the water. Some kind of research they did."

"It's beautiful out here."

"And a little creepy, right?"

"Well, it's certainly isolated. The kind of place to film a scary movie, like *Psycho*." Sam laughed, feeling like that wasn't a good thing to say. "Do you watch scary movies, or do you like them?"

"I get scared when the flying monkeys are on the *Wizard of Oz*."

"Oh no, not the monkeys."

"I guess I haven't seen too many movies. Whatever they show on TV, like the old *Frankenstein* movie, or the one with the birds that attack. It's been a while since the last time I went to a movie theater."

"We had a theater by our house in Michigan, so I went a lot. I guess the closest one from here is Murray?"

"Yes, Cheri Theaters. That's where I saw *Mary Poppins* when I was about five or six years old."

"That was the last movie you saw?"

"I think so. At least the last time I saw one in a theater."

"We should go sometime. If you want to, I mean."

"Oh, sure." Raine didn't know what else to say; she wasn't sure if he was asking her on a date, or if he was making conversation about movies. Maybe he simply liked movies. Either way, she had to change the subject. "So, the cabin is down this trail, and it looks okay, so follow me."

The trail was steep going down, but the horses did fine. No signs of snakes or snapping turtles at this point. The trail opened to a small meadow with wildflowers coming up, a few in bloom. The trail disappeared with the brush, but now and then, Raine could make it out.

"I see a lot of deer tracks down here."

"Yes, that is mostly what keeps the trails passable. We don't ride here very often. I don't know when my dad was here last." Beyond the clearing, the trail picked up, crossed a small creek, past a huge sink hole, with fallen trees and another small stream. "This is it."

The fireplace and foundation stood, and some of the beams used in the structure were on the ground. No walls, no roof. There wasn't much left of the cabin, and what remained was overgrown with vines and rotten lumber. Behind the cabin, was a limestone ridge at least a hundred feet straight up. From the top, there was a beautiful view of the lake at sunrise.

Sam got off his horse to look around, as did Raine. She held the reins of both, checking the ground for snakes and turtles. The spot where Magnus built the cabin was slightly elevated, and the tall trees surrounding it prevented brush from growing in the area.

"It is peaceful out here," Sam said. He stood on the raised foundation, a stone base about two foot high and sturdy enough to support him. He made his way inside, near the old fireplace and found a rusty kettle. "Look what I found."

"There's stuff in there?"

"Not much. Some old empty jars, a metal frame. Maybe that was a bed, I suppose." In the distance, a bird emitted an unusual cry, reminiscent of a crow but considerably louder. A disturbance in the densely forested area behind the cabin caused Raine to startle, the sudden stir causing a dozen or more small birds to take to the air, spooking the horses. Raine held them, soothing them by calling their names.

"I think I'm ready to head back, Sam."

"Yeah, me too."

The horses took them back to the farm, side by side, mostly in silence. Above the trees, two white egrets circled. Raine smiled. "What a sight."

"That's what all the commotion was about? Two birds?"

"Maybe." Raine admired how Sam found the swamp as peaceful as she did. A spooky place, but it was far from the rest of the world. No school, no bickering between Lucy and Eva, no worn-down house with a leaky kitchen sink.

"It's like a sanctuary. I'll bet that's why Magnus built a cabin down here."

***

On the following Tuesday morning, Lorraine dressed differently than she normally dressed for work at the nursing home. She opted for black dress pants, shiny shoes, and a top with a combination of red, blue, and black hues. It was an outfit she'd purchased three years ago for Caroline's visitation.

Lorraine and Raine said nothing to David as he entered the kitchen—hair brushed back, brown dress pants, striped dress shirt and tie. He checked the papers in a worn manila folder, making sure everything was there that Sam had found in the library. He looked so much like his father, and it was more than the fact he wore his father's dress clothes. Lorraine thought of giving him a complement, something she didn't do enough, but she didn't want him to feel self-conscious about his appearance. Instead, she simply said, "Raine, grab your things; we'll give you a ride to school."

Lucy and Eva stood waiting at the end of the drive, and they jumped into the back of the pick-up with Raine. There was no seat in the bed of the truck, but they held on to a rope tied to the frame, and should David hit a bump, they wouldn't go far. It was fun; even in the cool morning air, it was nice to ride with the wind all around, in the safety behind the cab where it was still. Aerodynamics were fantastic.

Billy sold the couch, the lamps, and most of what David took to Paducah. After paying him his cut, David cleared well over six hundred dollars. Altogether, they had enough to pay the total amount in arears and the late fees. The meeting, he thought, would be to negotiate a new loan, one with a manageable payment. Going forward, David would work harder. He would invest in livestock to sell in the fall and plant fields that hadn't been worked in years. Putting up a little upfront along with a summer of hard work, and the farm would be back on track.

David and Lorraine entered the bank at nine o'clock sharp, greeted by a short, balding man in a dark green leisure suit. "Mrs. Sommer, glad to see you this morning. And David. I'm surprised to see you."

"'Morning, Ned." David stood behind his mother, one hand in his front pocket and the other grasping the manila folder.

Lorraine and David took seats across the large desk of Ned Baker, vice-president of the Lake Trust Bank. Lorraine held another large manila folder in her trembling hand, but it was Ned whose waxy forehead gleamed in perspiration of fear.

"Thank you both for coming in this morning, and I'm hopeful to quickly resolve this matter." Ned shuffled papers on his desk until he pulled a three-page contract stapled at the corner. "Here is the loan Gil signed with my father. You are behind on the payments, and of course, the interest and fees have added up substantially."

"Yes, we are behind on payments, and those can be paid today as well as the late fees." David took a deep breath in, puffing his chest out and leaning back in the seat. It felt good.

"Thank you, David," Lorraine began. "I have a copy of the loan and of the figures you sent in the letter. And as I told you on the phone, we would like to refinance the balance and combine all three loans."

"I wish that were possible, Lorraine." Ned folded his stubby fingers in front of himself. With a shake of the head and light chuckle, his pleasure was obvious in what he said next. "In order to secure refinancing, the payments must be on time, late fees paid, and other loans must be timely as well. The primary loan is not overdue, but the second mortgage is one payment behind, in addition to the late fee."

"And we are prepared to pay those today."

"Well," Ned said in a condescending tone, "in addition to that, to refinance the primary mortgage loan, there must be a profit shown on the farm balance sheets, and as you know, there hasn't been a profit on the farm for years."

David placed his hand over Lorraine's trembling one. The words spoken were painful, but the smirk on Ned's face was malicious. David was, in title, the owner of Cypress Hill, but since coming home from Vietnam, he'd had little to do with running the farm. "What are our options?"

"Unfortunately," Ned said with a stifled chortle, happy to see David, who knew nothing of the bank's dealings, taking the lead, "it doesn't appear you have any. Unless the balance owed shows up at the bank by the end of the month, we are prepared to foreclose on the property for the loan taken out in 1966. Now, if it sells for more than what you owe, you'll have a nice chunk of money to get you through for a while."

David pulled papers from a worn envelope and looked over the survey Sam found in his father's desk. Ned continued to talk, but he was focused on the document, his father's signature at the bottom, the amount borrowed, the description of the land. Another page was the deed for the land, and the survey referenced the deed by block and lot number in the loan agreement. It was not too complicated.

Cypress Hill started with thousands of acres, and bit by bit, it had been sold off since after the Civil War. Gil Sommer had the land surveyed and divided into several parcels. The house and barns were on one, the north field and cemetery another, Maggie and Bryce's farm was surveyed and gifted to them, then several other lots.

Only one lot was held as collateral for loan taken out to pay for Caroline's treatment. This lot was near the Clarks River, about fifty acres, a small piece of land on the remaining acreage they owned. It was a heavily wooded, wet tract of land, useless except for hunting and fishing, puzzling David. Additionally, the access road which ran along the Cypress Creek was not included in the parcel, nor was the old cabin. Basically, it was a useless tract of swamp, not fit for farming or development. Part steep terrain, a limestone ridge full of sinkholes, caves and gullies, part marsh, with Cypress Creek spilling over onto at least half the lot. Gil Sommer must have known this, as well as Ned's father. A grin crossed David's lips.

"And who are the buyers for this land?"

"You know I can't disclose that information," Ned said, leaning back in a large leather chair. He pulled a cigarette from his front pocket and slipped it in his mouth, revealing his yellowed teeth. "Care for a smoke, David?"

"No, thank you. I'm trying to quit."

Lorraine's head rose at those words, turning to look at David to make sure he wasn't joking. He had given up cigarettes? "You are?"

"So, there is a purchaser." David scrutinized the documents, recognizing that his father must have had a purpose for this. Was it conceivable that Ned's father extended a loan to Gil for swamp land? Considering their friendship, it could have been a benevolent and compassionate gesture. "Could you share your map of the land with me, Ned?"

"I'm sure it's the same as yours, but here." He handed him a paper, and David laid the two side by side for comparison. "My father had surveyors verify the boundaries."

"These are different. The boundaries are the same, but the land on your survey is marked field. It's not a field. Looks like I have the original survey with a topographic map, and the deed references the survey that I have, which is noted on the copy of the loan."

"What are you saying, David? That I don't know what I'm doing?"

"I'm saying you have an erroneous survey, Ned." Ned grabbed his survey and studied his copy again, gripping the document so firmly that his short fingers bent the paper along the edge. "What you have, Ned, is a loan on useless swamp parcel locked inside Cypress Hill property. There is no access to the land without our consent, and the land cannot be developed. It's swamp land, full of caves and very old bald cypress trees."

"You mean the type of tree the state is preserving? They would never approve development of this land." Lorraine sat up straight. "David, are sure about this?"

"Absolutely. Look, here's the full map and the other parcels Pa had divided on the property. The house is one, then six tracts of land behind it, Maggie and Bryce's land across the road, but the parcel he took the loan out against is over here—see, these other tracts include the river front in one, cypress swamp on this one, and another has the access road."

"That means that property is useless to anyone but us."

"Us, and the Kentucky Department of Fish and Wildlife."

Lorraine smiled, her eyes glazing over, whispering to herself, "Gil took care of us."

Ned studied the papers, shuffled others around on his desk, looking for another survey copy. He checked it, pulled out a magnifying glass, then slammed his hands on the desk. "Son-of-a-bitch."

"Hey, watch your language in front of my mother," David said, but he couldn't help a lopsided smile. At that moment, he thought of Sam. If he hadn't found that survey, the meeting today would have taken a totally different turn.

"Oh, pardon me, Lorraine. This is not at all what I thought."

"Yes, you thought you'd make a lot of money building houses overlooking the river, maybe a boat dock, right?" Lorraine's shaking hands turned into fist on her lap, her lips tight in a frown. "We trusted you, Ned. How could you?"

"The fact remains that you are behind on your payments." Ned thought about it and sighed.

"How much is that, exactly?"

"$822.10."

"And the balance due?"

"Another $3,250," Ned looked down his nose at the papers, "and 43 cents."

"You were going to foreclose on our property for $822.10 in late payments? And not even bother to let us keep the remaining loan amount?" David leaned back in the chair and threw his arms behind his head. "Ned, I don't know what to say. Just wrong. This is just wrong. What if I just brought you the total amount? $4072.53."

Ned and Lorraine looked at David. Ned clicked buttons on the calculator, then double checked. David was exactly right. $4,072.53.

"The bank has the right to demand full payment of the loan, of any loan, really, seeing how the payments are in arrears. The payments are regular, but at the time, the payment was short, and the fees and such add up."

"Unbelievable," Lorraine said. "You'd better be in the front pew on Sunday, Ned, praying for forgiveness. Where's your compassion, for Christ's sake?"

"When did you join hands with the devil, Ned?"

"Well… I…"

"When do you need the money?"

"You'll have to come up with the amount in arrears immediately."

"That's $822.10. I have it today. What about the rest, to pay off this third loan."

"The sooner, the better," Ned said, wiping his forehead with a handkerchief. "The other loans are in question as well. The board just met and won't meet again until next quarter. Even if this loan is paid off, they may review the other two loans and demand payment in full."

"And when is that?"

"End of June." Ned avoided eye contact, gathering the papers on his desk. He stood, holding out his hand to David and asked, "Would it be okay if I make a copy of the survey you have?"

David looked at the survey, looked at Ned's hand, then his beady eyes, and said, "No, but I will get a copy for you. I'm not letting this out of my sight."

Lorraine and David walked out of the bank and around the corner before making eye contact. When they did, both had wide grins. Lorraine skipped a step, getting ready to give David a big hug.

"Be cool, Ma. They're watching." He didn't see Ned and his assistant peering out from the bank window, but he felt eyes on his back.

"You did it, David! Oh, my heavens," Lorraine looked up to the sky, "Thank you, Gil! I knew you would take care of us!"

"Ma, we aren't in the clear just yet. We paid the $822 but need to pay off the balance before the board meets. Ned is talking like the other loans are in jeopardy if we can't come up with the full balance."

"Have some faith, David. I feel things are finally turning our way."

Chapter Twelve

"We need to go back to the apothecary and demand those witches help us," Lucy said, her jaw tight and eyebrows furrowed. "I know they know how to get rid of ghosts."

"Are they really witches, Lucy? They didn't seem very scary."

"Witches or not, I think they know how to banish spirits."

"Do we really need to get rid of him?" Raine said.

"Uh, yeah," Eva said, popping gum. "It's a ghost—why wouldn't you get rid of it?"

"He did help us find the bible with Sommer lineage. If anything, we could do a report on how our family founded this town." Raine waited by Sam's locker, although she couldn't figure out why. He was just a boy. "And for the Civil War part, we could mention how Franz and Adalbert were on different sides of the war."

"I suppose he did help find the bible," Lucy mused. "Maybe we could do something to calm him down. At least, ask the ladies today when we finish sorting boxes in their attic. There are just a few left, and maybe there will be something in them about Cypress Hill."

"What's up, ladies?" Sam gave a big smile to Raine. He might be just a boy, but when he looked at her like that, Raine forgot to breathe, and her tummy felt weird.

"We are going to the apothecary." Raine couldn't keep from smiling, something that didn't get past Eva and Lucy.

"Cool," he said, reaching for the crescent moon pendant hanging around her neck. "I like your necklace."

"Thanks." She'd forgotten she was wearing it outside her blouse, and for a fraction of a second, she thought he was reaching for her blouse, but that would be ridiculous. Raine blushed and took a deep breath to compose herself. Being around Sam had the strangest effect on her.

"Well, let's go to the apothecary."

Eva and Lucy walked ahead of Sam and Raine, giving Sam and Raine a chance to talk. Raine wasn't outwardly sociable like her two friends, and while being around Sam was nice, it also made her nervous.

"What does your father teach at Murray, Sam?"

"Accounting and finance," he replied. "A very boring subject for most."

"Is that something you want to do?"

"Heck no! I want to be a physical therapist, work with people who have injuries."

"That's cool," Raine said. "My dad had physical therapy when he came back from Vietnam."

"He was injured?"

"Yes, but he's better now."

"I had a friend in Michigan. He was hit by a car in second grade and paralyzed from the waist down. The physical therapist would come to the school to help him navigate in a wheelchair."

"Is that why you want to be a therapist?"

"You bet!"

A new sign hung over the apothecary—a new name. Sage Sisters. The woodwork on the front has been painted a deep green since Raine last visited, and stepping inside, the store had been filled with all sorts of gifts, snacks, jewelry, and more.

"Wow," Lucy said, inspecting a table of gemstones in small baskets—amethyst, jade, turquoise, citrine, rose quartz, and more.

"Far out," Eva said and went to a display of suncatchers by the window, sending prisms across the store as they spun.

"It's changed so much," Raine said, looking at necklaces and grasping her own crescent moon she wore. There were earrings and bracelets now. She didn't have pierced ears yet, but if she did, she would want earrings to match her necklace.

"Hello," Ashlyne greeted them from behind the counter. She opened her arms wide, gesturing to the new items across the store. "What do you think?"

"It's fantastic!" Eva said, the others nodding in agreement. "I love that you sell jewelry now. And wow, look at these denim purses! Very cool."

"These are made by a local artist in Murray. She makes denim hats, too."

"I love it!"

"We are still adding to our inventory. Expecting a few clothing imports, leather purses, that sort of thing." Ashlyne looked around, proud of what she and her sister had created. "Our grand re-opening is Saturday at ten o'clock, and you are all welcome. There will be prizes."

"I'll let my mom know this is where she can buy my birthday present." Eva eyed a purple lava lamp, something she'd wanted for a while.

"That reminds me... Dad's birthday! I need a gift for him."

"I may have something for you to give him, Raine. It was a sample sent to me with an herb order, and I have no use for it. Perhaps your father could put them to use." Ashlyne pulled out a small burlap pouch, opening it and pouring a few seeds in her hand. "I have no place to plant pumpkin seeds since I live upstairs in an apartment. Maybe your father could plant them on the farm? It could be a project for both of you."

"A pumpkin patch," Raine said. "Weird, I just remembered a dream I had about a pumpkin patch in the side field at our house."

"It must be a sign that you are to plant these seeds." Ashlyne waved a hand over the bag before handing it to Raine. "May it bring you good fortune."

"I have money. I have five dollars, but it's at home. Can I pay you later?"

"Oh no, dear. These were free to me, so they are free to you."

"Thank you. I still want to buy him a birthday gift.

"When is that?"

"Um, next Sunday, I think. We're having a surprise party for him. You should come! My grandmother always makes a big deal for his birthday."

"Sunday." Ashlyne walked around the counter, to a display of hats hanging on the wall. "What time?"

"I'll have to check, but probably after church, like one?"

"I think I could make it." Ashlyne walked around to the wall across from the counter. "How about a new hat for your father?"

"No, he has plenty of them."

"Hmm… what about a leather portfolio, to keep important papers."

"That would be perfect! Better than the manila envelope he uses, but five dollars won't cover something that nice."

"This one is only $4.99." She reached for a dark brown leather portfolio, opened it to show pockets on both sides and three rings in the center.

"That seems perfect! Can you hold it for me?"

"Absolutely, Raine."

"There's something else we need," Lucy whispered. "Remember our house guest?"

"House guest?" Ashlyne mirrored.

"The ghost. Is there anything you have here," Lucy pointed to the crystals and incense section along the side wall, "anything that will help him, um, move along?"

"Or at least calm him down?" Raine added.

Ashlyne took a deep breath and smiled. Her experience with unwanted ghosts was minimal. She did have a simple way to release negative energy, and ghosts were pure energy. "I might have something to help."

The four listened while Ashlyne explained how to clear negative energy by burning sage, juniper, and cedar. Lucy eagerly purchased two bundles of herbs and a large shell for this task, as well as three stones.

"The Potawatomi have a similar ritual for cleansing. Is this where you learned your technique, Ashlyne?"

"What I've described is a saining ritual that my grandmother would perform to clear negativity, but yes, that is similar to indigenous smudging or smoke ceremonies."

"Kind of like Catholic church," Lucy said.

Sam looked at her and tilted his head sideways. "They smudge in church?"

"Yeah, well, they burn incense in that thing the priest swings around. He walks up the aisle with it, and I think I've seen it done before reading the Gospel. I can't remember—we don't go there much."

"They don't do that at our church," Eva said.

"Be very careful," Ashlyne warned. "Remember to focus on clearing negative energy and open the windows to give it a place to go."

"Will do," Lucy said. She and Eva headed up the stairs to the attic.

"Raine," Ashlyne said, "are your ears pierced?"

"No, not yet." She smiled, took a deep breath, but couldn't finish what she was going to say. Her mother planned to take her, but time got away from them. She passed months before the doctors expected her to go. Ashlyne understood.

"We were thinking of doing a demonstration here on Saturday. Maybe your father would allow us to do it for you, but you'd need to ask him if it's okay."

"Really? I'm sure he would let me."

"You'd be doing us a favor."

Upstairs, Lucy and Eva began sorting papers. When Sam and Raine arrived, they pulled another box filled with the first Cypress Grove newspaper—a single page, folded in half. It was released weekly, with local news, help-wanted ads, new items available at the mercantile, death and wedding announcements. Half the cover page was national and regional news, including the completion of the L&N railroad in 1859 and the hopes that John Breckenridge would win the 1860 election. In 1861, the headlines announced the inauguration of President Lincoln.

"These are significant and directly related to the Civil War," Sam noted.

"There's more—here's one about the start of the Civil War, with the attack on Fort Sumter, and another about Gettysburg." Raine held several more pages in her hands. "I think someone saved papers about the war."

"You're right. Not all the weekly papers are here," Lucy said.

"It's possible they didn't print it regularly during the war," Sam said. "Although… look! Here's an article with a photo of a hospital—and look at the walls."

"The cherubs," Lucy said. "This is it!"

"It's Cypress Hill!"

"We got it! We found proof that Cypress Hill was used as a military hospital."

"Thank God," Eva said, sitting in a cushioned chair by the window. "Are we done now?"

"No!" Lucy shouted. "Why don't you help us, Eva. Maybe go through another box. Here, this one has photos. See what you can find."

Eva sighed and slowly moved from the relaxing chair to the table in the middle of the room. She opened the box marked "photos" and started putting them into stacks—individual people, groups of people, buildings, and everything else in the fourth pile of photos. She couldn't help but notice all the photos were of white people, until she was almost at the bottom of the box. There it was—black people, maybe slaves, working in the fields, with Cypress Hill in the background. The photos were printed on heavy paper like cardboard, which was how she knew they were very old. She handed Sam two photos. "Look at this."

One photo was two women and a child in cotton fields near Cypress Hill. Eva looked at their faces, studied their features, the dresses, and head scarves they wore, and the children. A hundred years ago, this could have been her life. She could have been working in the fields, or as a housemaid, or worse.

While the photo didn't prove they were slaves, and it didn't have a date stamp, most likely, it was taken around the same time as the Civil War. Another photo, a black woman and a child, had *Della Lewis and Isaac* written on the back. "Maybe this something we can use to support the theory that Adalbert held slaves at Cypress Hill."

Lucy and Raine looked at the photos, looked on the back for any information, studied the attire. "These women could be slaves, the photo doesn't have a date, but it could be pre-Civil War, and that certainly is Cypress Hill. Still, there is nothing to confirm they were slaves."

"I'm going to Murray this week, and they have slave records in the school library. I'll check for a Della Lewis, or any slaves held by the Sommer family.

"It's still just a theory." While still uncertain of the facts, nausea churned within Raine as the realization loomed that her family most likely once owned slaves. The clearer the truth, the more profound her physical discomfort became. The questions weighed heavily on her mind. *How could they engage in such actions? Could they be relatives of Eva?* Her family's presence in Cypress Grove paralleled that of the Sommer family, but something about it felt inherently wrong. "Not all blacks were enslaved."

"You all right, Raine?" Sam asked.

"Yeah, just a little surprised. I can't believe my family-owned slaves." She sat down, feeling like her legs would go out from under her at any moment.

"Owning slaves was quite common in the south, especially on large estates like Cypress Hill was once. It's how things were back then, like how my ancestors were forced onto reservations."

"They were?"

"The Potawatomi, yes. It's the past, Raine. It's not your fault Adalbert owned slaves and fought on the Confederate side, just as it isn't your fault how Native Americans were treated."

"Yeah, Raine. This was a long time ago." Eva looked at another photo of a slave woman, wondering who she could be. "I would like to borrow one of these photos if possible. I want to show my granny."

"Where's your grandmother?" Sam asked.

"She's at the nursing home, the one where Mrs. Sommer works."

"How old is she?"

Eva laughed. "Like a hundred. She's my great-grandma, but I've always called her Granny, I guess because my grandmother died before I was born. I never knew her."

"And you're just now mentioning this?" Sam laughed and shook his head. "Let's do one better and go visit her, take the whole box. Would she be able to see these photos, maybe recognize the people?"

"We could ask her."

"Let's go!" Lucy was first down the stairs, seeing Sorcha and Ashlyne at the counter.

"Are you done for the day?" Sorcha asked.

"We'd like to borrow these photos if that's okay. We're going to visit Eva's great-grandmother at the nursing home," Lucy said, her eyes wide and a smile that said they'd found what they needed for their project.

"Absolutely," Ashlyne smiled, "everything okay?"

"We found what we need for the project. We found a photo of the hospital at Cypress Hill!"

"That's wonderful! It sounds like your report is coming together."

The nursing home was on the opposite end of town from Cypress Hill, near the railroad tracks. With the sisters' permission, they packed the box of photos in Sam's backpack and walked to where Eva's great-grandmother resided—Fern Valley Retirement Center.

Eva led the way through the main doors, past the reception desk, and down a long, sterile white hall, to the second to the last room on the right. The facility reeked of urine and astringent cleaner, with nurses in stark white uniforms pushing medicine carts in the hall. Elderly women sat slumped over in wheelchairs along the side of the hall, one with her hands on the wheels trying to push, moving only half inch at a time.

"Granny—it's Eva!" Mrs. Ellen Collins was sitting in her wheelchair by the first bed, watching a small black and white television with the volume turned up high. Another bed was empty, and someone was sleeping in the third bed by the window.

"Who is it?" the elderly woman replied.

"Eva. It's Eva, Marilyn's daughter." Eva had to speak louder than the television, then turned the volume down, telling her friends, "Her hearing is bad, and memory is slow, but she will eventually remember who I am."

"Eva? Hello, child! So good to see you today," Mrs. Collins beamed, and she spoke with a slow southern drawl. "Who'd you bring with you?"

"These are my friends. You remember Lucy and Raine. Her grandmother works here—Lorraine?"

"Oh, yes, yes. Lorraine. She works in the kitchen."

"And this is Sam." Eva pulled Sam closer by his elbow.

"Is this your beau?"

Eva blushed, as did Sam. "No, Granny. I'm too young to date."

"Well, he sho is a handsome one."

"Granny, we have some pictures to show you." Sam handed Eva a stack of photos. "We're wondering if you might remember anyone in the photos."

The old woman held a photo with her gnarly, arthritic, trembling hands. "Hand me my glasses—let me take a gander."

"We're working on a history project about Cypress Hill," Raine said. "If there's anything you remember about the place from when you were a child, it might help us put the pieces together."

"They had slaves on that hill, ya know." It was a statement, not a question, and it stung Raine with a tingling from her feet all the way up her spine. "Not a bad place, though. They treated 'em well, from what Momma told me."

"Was your mother a slave?" Lucy asked.

"She was born into it, yes, and her mother a slave, and her mother before that. Lookie here, I've seen this photo before." Ellen Collins gave a toothless grin, looking close at the image of three children and two older women. "That's my grandmother, Rebekah Merriweather."

"Are you sure?"

"I'd never forget what my grandmother looked like. One of them children must be Evalyn, my mother."

"Evalyn… E-V-A, like Eva?" Sam asked.

"Yes, I'm named after Granny's mother." Eva took the photo and looked at it closely. She was drawn to this photo the first time she saw it, and this must be why. Seeing her ancestors for the first time was a feeling she couldn't identify. Exciting, but also sad, knowing they were enslaved to the Sommer family more than a hundred years ago. "Who is the older woman?"

"I'm not sure." Mrs. Collins studied the next photo, Rebekah with a young girl. "This must be a few years later. My grandfather went off to fight in the war and she never saw him again."

"How sad that you never knew your grandfather," Raine said. "And you are certain they were slaves at Cypress Hill?"

"Oh, most definitely. I grew up on land from the colonel, over on Merriweather Road."

"As in Rebekah Merriweather… I had no idea the road was named after our family, Granny."

"What do you mean, land from the colonel? He gave his slaves land?"

"Yes, our place on Merriweather, and another family, over on Lewis. Did that before he left for Europe. I remember my pa moving us into a new house when I was 'bout ten."

"Oh, wow," Raine mused. "Adalbert gave his slaves part of the farm."

"Della Lewis… the woman in the photo. If Adalbert gave the Lewis family land, that would confirm they were former slaves."

The realization of her family's part in slavery was becoming clear. The Sommer family and Cypress Hill existed because of slave labor. This did not sit well with Raine. She tried to take comfort in the fact the colonel gave land to former slaves, but was that enough? How did he treat his slaves before the war, and if he truly cared for the slaves he owned, why did he fight for the Union?

"I remember seeing old maps of the land. I put them in the drawer for your father, Raine. We should check with him."

"This is going to be such a good report! Mrs. Weismann is going to love that we found all this out," Lucy beamed, scribbling down all Mrs. Collins talked about, with Sam taking notes of his own. "So, the Sommer family-owned slaves, and when they were freed, he gave them land?"

"Why, yes… of course, he did. He was a fine gentleman, the colonel." Mrs. Collins looked at another photo, this one of a man leading a white pony, two small children on its back. With an audible gasp, she covered her mouth and swallowed hard. Tears pooled in her eyes as she held the photo to her chest.

"I think my grandmother is getting tired."

"No, I'm okay," she said to Eva.

"Okay, but let us know when you want to lie down."

"This photo… that's my pa, with me and my sister, Polly, up on our pony. I can't remember the damn pony's name." Ellen Collins went through every photo in the box, finding several more photos of her family from the Civil War times through the 1920s. Some were taken at Cypress Hill, others at her childhood home. She identified some of the Lewis family, who were slaves from the Memphis area who traveled north and worked for the Sommer family after the war.

Lucy and Sam asked questions about the war, what she was told about it growing up. Mrs. Collins was born in 1874, almost ten years after the end of the war, yet the hardships continued as the country began to rebuild. During the Civil War, the men were off fighting, and the women remained, bonded in the struggles they faced in those times. Some men returned, others did not.

Ellen shared many stories about the war. Despite her sharp memory, there were occasional lapses in recalling specific times and names. She recounted tales her mother told her of the ballroom's first official ball, and later, she worked there, serving post-war era.

"The women took care of them injured soldiers," she recalled. "My pa was one who came up on the Hill. That's how he met my momma."

"You mother worked in the hospital?"

"The one in the ballroom, yes. Everyone helped much as they could. It was a military hospital not long after the war started. The missus cared for soldiers on both sides. She and that healer woman."

"Healer woman?"

"Some called her a midwife, some said witch, but I said she a healer. I went to her, I took Irene there, too."

"Took her where?" Raine had a hunch. "The apothecary?"

"Yes, Saoirse Hughes and her daughters, Claire, and… oh, what was the other one's name?"

"They really are witches," Eva whispered.

Mrs. Collins laughed. "No, of course not. But they could do magic with the cures. Used herbs and such—that's all we had at the time. Medicine women. They cured Irene's tuberculosis by breathing fumes of apple brandy in a charred keg."

"Irene was my grandmother," Eva told the others.

"Isabella. That was the other girl's name. The Hughes sisters who fought all the time." She shook her head and laughed. "They'd get into it all the time as young 'ens. As teenagers, they fought all the time. They'd make up, and fifteen minutes later, they's the best of friends. This went on for years—until the incident, you know."

"What incident?" Eva asked.

"The boys who drowned in the lake. That was long, long time ago, long before y'all's born. It sho was somethin' at the time."

"What else do you remember about Cypress Hill, Mrs. Collins?" Sam asked.

Ellen revisited memories of her work as a cook at Cypress Hill. As a child, she'd help her mother in the kitchen when Franz entertained, then when older, she catered for Raymond and Adeline, frequently serving meals in the expansive dining room before the commencement of dances. Her husband worked for the Sommer family too, and her sister had been Gil's nanny and later took on the same role for David. The intertwining histories of the families spanned many years.

It was close to five when they left the nursing home. Raine and Eva walked together in silence, each reflecting on what they'd learned and the impact on their individual lives. Lucy chatted with Sam about the project until the corner of Cypress Hill and Millstone Place, where Raine went up the hill to her home, and Lucy, Eva, and Sam went the other direction to their respective homes. Eva would hold the box from Sage Sisters, as she wanted to show her mother the photos she'd found of their ancestors.

Contemplating life at Cypress Hill, a former plantation with a history of slave ownership, Raine struggled with the knowledge that her great-great-great-grandfather held slaves for labor. If he hadn't purchased slaves, his father before him did. While she had always acknowledged this as a potential reality, she found it difficult to accept the notion that her ancestors had engaged in such practices.

Sam's perspective, however, held truth. Long ago, this was the custom in Kentucky as it was in much of the southern United States. Raine couldn't help but recall how recently it was that black individuals were barred from using the same water fountain at school—a reality that only shifted when the Civil Rights Act of 1964 came into effect. Even after the town's "White Only" signs were removed, people of the town continued to silently practice segregation.

When Eva and her mother moved back from Chicago, Eva had only heard of segregation. She walked into the classroom like she owned the place, and that was what Raine liked about her. The signs came down the same year, fortunately for Eva. Raine's heart ached for the pain that such ridiculous laws caused others, and to think her ancestors played a role in causing this pain filled her with sadness.

Next to the garage, a white van with the distinctive Harley-Davidson logo was parked with the back doors open, a ramp extending out. A tall man handed David an envelope, its contents meticulously inspected. David diligently counted the money before he securely returned it to the envelope. A handshake sealed the deal. David and the gentleman pushed the motorcycle up a ramp, seamlessly guiding it into the van's cargo space. The van and the motorcycle were gone by the time Raine reached the top of the hill.

"Hey, Dad, who was that?"

"That was the Harley dealer from Louisville. He bought your grandpa's motorcycle."

"I thought you loved that bike." Then it suddenly occurred to Raine what had just happened. Her father sold the motorcycle to get the money for the bank.

"Well, I did, but I can't ride it anymore. The kick start is on the left, and with my bad leg, I should look for a bike that starts on the right. I'm thinking of a shiny new Harley with an automatic start if I decide to get one."

"Okay, well, that's nice of him to come pick it up."

Raine, Lorraine, and David were having dinner—slices of ham, biscuits, baked beans, and fruit Jell-O with Cool Whip for dessert. They ate together more often lately, talked more during meals, and overall did more together. Raine tried to remember when the change came about.

Since her mother died, there had been many phases. At first, Raine stayed in her room, and her father was gone a lot. He didn't plow or plant the fields that year. She now knew he was at the bar, then, after months of going to bars, he began to bring the alcohol home, staying in the living room most of the day. Eventually, it got so David never left the living room, except when he had to go to buy more liquor, or when he performed the chores that demanded he do, like feedings.

This year, things seem to be changing for the better. The two fields behind the barn were plowed, and it was only April. Raine was hanging out with her friends more outside of school, and for the first time, she liked a boy. She would be sixteen in the fall, old enough to date if she wanted.

"You still working on the history project, Raine?" Lorraine started clearing plates, while David and Raine ate Jell-O. "Anything new come up?"

"Oh, yes. We took a box of pictures over to Eva's grandmother, Mrs. Collins, and she recognized some of the field workers here at Cypress Hill."

"What photos do you mean?"

"There was a box in the attic of the apothecary. Did you know Cypress Hill had slaves?"

"I'd assumed they did, Raine. It was a large plantation before the war, and Colonel Sommer was a Confederate soldier."

"You knew this?"

"It's not something we often talked about—your grandfather and I—but it was generally accepted that's how it was done."

"Why am I always the last to know these things?" Raine sighed, then licked her Jell-O dish, leaving a dab of whipped cream on her nose.

"In that case, so you are not the last to know, tomorrow afternoon, your grandmother and I will be over in Murray, so you hang out with Lucy until we get home."

"I can stay here alone, Dad."

"I know you can, but I'd feel better if you weren't alone."

"Raymond will be here." Raine rolled her eyes. Later that night, when her grandmother and father were watching television, Raine called Lucy and went into the pantry. They planned the smudging for after school when they'd have an empty house.

Chapter Thirteen

Raine cleared her desk of the sketchbooks and colored pencils and made room for what Ashlyne gave them. Lucy thought it best to start with the living quarters on the north side, so the smell of burning white sage, juniper, and cedar, which smells much like marijuana, would have time to dissipate before Lorraine and David returned. Lucy dumped her bag on the desk and pushed around for the dried bundles, feather, and abalone shell.

"Let's get started." She lit a candle, then the sticks, and fanned until it glowed, just as Ashlyne described. Starting with her bedroom, they waved the smoke to each corner, closet, and crook in the room while chanting the incantation. "Ashes to ashes, dust to dust, spirits take flight with wanderlust."

"Did you make that up? Ashlyne said we don't need an incantation, only focus on getting rid of the negative energy."

"Yeah, but remember what Sorcha told us? It's like we're praying in rhymes," Lucy said, her voice more confident than she felt. "We got this."

They smudged the upstairs first, Raine's room, then the bathroom and the room her parents had shared. The door to that room had remained closed for most of the past three years, and placing her hand on the crystal doorknob felt strange. One of the last times she entered the room, her mother was lying in the bed, too ill to get up. Caroline died a week later.

The room was bright and clean, with light blue and white wallpaper, white furniture, and a photo of David and Caroline on their wedding day. Baby photos of Raine with her mother were on the dresser, next to a jewelry box. She lifted the lid, and it played *Love Me Tender*. Raine opened the window, and Lucy fanned the sage.

"Come on, let's get in your dad's room." Raine hadn't been in her father's room for more than ten seconds since he'd come home when her mother was ill. She opened the curtains, cracked the window so the spirits could leave, and looked around. He still had Twiggy posters and football trophies from high school and photos of the family.

There was a display of medals modestly sitting on top of his dresser where only David would see. Raine noticed the Purple Heart and knew that was for being injured in battle, but the others were not familiar. There were circles, stars, and crosses. She picked up one and ran her thumb over the medallion. She looked at the ribbons, so many. Then she saw it. There, for no one to see in his bedroom, in another frame behind the other medals, was the Medal of Honor. The large, star-shaped medal hung on a blue ribbon, carefully mounted behind glass for protection.

This was where he was for the first part of her life, she thought. Fighting for our country. She didn't know a lot about his time in the military, but she knew this medal was something that wasn't given out often. She ran her hand over the glass, feeling pangs in her heart for the things she didn't know, the things she would never understand about her father. Who was he? Why had he never talked about the war or these awards?

"Raine, let's get this done." Lucy was down the stairs with a trail of smoke behind her. Although neither had smelled marijuana before, Eva had, and Lucy was so glad she'd mentioned that. She'd rather get caught practicing witchcraft than smoking pot. Lucy waved smoke as she walked down the creaky stairs, and repeated the chanting and smudging in Lorraine's room, the living room, the tiny bathroom under the stairs, and the kitchen. Raine lit a honeysuckle candle that was on the kitchen table and opened the windows and the screen door to the porch.

Opening the library doors from the living room, then the pocket doors into the foyer, they continued into the entryway, through the music room, the ballroom and solarium, then back inside to the dining area to the doors of the main kitchen. With a quick glance and a nod to Raine, she pushed open the door. Mice scattered along the edges of the room and found their tiny holes. A mildewed, sour smell hit them as soon as they stepped inside. They stepped back and turned their heads.

"Auugh…what died?" Lucy asked.

"Is that from being locked up for so long, ya think?"

"No. Seriously, what died? Over there." She pointed into the kitchen at small bones and bits of fur where the refrigerator would go, if there was a refrigerator.

"Oh, gross! That's why there's kind of a barn smell in there, I guess." Raine made a face and covered her mouth to filter the stench. She propped the kitchen door open, then the side door in the breezeway. The windows did not want to open, but they managed to get one to lift a few inches, then the breezeway windows were slats, each with a crank to open them like wooden blinds. The screens were torn near the bottom where cats and critters had unsuccessfully clawed to get out.

"At least this smudging will cover up the rotting corpse smell." They walked into the kitchen, mostly a cavernous shell with whole tree trucks for walls from decades past. The cabinets were open, revealing mostly bare shelves, only a few plastic containers and old Kentucky Derby glasses. No curtains and no lights. Lucy flipped the wall switch several times then tried two other switches in the room. "Just making sure."

"Let's gets this smudging done. I'm starting to get creeped out." Just as the words left her mouth, a door slammed upstairs. "He's here…"

"Okay, I'm done. Let's go. Maybe this wasn't such a good idea."

"Hey, you're the one who thought a séance was a good plan."

"That was before swarm-thing came." She headed towards the breezeway.

"No, Lucy, wait. We need to do this." Raine pulled the black tourmaline out of her pocket and handed one stone to Lucy and squeezed the other in her left hand. "Hold this in your hand. It will protect you."

"Okay… but I don't like this." Lucy looked up the stairs with unease.

"Let's smudge his ass." Still holding the tourmaline, Raine picked up the sage and relit the end. It took a couple tries before it stayed lit, and smoke curled up to the kitchen ceiling, vaulted with more large wooden beams. With the sage mounted in the shell, rock in one hand with the feather and sage in the other, Raine began to stir the smoke.

"So, it's a 'him' now?"

"It must be. He didn't say a word, just moaned, made a mess of everything, and left. Women are more vocal when they're angry and stick around to see the damage they caused." Raine wasn't sure what made her say that and shook the notion out of her head.

Lucy was right, the burning sage did help cover the dead animal smell. They looked more closely at the carcass, and Lucy said, "I believe it was an opossum." They smudged the kitchen, then went back to where the staircases led upstairs. They continued fanning the smoldering sage, reciting the incantation in every room, finally standing at the foot of the stairs. Their gaze traced the curved staircase to a balcony at the top, with the hallways on either side appearing dark and inhospitable.

"Raine," Lucy repeated, "Raine, are you all right?"

A hand on her shoulder made Raine jump, and it was a few seconds before she realized where she was and what she was doing.

"Yeah," she said. "Let's get the son-of-a-bitch."

"Wow, I thought he'd gotten to you for a second. Like a possession or something, but okay."

A chill came over the girls, although the house was warm and stuffy, and the faint smell of cigar mingled with the sage. Lucy reached for the shell holding the smudging stick and the wind blew the smoke from her, towards the window.

"He's coming," Raine said.

A low groan followed by a slow chuckle filled the foyer, vibrating the girls to the bone. They continued to repeat the incantation, Lucy waving the smoke around them, counterclockwise. The double pocket doors to the library slammed closed on their own, and the swarm thing appeared, circling the ceiling a few times before slipping between the two doors. The shell in Lucy's hand trembled and she continued waving the feather through the smoke, both girls now silent. He was gone.

"Holy cow, let's get out of here." Lucy pushed on the doors to the library, unable to budge either side. She handed the smudge shell and feather to Raine and tried again, this time grunting, but to no avail. "Oh my God, we're trapped in here!"

"Lucy, it's locked at the top." Raine pointed to the slide bar. "And there's the front door?"

"Oh." Pulling down on both at the same time, Lucy pushed both doors back into their pockets. Her sneakers squeaked on the marble floor in the foyer, causing her to jump. "I've had enough. Let's go."

"Lucy, we still have to go upstairs. Let's do this now and finish what we started." Raine looked at Lucy, from her ponytails and Dr. Pepper t-shirt to jeans and riding boots. She was supposed to be the séance expert in the group, and now she was ready to run.

Lucy was trembling, and that was when Raine realized that under the whole witch-like persona, was a fifteen-year-old girl just wanting to be different in a world of other fifteen-year-old girls doing the same things. "Fine. You keep the sage—you fan the smoke."

Mahogany banisters curved around the foyer to an upstairs balcony with tattered and faded burgundy carpet in the center. The stairs creaked like in the other part of the house, echoing in the cavernous entryway and house. Raine continued to fan the smoke, with both repeating another incantation, "Smoke has cleared this sacred space, leaving light and love in its place." Simple, yet effective, just like Sorcha said. They repeated each incantation three times.

Raine thought about Aunt Melinda and her attitude towards this sort of practice, and in a way, she understood more today than she did before. Prayers are like incantations—they are both intentions set free to the universe, to the energy surrounding us. Like the Boy Scout motto and slogan, or mission and vision statements. It was not witchcraft. It was an affirmation of what you want, or a statement of gratitude—that was all.

It seemed silly to think that these types of statements of intention were only appropriate in a church, as Aunt Melinda believed. She believed if these "prayers" were not sent to *her* God, then they must be evil. She'd heard stories about the ladies at the apothecary. Aunt Melinda still called Ashlyne's grandmother a witch, blamed her for the terrible accident at the lake. Even if they were witches, they were not evil. Raine didn't believe for a minute that Ashlyne or Sorcha would do anything to harm anyone, and she couldn't believe their beloved grandmother would, either. These words Raine and Lucy spoke were for good, to free the spirit trapped and to clear the house where she and her family lived.

They walked along the shorter hallway to the north side, cleansing each room until they backtracked along the balcony again, and *bam!* A door slammed at the end of the south wing, above the ballroom. Lucy's hands grabbed onto Raine's arm, and Raine struggled to hold the large shell. The smoke drifted up to her face, making her eyes water.

"Raine, let's go. I don't feel comfortable with this—"

"Are you kidding? This was your all your idea in the first place. Let's ask the ghost for help, you said. Let's get them to help with our project." Raine grasped the feather and shell tightly, determined to complete this mission. "And you are the one who asked Ashlyne and Sorcha for help. This is what they said to do."

"You're right. Let's just do it and go," Lucy said, her voice low and a bit shaky.

"Yes." Raine took a deep breath, closed her eyes, and tried to focus.

The first two rooms on the left at the top of the stairs were empty, aside from a chest of drawers in one room, and the next room was more like a large closet of some kind. Two more rooms on the right also mostly empty, just old stuffed chairs and a stack of framed wall hangings, and that was where the hallway became intimidating.

The door at the end of the hall remained closed, leaving the hall darker than anyplace else in the house. A low growl was barely audible from inside, and the girls heard it. Grrrrrmmm….

The girls stood side by side where the balcony ended and the hall began, and they peeked into the first room on the right. It was a large bedroom, with a canopy bed still in place, a bench at the end of the bed, a dresser and a chest matching the bed. This room had its own bathroom with a shower.

"Wonder why the furniture in this room isn't covered in white sheets like the rest of the house," Raine said. "It's nice."

"I'll keep my bunk bed in a room shared with two sisters, thank you."

They smudged the large bedroom on the right side of the hall and two more bedrooms on the left. There was a bathroom with a clawfoot tub, the last room on the right. They stood about six feet from the tall door at the end of the hall and tried to build up the nerve to open it. From the gap at the bottom of the door, a shadow passed quickly and subtle enough to make Lucy blink.

"Did you see that?" Lucy whispered, and Raine realized that Lucy had been clinging to her arm the entire time.

"Smoke has cleared this sacred space, light and love are in its place. Smoke has cleared this sacred space, light and love are in its place."

Lucy joined in the chant and they stepped towards the door. Raine handed the shell and feather to Lucy and reached for the crystal doorknob, original to the house, she thought, then she realized that was a very odd thought to have before opening the door to an unrested spirit. She then turned it slowly before pushing the door open.

The girls were blown back by the force of the entity, the swarm knocking them to the ground as it shot out of the room, against the walls, under the chandelier in the foyer, and downstairs. Lucy dusted the embers from her shirt and pants, stamping out any that had fallen to the floor.

Raine said, "Well, at least he's gone."

"Do you think he's really gone, Raine, for good?"

"How would I know?" She was still holding the sage in the shell. "That is definitely not Raymond. That, I know for sure."

"Isn't that what we wanted? For him to leave?" Lucy looked around, wide-eyed, with trembling hands. "Whoever he was, he's gone. Now, let's go."

Raine took a deep breath and nodded. "We need to smudge that room first."

The sage still had a small glow, easily seen in the dark hallway. Raine blew on the sage until it smoked freely. Assuring no embers remained on the floor, they pushed the door open all the way. It was another fully furnished bedroom, no white covers on the bed or dresser. A cigar odor lingered in the bedding and curtains, and Raine cautiously stepped inside. The dresser to the left of the door had a white marble top, with intricately carved legs. It had ladies' things—hairbrush and comb set, mirror, a crystal dish with some jewelry—pearl earrings that looked familiar to her. She'd seen them, in the library, on the woman.

Raine walked to the right, where a portrait of a bride and groom hung in a circular frame, and Raine guessed it was from the late 1800s or early 1900. The wedding dress was ankle-length, and the woman's long hair was pinned on top of her head.

"This must be Adeline and Raymond," Raine said.

"Possible. It's the same woman in the photo downstairs."

"Maybe we could find out more about them." She looked around the room for other clues in this room. From the dusty, outdated décor, the room hadn't been used for decades. There was a tall dresser that had small drawers at the top and larger drawers near the floor. Raine walked the circumference of the room, around the four-poster bed with matching carvings, and waved puffs of sage as she and Lucy repeated the incantation.

There were no more run-ins with swarm-thing. Swarm-man. Raine wasn't sure how she felt about that anymore. Maybe he wasn't all that bad after all. It could be one of her ancestors, Adalbert, or even Magnus. Maybe he doesn't know how to be a peaceful ghost physically, but spiritually, he was kind. He hadn't caused harm to them, not really. He was just… wild.

Lucy stood at the door with her arms folded tightly, while Raine looked around for clues to his identity. In the far corner, was an armoire. Raine pulled on the handle, and it was locked. Under the window, was a cedar chest covered with a lace cloth. Raine carefully folded the cloth and moved it to the floor. She clicked the button to open the lid and it was locked too. She checked under the chest, then stood and ran her hand across the top of the armoire for a key. Nothing. Then, without touching it, the lid to the chest popped open, squeaky hinges echoing on the high ceiling as the chest fully opened.

"Holy crap. Raine, let's go. Seriously."

"I think he wants us to look in here." Raine turned her palms up in surrender, then knelt to see what treasures she could find. "Hey, Lucy, check this out."

Inside the cedar chest was like a time capsule to the late 1800s, with sepia-toned photographs, postcards made of heavy cardboard, and a yellowed lace gown with a sky-blue skirt. She ran her fingers over the tiny pearl beads sewn into the neckline, blue ribbon woven around the sleeves, so carefully handmade years ago. Raine glanced at the photo on the wall and realized it was the same wedding dress. Under the dress was a leather-bound notebook and Raine picked it up, carefully untied the cord and opened it to the first page. She stood and set the book on the bed, turning pages to see years of notations inked in longhand swirls and curls.

"Does it have a name in it?" Lucy asked.

"Yes. There's a note on the first page. It says, *To my daughter, Adeline Mae Lischka Sommer, Congratulations on your marriage. Treasure every moment with your Kentucky family. Love, Mother.*" Raine closed the book, skimming the Celtic cross stamped on the cover with her finger. She opened the top drawers of the dresser, found a linen handkerchief, and she wrapped the diary before holding it out to Lucy. "We're taking this. It may give us an idea who swarm-man might be."

As the words left her mouth, the cedar chest lid dropped, and the lace cover flew up to the ceiling then floated above, gently falling to rest perfectly on top the cedar chest as it was before. The bedroom door slammed closed and opened again, very slowly, with a high-pitched squeak in the hinges. A man's upbeat laughter in the distance echoed in the cavernous foyer.

"Is he laughing at us?" Raine looked out of the corner of her eyes at the door. "It sounds like he's laughing at us."

"Let's go, Raine. Seriously. This is freaking me out." Lucy backed away, shaking her head, and pushing the journal back to Raine. "I don't want that, either."

"It's just a notebook. What can it hurt?" Raine sighed, shoved the journal in the back of her pants, and picked up the smudging shell and feather. "Come on. Let's go. We smudged everything but the attic."

"And the cellar," Lucy said. She was halfway down the staircase to the foyer before Raine was out of the bedroom. "You are on your own. I'm sorry, but I'm out."

"What cellar?" Raine called down the stairs. The entire house was to be smudged, including the cellar. Lucy was nowhere to be seen. "Lucy? What cellar?"

After Lucy left in a state of panic and shock from the ghostly events, Raine picked up the earrings from the dish. Although she couldn't wear them until her ears were pierced, maybe her father could sell them at the flea market.

Raine finished smudging the attic. It was dark and dusty up in the three rooms, but no more signs of ghosts. One room was a nursery and playroom, filled with old toys and cribs, another a room with four twin beds, perhaps for nannies or housekeepers, she wasn't certain. The third room served as storage, housing wooden crates, aged trunks, and shelves decked with an assortment of decorations and miscellaneous items.

In awe of this hidden space, she stumbled upon a small box on a shelf. Upon opening it, she discovered a string of white beads, perhaps pearls. Swiftly tucking the box into her front pocket, she hoped that it might hold some value and her father could sell it. Looking around, she realized there were many things her father could sell.

Moving among the crates, she uncovered a stack of paintings, the initial one bearing a resemblance to the artwork in the library, particularly the one painting that kept showing up outside her room. Wiping away the dust, she carried it downstairs to the library, placing it on the floor beneath the others. With matching frames, they should be hung side by side. She would ask if her father could sell those at the next flea market.

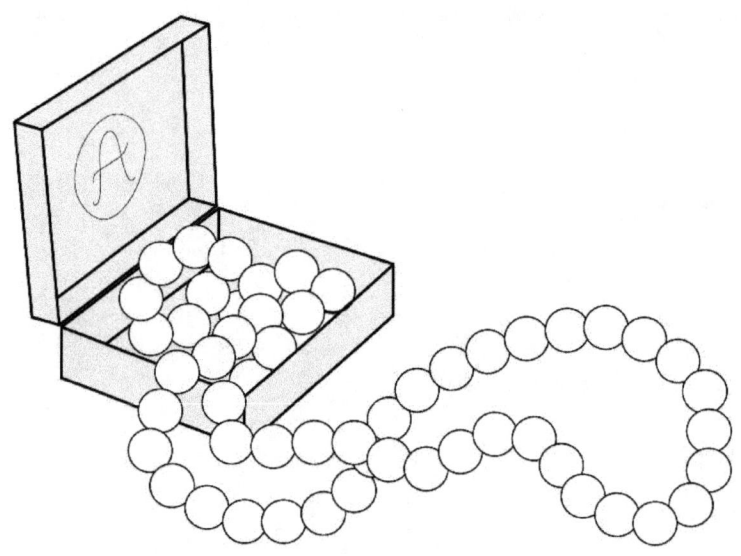

Chapter Fourteen

Lorraine and David arrived at the bank on early in the morning with enough cash to settle their outstanding debt and the third loan. They planned to pay at the cashier counter and had no appointment with Ned Baker. Lorraine joined David, as they would stop by the A&P, and if they had time, Lorraine needed to run into K-Mart for a couple of items.

"I'd like to pay on this loan. I have paid the $822 in late payments and the late fees on the mortgage, and I'd like to pay off the balance of this loan as well as make next month's payments on the other two loans." The clerk nodded and began counting the money. "And I'll need receipts for all three payments."

"David, I don't know how you pulled this off, but thank you."

"Ma, there's always a way. We'll be fine." He hadn't told his mother about selling the rare motorcycle his father prized, but he knew she'd understand. No need to mention it. The rest of the money came from Billy selling nearly everything he'd taken to the flea market, and two truckloads he dropped off at his store.

"I pray you are right."

The short, balding man they'd known for years greeted them at the counter. "David Sommer, good to see you in today."

"Good morning, Ned." The words oozed of dislike for the man who'd tried to take advantage of his family. Between selling the Harley and the antiques, David walked into the bank with more than $4000, which surprised David as much as Ned. He needed more by the time the board met in June. However, that was not going to take away from the satisfaction of seeing the shock on Ned's face.

"Lorraine," he said, "so good to see you both, and just in time."

"We're all caught up and paid ahead."

"Yes, well, I hope it's enough to satisfy the board. Please, come to my office. I'd like to introduce you to the newest board member."

Lorraine and David looked at each other. David shrugged, following him down the hall to a large office. There, sitting behind a huge cherry desk, was Liam Baker.

"Well, well, If It Isn't David Sommer." Liam didn't bother to stand. Instead, he leaned back in his chair, fingertips to fingertips, with a smirk that implied a sinister plan. He wore a slick new suit in dark blue, with a crisp white shirt and tie. There remained a greenish-blue hue below his left eye from where David had punched him nearly a month ago.

"Liam," David said calmly and nodded, trying to put the pieces of their game in order. It was just a chess match, and the Bakers were setting a trap for David and the Sommer family. Besides having Liam on the board, he knew there was more. "I see you've made a career change—musician to banker."

"We all must grow up sometime, hold a responsible job, pay our bills. Isn't that right, David?" Liam eyed him head to toe, deliberately focusing on David's worn boots, still dirty from morning chores. Liam knew which buttons to push and targeted David's weak point. "How's the leg?"

"It's fine. How's your face?"

Lorraine reached for David's hand, squeezed into a fist and so tense, it felt like steel. "Liam, it's good to see you. I hope your mother is doing well. Please tell her I said hello."

"Certainly, Mrs. Sommer. You are looking lovely today."

"Thank you." Lorraine wasn't oblivious to Liam's snide comment. Her clothing was outdated and there were grease stains on her shirt from frying bacon that morning. While she wasn't ashamed of her appearance, she understood Liam's intention with his fake compliment. "Oh, I almost forgot, I brought strawberry jam for your family. As a thank you for being so understanding about our predicament."

Kill them with kindness, that was always his mother's way, but David wore no smile. Calming himself with deliberate, measured breaths, he abruptly departed, leaving with seemingly kind words that carried a subtle sting, "Have a fantastic day."

Once in the truck, Lorraine remained quiet, as did David. They stopped at the supermarket in Murray and stocked up on groceries—pasta, rice, dry beans, canned goods—things they didn't grow or raise on the farm. It was the first time in a long while that they shopped without worrying about not having enough cash at checkout. They took their time, making sure they picked up extra sale items, while still cognizant of how much they spent.

"Hello." Annie was shopping at A&P as well. She'd changed her appearance recently. She'd cut her hair, had on less make-up, both of which made her look ten years younger. "What a nice surprise seeing y'all here."

"Hi there, Annie," Lorraine greeted her. "I really like your new haircut. It brings out your eyes."

"Thank you, Lorraine. It was time for a change."

"You not working today?" She normally worked afternoons—David should know, since he'd been at Mack's nearly every day for the past three years. "Or did the old man finally give you a day off?"

"I'm going in late today." She stood up straight, adding another inch to her short stature and added, "I took an assessment test at Murray. If I score high enough, I'm going to college!"

"How exciting!" Lorraine gave her a hug, "Congratulations."

It occurred to David that in the bright grocery store lights, Annie's youth was evident, whereas in the dim bar room, she appeared much older. And college was always a good thing, he believed, and was impressed by her ambition. "That's pretty cool. What type of classes are you planning to take?"

"Basic classes for now but, eventually, business classes."

"Interesting. You'll be great at that with the experience you have at Mack's."

"Yeah, he's encouraged me to take classes. I've been helping with the books for years. I guess it's time I find out if I'm doing it right."

David listened as Annie and Lorraine chatted, pushing carts up and down the aisles at A&P. College was something he'd never considered for himself, and at this point, he felt he needed to focus on the farm, not school. He'd leave the college experience for Raine.

Lorraine and Annie spoke in hushed tones, and David had an idea why. His birthday was next Sunday, and she was most likely inviting Annie. He found it endearing that his mother did this every year for his birthday, and she always had. She made a big deal out of it, no matter what else was going on. He' play along, acting like he didn't suspect anything was happening, but really, a surprise party every year wasn't much of a surprise.

When Annie headed to check out, David waved and said, "See you soon." Both women stared blankly at him, wondering if he knew about the party next Sunday. "I might stop in for a beer tomorrow night, at the pub."

"Oh, yes. At the pub," Annie said. "See you then."

"Are you seeing Ashlyne this weekend?"

"I might." David hoped he would see her today. "The grand re-opening of their store is Saturday. Why don't you go with me, Ma?"

"That would be lovely."

Once home, David went to the office to file the receipts from the bank. He was starting to feel like things were more organized, at least the paperwork. His taxes were nearly done, thanks to Sam's mother, Colleen. She'd helped Mack with his taxes this year, and David met with her at the pub. She helped him get the correct forms in place and took a couple of phone calls to answer his questions on filling them out. Best of all, she understood his tight financial situation and agreed to work pro bono. She said it was the right thing to do as the Sommer family has been so kind to her son since they moved back to Cypress Grove. That, and she thought what her great uncle tried to do was horrific.

The next flea market was on Mother's Day weekend, and Billy had agreed to sell what he could, but they needed something more. He had to come up with thousands before June, else Liam would certainly try to foreclose on the farm.

Raine came in from the main house carrying a large frame.

"Hey, pumpkin. What is that?" David asked.

"I found this in the attic." She pulled the jewelry box from her pocket. "Maybe this would sell at the flea market or something. I think they are pearls like the photo on the wall. Oh, and I found another painting of trees up there too – it matches the one down here."

"Where's Lucy?"

"She left about twenty minutes ago. We tried to get rid of the dead animal smell in the old kitchen, but I don't think it worked."

"Is that what I smell?" David opened the small box and lifted a strand of pearls, raised his eyebrows, and nodded. "Nice. I wonder how much these would be worth."

"You should ask Ashlyne. She seems to know a lot about this stuff."

"Good idea."

Lorraine was fixing dinner—spaghetti and meatballs. It smelled so good, much better than the dead opossum in the other part of the house, and Raine realized she hadn't eaten much for lunch. She felt Lorraine could use her help, but first, Raine took the steps two at a time to her room, closed and locked the door. She pulled the diary from her back pocket and started to read.

Her great-grandmother's diary, with the first entry on May 27, 1902. She wrote about the wedding held a few days before, a simple ceremony at the non-denominational church here in Cypress Grove. While she was Catholic, St. Joseph's Catholic Church in Mayfield was the closest Catholic church at the time. It was too far for some of the guest to travel, and because Raymond grew up in the local church, they compromised. Father Conrad from St. Joseph's traveled to Cypress Grove and performed the ceremony alongside Pastor Horace Redman. Afterwards, they all returned to the ballroom for dinner and dancing.

There was a reception at Cypress Hill following the ceremony at church. It is a beautiful home, but with the white lilies and roses gracing each corner of the ballroom and pink roses on the table, it was breathtaking. Franz and Margaret had arranged it all and thought of everything, from the carriage ride following the ceremony to gift bags for the guests as they departed.

Adalbert made it back from Europe in time for the wedding. Having spent the past few years abroad, he returned in good spirits for a man of his age, but perhaps it's his companion, Isaac, who keeps him smiling. He brought us gifts from his travels, including two paintings of his own. We will keep those displayed in the house for years to come.

It's only been three days since we were wed, but already, I know coming to Kentucky was the right decision for me. It is a challenge, having left all my friends in Virginia, but already, I've made friends with a young woman, Saoirse, at the apothecary. We are the same age, and of course, our mothers are both hoping they will be a grandmother first.

There is also a woman on staff whom I've become very close to—her name is Ellen, and while she is ten years older, we both married this spring. We have so much in common, considering there are so many differences in our lives. I hope we can bring her on full-time soon, and perhaps her husband as well, but more than that, I am certain our friendship will continue.

"Holy cow," Raine mused. "Eva's great-great grandmother was more than an employee. She was friends with Adeline… I wonder why she didn't mention they were friends when we visited her. She made it sound like she was a worker."

Raine put the diary under her mattress for safekeeping. When she opened the door, the painting from the attic was outside her room on the floor, against the door. "What the… no way."

Carrying the painting down to the library, she sat it on the floor where she'd left it. Her father had turned off the lamp, which still had the long extension cord, to work at the desk. He wasn't in the living room, either. "Grandma? Where's Dad?"

"He said he had to go into town, I assume to Mack's for a beer."

When her grandmother said that, it occurred to Raine that her father hadn't been drinking as much. She looked in the living room, now free of beer cans, ashtrays, and it was… clean.

"Did Dad stop smoking?"

Lorraine turned, a puzzled look on her face, "Yes, maybe so. I haven't seen him with a cigarette for several days now."

"Or a beer," Raine added. She smiled, Lorraine smiled, and together, they said her name.

"Ashlyne."

***

David parked behind Mack's, near the apothecary. He wasn't sure if he should go in to see her, still dressed in his worn jeans and dirty boots, but she knew he was a farmer. She had never judged him for his dress before, and she wouldn't do it now. With the small box in his hand, he got out of the truck and crossed the street. Then, his heart sank. A shiny new blue Cadillac drove through the quad, two people in the car. Liam and a dark-haired girl. *Why on earth would Ashlyne go anywhere with him,* he wondered. David stood on the corner near Michael's doctor's office, which was closed. No point of going in now, and he sullenly turned back to the truck.

"Where are you going?"

He turned to see Ashlyne standing at the side door, hand on hip, wearing bell bottom jeans and a halter top short enough to show her belly button. Her dark hair blew in the wind, revealing sparkling earrings. He couldn't help but grin, first, because she was stunning, but more than anything, just relieved it wasn't her in the car with Liam.

"Hey," he trotted over to her, limping the last few steps due to searing pain in his left leg. "I thought I just saw you leave, but I guess it wasn't you."

"Not with Liam—no way. He came in with her. I think that is Sam's mother. I think he brought her in here to make a point. Are they dating?"

"What a jerk." Then David started laughing. He laughed out loud and slapped his hand on his thigh.

"What in the world are you laughing at?"

"Sam's mother," he said, "is Liam's cousin. He used his own cousin to make you jealous."

"You think Liam wanted to make me jealous?"

"Definitely." David shoved his hands in his pocket, not sure if running to Ashlyne to look at a strand of pearls made sense. It was the only excuse he could think of to see her, because he didn't need her opinion on the necklace. Billy could give him a price for selling it.

"So, were you coming to see me?" She smiled, allowing him to open the door for them to go inside.

"I was. I'd like your opinion on something Raine found in the attic, maybe see what it might be worth at the flea market."

"I'd be happy to take a look." Sorcha was talking with a couple about teas behind the counter, offering samples to boost sales.

"Oh, I didn't think. You are probably busy, with the re-opening this Saturday."

"I'm not busy. We are ready, so I have the rest of the night to relax."

"Okay, if you're sure. Ma has dinner on, so I'll be quick." David took a seat on one of the overstuffed chairs at the back of the store, noticing the whisky prescription hanging on the wall next to the pharmacy window. Within minutes, Ashlyne handed him a steaming cup of coffee and sat on the armrest. "Say, would you like to join us for dinner tonight? Spaghetti and meatballs."

"It sounds wonderful, but Michael is upstairs cooking chicken stew for us. Maybe another time?"

"Oh, of course." David sipped the coffee and set the cup on the table next to him. Ashlyne leaned over him, setting her cup next to his. He noticed she wore a light floral scent, and was intoxicating. For some reason, at that exact moment, he heard Caroline's voice in his head whispering, *She's the one, David. She's the one for you.*

"Show me what she found."

He handed her the small green velvet box. Lifting the lid and the strand of pearls, she carefully inspected the beads and the clasp. "It looks like a gold clasp, but I'm not an expert on pearls. I've never seen any this shade of ivory—they are beautiful."

David nodded, mesmerized by her gentleness with the necklace. It was the small things—her petite hands holding the pearls, her eyes reflecting the lights, her hair dangling as she looked down. It wasn't likely the pearl necklace would be enough to save the farm, even if they were real. Really, it was just an excuse to see Ashlyne. He knew it, and he was pretty sure she knew it. Her delicate fingers pushed a lock of hair behind her ear, and she looked at him with golden eyes, warm and welcoming. She really is the one.

"Would they sell at the flea market?"

"Most likely, but you should get a professional jeweler to appraise them first. If they are real, they could be worth hundreds of dollars, maybe thousands. Pearls this size are rare, so it's most likely manufactured pearls."

"Thank you, Ashlyne. Maybe we'll just hang on to them."

"Tell me, David. What is really going on? Why are you selling the antiques from Cypress Hill?"

He looked away, embarrassed at the financial situation he found himself. How could he ever think a woman like Ashlyne would be interested in a man like him? He could barely take care of himself, much less his daughter or the farm. "There's a little cash flow issue on the farm, that's all. I'll work it out."

"I'm sure you will. Is there anything I can do to help? I know a lot of buyers, quite a few people in antiques, people from college."

"You'd do that for me?"

"Of course," she said. Seeing the surprise in David's eyes, she did what she'd told herself she wouldn't do again, not to David. With a slow breath, she connected to him, intuitively, looked inside to feel his soul, to be sure he was as humble and honest as he seemed. The warmth that surged within her validated her initial belief that he was indeed a genuinely good man.

Drawing nearer, she whispered, "I think I'd do just about anything for you."

Chapter Fifteen

Overlooking the back yard, Raine worked a drawing of Cypress Hill and the former slaves—that was how she would refer to them now—former slaves who once worked in the field. She was relieved to have the project almost over, at least the research part. Digging up the dark family history, albeit with a gentle end with Adalbert's gesture of land for the slave families, it was exhausting. She thought about slavery, and how for centuries this went on all across the world – and still does in some parts – and wondered how anyone could possibly think it's okay to *own* other humans. It's unfathomable.

She sketched at her desk after breakfast, happy to have a few days to finish. Sam and Lucy were coming over to put the presentation together after school, and this was her main contribution to the project. Eva wouldn't make it, with dance recital taking priority. Raine felt that she and Eva got off easy, with Sam and Lucy doing most of the work, so the drawing needed to be really nice.

She hoped others wouldn't think less of her because her ancestors were slave owners, if that were even possible. Although she lived in the largest house in town, she felt everyone knew her family had no money and were deeply indebted to the bank. She felt exposed by the project, vulnerable to the judgment of others. Then again, there were some who would be proud to know she was a descendant of slave owners, like Priscilla Hopkins. That girl made Raine sick to her stomach. If slavery still existed, her family would have slaves today.

The idea of someone being a lesser human, deserving of being owned and controlled by another, just because of the color of their skin, was unimaginable to Raine. She read the paper, she watched television news, and she was aware of the current racial tension across the country. She saw it in her tiny corner of the world, and the history they'd discovered in this project had made Raine that much more aware of her family's part in the history of slavery.

She hoped the slaves who once lived at Cypress Hill were well cared for, unlike so many, who were abused and tortured by their owners. It had nothing to do with the project, but the fact that Mrs. Collins mentioned the former slaves were given land when freed made Raine feel a little better about Adalbert owning slaves. Maybe he'd changed, realized how wrong it was holding slaves, and tried to make things right with the ones he owned. She hoped it was the case.

The diary was on her desk, left out from the night before. She opened to the next entry, where Adeline was writing about the buried treasure Adalbert talked of.

Raymond's grandfather appears to be becoming confused. Old age, I suppose, but he keeps talking about a treasure on the property, something of value left for his heirs to find someday. He says it is hiding in plain sight, where no one would see. Under the trees. I believe he may have dreamed of a treasure, or remembering something he'd buried as a child, some marbles, or a whistle, but I highly doubt there is a valuable treasure out there.

"Raine, come on if you want to go with me," Lorraine called. She quickly put things away and headed down the stairs.

Still, the words echoed in her mind—hiding in plain sight. What did that mean? Lorraine drove down the cobblestone path to where Eva and Lucy were waiting. Raine looked back towards the house, with so many trees on the property, at least a dozen in the front yard. How would anyone know which tree? They were all in plain sight.

In history class, the schedule for presentation was posted on the wall. The written paper was to be turned in by Wednesday of next week, and the presentations were the first week of May. Lucy was confident. Sam was nonchalant. Eva and Raine were like deer in headlights, unsure what their role would be during the presentation and not really knowing what Lucy and Sam had put together.

Noticing Raine's unease, Sam turned to her and whispered, "We got this."

"I hope so." His deep brown eyes warmed her heart, and she took a deep breath, smiling at him. She kept her hair behind her ears today, a colorful scarf around her head. It was mostly because she hadn't washed her hair the night before, but it was also the latest trend around school. It matched a solid green shirt she'd found in her mother's room. Lately, Raine paid attention to stylish trends.

Reaching for the ends of the scarf, Sam whispered, "I like the way you have your hair today."

"Thanks." Raine felt the heat rise in her cheeks and knew her face was turning pink, which always made the freckles stand out more. Sam smiled and turned around when Mrs. Weismann started speaking.

"Are you flirting with Sam?" Eva murmured.

"No!" Raine hoped he didn't hear Eva ask her that question. It was ridiculous—why would she flirt with Sam? It wasn't like he liked her, she was pretty sure. He'd spent so much time with Lucy on the project, and they had more in common than she had with him. Lucy could be charming when she isn't shouting orders, and pretty, and she was smart, like Sam. Raine believed Sam couldn't be interested in a girl like her.

She prayed he was right, however, that the project would receive a high grade. This was almost a third of her grade, and she needed every bit of it to pass the class. It wasn't that she didn't put in the effort at school, but it was more difficult for her. Lucy and Raine heard the same thing in class, had the same books to study, but Lucy got an A and Raine got a D. Now, she needed tutoring in algebra, and she didn't know if her father could afford it.

After class, the four met at the lockers in the hall. Lucy and Sam chatted at his locker, while Raine and Eva went down the hall to their lockers. After a few minutes, Lucy and Sam caught up with them.

"Are we ready to head over to your place, Raine?"

"I need to go to Sage Sisters to pick up Dad's birthday present. Ashlyne is holding a leather binder for me."

"Okay, I'll walk with you if that's okay," Sam said.

"You two go ahead. I'll walk home with Eva. I need to stop by my house and get the poster board for the project. Let's meet at your house then, say at four?"

"Sounds good to me." Sam stood next to Raine, at least six inches taller, and when she looked at him, she had to tilt her head back. She nodded. That was when Sam put his arm around her shoulders, turned and walked with her towards the doors. "Okay then, we'll see you at four."

"Wooo, somethin' happenin' there, right, Lucy?" Eva giggled, understanding Raine was the first of the girls to have a boyfriend.

"Eva, that's been happening since Sam transferred here. Raine just didn't realize it until now." Lucy looked at Eva, tilted her head and added, "I always thought you'd be the first."

"Me? Hell no! I ain't got time for no boyfriend. Especially now, getting ready for this recital, and then my trip this summer. I got a lot going on."

Exiting through the doors, Raine and Sam strolled side by side, his arm draped comfortably around her shoulders. Although she didn't mind the closeness, her nerves tied her tongue in knots, rendering her unable to speak. The situation dazed her—what did this mean? Was he her boyfriend? These thoughts buzzed through her mind, leaving her at a loss for words with Sam's comforting touch.

"You okay with this?" he finally asked.

Gazing at him, she admired his handsome features—the dark hair framing his angular face and the warmth of his broad smile. She couldn't help but notice the attention he garnered from others, feeling a sense of pride that of all the girls in the school, he had chosen her to walk beside. "Yes." She couldn't help but giggle a little, then looked away.

"Are you blushing? Raine, what am I going to do with you?" He pulled her closer, leading her off the sidewalk to stand underneath a pink flowering dogwood tree, the blooms bright against a teal blue sky. Face to face, his hands around her waist, he leaned forward and gently kissed her.

Raine had never been kissed before. Recalling late night talks with Lucy about when they would have their first kisses, she closed her eyes. She was hesitant to open them after he kissed her, and all she managed to do was utter a quiet, "Thank you."

"Uh, you're welcome?" Sam replied. Realizing the first kiss jitters may have gotten the best of Raine, he asked, "Is this the first time you've been kissed?"

She opened her eyes then, looked around at a few kids watching them, and said, "No. Well, yes, first boy kiss, but does it matter?"

"Not at all, but I think we should kiss again. For practice, you know." He kissed her again, this time a little longer, and Raine didn't care who was watching at this point. Her hand moved around his neck to steady herself while they kissed, then he pulled back and muttered, "Just so you know, that was my first kiss too."

***

Sage Sisters held a grand opening on Saturday, or rather a grand re-opening, for the apothecary. A new phase, a rebirth of the same type of general store, but a different type of medicinal products. Ashlyne ran ads in as many papers as she could fine—the Mayfield Weekly, the Paducah Gazette, the Murray State News, and local church bulletins. Sorcha put together a raffle for three prizes—a tea pot with a bag of loose tea, a book on stones with three gemstones, and the grand prize, a gift basket with a little of everything.

There were people waiting outside on the sidewalk when Ashlyne opened the doors, exactly when the cuckoo clock rang ten times. Sorcha, Michael, and Ashlyne waited inside to welcome the new and returning customers.

"Mrs. Sommer, so good to see you. I'm happy you made it to the opening," Ashlyne greeted Lorraine with a hug.

"Thank you, Ashlyne. I love what you've done with the place!" Lorraine brought the girls with her, who immediately began looking at the clothing and jewelry. "David said he'd be over later, after tending to chores."

"Be sure to write your name on these tickets and drop them in the box for the door prizes. Is there anything you were looking for today?"

"No, nothing in particular." Lorraine hesitated then, pointing her index finger at her temple, said, "Oh, there is something I wanted to ask you."

"Sure, anything."

"I know you are a history teacher, but how are you with algebra?"

Ashlyne grinned. "I can manage at high school level if that's what you mean."

"I'd be grateful if you could tutor Raine. I'll pay you, of course."

"No need to do that. Have her stop by after school and I'll help her with homework, or memorizing formulas or rules. Once she has those, it's not so difficult."

"You are a godsend, Ashlyne. Thank you!" Lorraine gave her hand a squeeze. "Please come by the house next Sunday after church. We're having a little surprise party for David's birthday."

"I'll be there."

Michael was serving samples of fruit smoothies, something most people in the area had not tried before, so he cleverly called them "milk shake smoothies", adding just a splash of coconut cream and honey. They were a healthier version of a milk shake, made with fresh frozen fruit instead of ice cream. He hoped it would become a trend in Cypress Grove.

Sorcha spent much of her time lately making the skin care products—lotions, soaps, body scrubs, perfumes—and created a Sage Sisters logo. Each item had a custom tag, listing the ingredients and why each worked like magic. She also bottled potions, which were mostly essential oils and smelled great, but she might have cast a little more into those tiny bottles. Those also had authentic labeling, including how to use the potions for your own magic.

"Are they really magical potions?" Raine asked.

"They are if you want them to be," Sorcha explained. "But there is nothing in that bottle but coconut oil, essential oils, flower essences, and other herbs. It's all natural."

"No magic?" Lucy winked. "Okay, I know what you mean."

That was exactly why they sold out of the jasmine love potion, the mulberry money magnet, and the lucky lavender potions. Sorcha might have been trained as a nurse, but she had developed a very clever marketing plan for the products.

Lorraine joined the girls and tried the hand lotion, rubbing it into her arthritic fingers. Closing her eyes and inhaling through her nose, the lotion smelled like flowers and lemon and her dry hands became slick and soft.

"The facial mask is delicious," Sorcha said. "Made from oatmeal, flax seed, coconut oil, vanilla, and a little honey. It does wonders for fine lines."

"You mean wrinkles? Does it work?" Lorraine asked. "Wait a minute… is this your grandmother's recipe? She gave this to Maggie when she had acne."

"This is different, but I have the acne treatment too. It's also edible but tastes horrible. Made with turmeric, green tea, apple cider vinegar."

"Yes, I remember it now. It worked so well." After looking around at jewelry, candy, handwoven rugs, windchimes, and more, Lorraine purchased a large-sized oatmeal mask. The girls wanted to stay and agreed to walk home when done. Lorraine ran into David as she was leaving.

"What did you buy?" he asked. He'd cleaned up after chores, wearing a crisp shirt the same color blue as his eyes and brown slacks. He left his shirt untucked and unbuttoned, with a Bagdad Seed t-shirt underneath.

"None of your business," she said with a mischievous smile. "It's definitely not wrinkle cream."

David shook his head and laughed. "Are the girls here?"

His mother pointed out the girls at the back of the store, patted her son on the chest, and said, "Ashlyne has created something delightful here. Be sure to tell her how special she is, David."

"Ma, come on."

"I know sometimes you think people know how you feel, but honestly, we don't. If you like her, tell her."

"I love you, Ma." He kissed his mother on the cheek as he moved past her. David glanced around and saw Ashlyne talking with an elderly couple about teas, so he took a closer look at old man Whitmer's wood bowls. Such incredible work, and he noticed the bottom of each bowl has his initials burned in, like a tiny hot iron was used, the way cattle are branded. David whispered, "I'll be darned. He's made them with brand awareness."

"Mr. Whitmer has become somewhat of an artist, signing each piece he makes now. He's been attending art shows in Nashville, Louisville, Atlanta." Ashlyne pointed out a small tag attached with information about Whitmer's work.

"I had no idea he was doing this. Working with wood, sure, but he's really found a niche, hasn't he?"

"He seems to have found a way to earn some money while doing what he loves."

"And you," David gestured across the store, "this is amazing."

"Thank you," Ashlyne beamed. "I'm so glad you made it today."

"You still have aspirin, I see, and so much more."

"There was a shop in Berkeley very much like this one. It had once been a grocery and still had many foods, but it shifted to meet the needs and desires of college students, selling premade sandwiches and pizza by the slice. That store was the inspiration for Sage Sisters."

"You did it. You've completely changed the store and somehow managed to keep it looking like an apothecary, with bottles of natural medicines, vitamins, and things. You are a genius, aren't you?"

"I wouldn't say that." Ashlyne tucked a strand of hair behind her right ear, tilting her head slightly. With that one simple motion, David's heart skipped a beat, and he found it difficult to take a deep breath. He couldn't take his eyes off her. "Did you see the postcards? Souvenirs of Cypress Grove?"

"No, I haven't."

Ashlyne led him to a shelf to the right, next to a section of books. There, in two wooden stands, were postcards—one of the fountain, the other of Cypress Hill. Larger prints of the same two drawings were on the shelf below, each signed and numbered by the artist. "Your daughter drew these in oil pastels."

"Raine did that?"

"Yes, she was working on art for the project a few weeks back, and I happen to know a printer in Murray who makes postcards, so I paid her to borrow the artwork. She has the original for the project, of course, but I thought it would be nice to have a young local artist's work to sell."

"She didn't say a thing about it."

"Oh, I hope I haven't overstepped. She was excited about earning some money, so I offered to help. I paid her ten dollars each for the drawings."

"That sounds like a lot of money, especially if she got to keep the drawings."

"I will make the money back soon enough. We've already sold one print of the fountain and a few postcards. I hope it encourages her to continue drawing."

"Is that so?" David glanced over at Raine and smiled.

"Maybe she could buy some watercolors, or other supplies, with the money. Although, she has been looking at earrings."

"She's never mentioned needing anything to me," David said, shaking his head. "Sometimes I feel like I'm so out of touch with my own daughter. She's growing up so fast."

"I think you are a wonderful father, and you know her better than you think."

"Well, thank you for saying that. And thank you for helping her."

"My pleasure, but as you see," a young woman reached for a postcard on the shelf, showed her husband, then grabbed the other to purchase, "it's Raine who is helping me."

"She did say she wanted her ears pierced."

"It so happens that we do that here. If it's okay with you, she could get it done today."

"Really? You do that here too?"

"Yes, we sure do. Michael does it back in his office."

David smiled, finding it amazing that Ashlyne not only knew what Raine wanted, but that she had taken an interest in Raine's artwork, her schoolwork, and most likely, other things she wouldn't talk to David about. He gazed at the woman before him, feeling things he had not felt for years. Things he thought he'd never feel again.

"Ashlyne," he said, taking a deep breath. He was falling for her, and he hoped she felt the same. He heard the words in his head, but his lips didn't speak. It wasn't necessary. Ashlyne heard those words in his head loud and clear.

"David," she said after a moment and smiled. "How about you find Raine, and we'll get set up to pierce her ears?"

***

Storms came during the night, waking Raine with loud thunder and bright flashes of lightning. She remained in bed but couldn't fall back to sleep. She'd cleaned her newly pierced earlobes with alcohol, just as Ashlyne instructed, and turned the small gold post earrings her father bought her.

She'd had a dream about her mother again. Raine was at Sage Sisters with Ashlyne and her father, and they were admiring her new earrings. Her mother was there, standing off to the side watching David and Ashlyne, and seemed to recognize the bond that has formed between them. Her mother smiled and nodded, delighted that David had found love again and Raine had a mother-figure in her life.

Raine lay in bed, a melancholy yet optimistic feeling surrounding her. She knew that is how her mother would look at things – she is gone, and they needed to move on with life, find happiness, embrace love where it grows. Her mother is watching over them, and this is how she communicates with Raine now – through dreams. Raine was absolutely sure it was truly her mother in her dreams, not a dream about her mother, but her mother's spirit showing up to tell her things will be okay.

"Mom, I miss you. I love you. But I really, really need you to help us save the farm. I don't want to leave this place, and I know money problems are a huge problem for Dad. Please, if there is any way for you to help, now is the time."

Chapter Sixteen

David knew something was up with his mother and his daughter. They were acting strange and had yet to mention his birthday during breakfast. A lot of whispers before they left for church services, and with the big fuss Lorraine was making over brunch, together with the fact that Raine ran the vacuum, he suspected something was happening. Most likely, Maggie and her family would come over, maybe the aunts, and they'd all eat until they couldn't take another bite. That was when his mother would pull out a big cake with way too many candles.

He skipped church to feed the chickens, clean the stalls, and set the horses out to pasture. He didn't want to smell like barn when they ate, so he went upstairs to shower. He shaved and donned a crisp, striped polo shirt paired with jeans. When it came to footwear, he faced a decision between work boots or his father's brown dress shoes, as his sneakers had worn down completely on the soles and emitted a rather unpleasant odor. He opted for the boots.

Down the stairs, he saw that Maggie and three of her children—Russel, Jacob, and Linda—occupied the couch, the television tuned to reruns of *My Three Sons*. The networks had no choice but to play reruns, seeing how the baseball strike continued and games were postponed.

"Wow, look at you. Happy Birthday." Maggie stood, giving her brother a strong hug around the neck. They had the same dirty blonde hair, hers hanging in waves down her back, and the same blue eyes. "You clean up pretty well."

"Thanks." David squeezed his sister, lifting her off the ground.

"Ma's outdone herself today, David. She's invited the aunts, Mack, Pastor Tim…"

"Ah, man… I knew she was up to something. Very busy and very quiet."

"Well, she invited your girlfriend too."

"Girlfriend? What girlfriend?" His eyes squinted and his head shook. His mother knew he hadn't dated since Caroline. "Who?"

"Ashlyne." Maggie smiled knowingly, nodding in approval. "You didn't have a clue, right?"

"Ah, man. She's not my girlfriend!"

"Well, David. You've always been a little slow in figuring these things out." Maggie playfully slapped him on the chest. "Anyway, that's why we came early. I wanted to make sure you were presentable."

"Presentable?" He rubbed his hand through his hair, glancing down at the boots. Maybe he should have picked the loafers.

"Yeah, you know what I mean. You look good, David."

More voices came from the kitchen. The doors to the screened porch were open and there he saw Raine, Sam, Lucy, and Eva sitting on the bench. The youngest member of Maggie's family, Ben, was running around the kitchen wearing a towel clipped to his shoulders with clothespins. Bryce appeared to be chasing Ben, making sure he stayed out of the way of the women—Lorraine, Petra, and Melinda—while they peeled cooked potatoes. Being so small that he could barely peer over the kitchen table, David scooped Ben up in his arms, playfully giving him a little jiggle before cradling him across the table, as if he were soaring through the air like Superman.

"Weeeeee!" Ben squealed.

"Happy birthday, man." Bryce gave a manly side hug, squeezing David around the neck and shoving him away. "Or should I say… old man?"

"Hey, watch it! You're only a few months behind me."

"Yeah, but I'm not there yet." They turned when the girls laughed, noticing Sam sitting close to Raine, head down, smirking. "Looks like you have a situation there, David."

"Nah, he's working on some history project with them."

"Man, you ain't got a clue, do you?"

"Why does everyone keep saying that?" Raine and Sam were sitting on the swing, Sam's arm resting on the back of the swing. Raine was at least a foot away from him, her hands folded on her lap. Raine kept her hair behind her ears today, careful to not get any caught in her new earrings. David looked at her, his little girl, sitting next to Sam. They were just kids.

Then, Sam reached for Raine's ear, gently touched her earrings, and said, "I like the earrings."

Raine blushed, squirming in her seat. The truth hit David like a slap in the face. Sam and his little girl. Then, she twisted her long hair down the front, something she only did when she was nervous. That's when David put it together. "Son-of-a-bitch."

"Remember when I first came over to see Maggie? Your father took me in the library and gave me a talkin' to. He had me so terrified, I wasn't sure if I'd ever step foot in this house again."

David nodded to Bryce, expressing full understanding of his role as father, and walked over to the porch. Bryce grinned, knowing full well what was happening. It wasn't long before Sam followed David into the library, and the doors closed. Maggie joined her husband in the kitchen.

"What did you do?"

"Nothin'. Why?"

"I know you too well, Bryce Mitchell. You put David up to the same tricks Pa used on you."

"Woman, I have no idea what you are talking about." Bryce put his arms around his wife, kissing her on the cheek. She giggled, resting her head on his chest.

The three sexagenarian sisters chattered about how to chop celery properly, finally agreeing to disagree. Mack pulled up the drive with Annie, opening the car door for her. Lucy went out to greet them and carried in a large sheet cake from Paula's and sat it on the porch table. It was decorated with blue roses and the words *Happy Birthday, David* written on the top. Bryce chatted with Mack while Maggie introduced herself to Annie. She'd seen her before, but Maggie wasn't a regular at the pub, like Bryce and David.

"Where's our birthday boy?" Mack called out with his baritone voice, hoping David would hear him in the next room.

"He's in the library, having a little chat with Sam Hudson, a friend of the girls."

"David's giving him the shake down? Shouldn't you be in there, Bryce?"

"What? No, no—Lucy isn't, no."

"Really?" Mack stared curiously at the three girls." I always figured she'd be the first out of that group."

"You know, I did too," Bryce said, tilting his head in thought. Lucy was tall and thin, blonde, with big blue eyes. Raine was beautiful too, with her long, wavy hair and freckles, but Lucy was the outgoing girl. Raine was shy, and Eva only thought of dancing. Perhaps, he wondered, Lucy had another guy. "Now, you got me thinking."

***

David closed the doors behind them, leaving the small lamp plugged in to the extension cord as the only source of light in an otherwise dark room. He gestured for Sam to sit in a straight back, wooden chair next to the desk, and he tilted the lampshade slightly, directing the light into Sam's face.

"Sam," David began, "I wanted to thank you for helping the girls on this project and sorting through the maps and such. It really helped me with something I was working on."

Sam gulped, unable to see David's face behind the lamp. "My pleasure, sir."

"I hear the history project is wrapping up, which is why I'm a little surprised you are still hanging around the girls."

Sam wasn't sure how to respond, so he sat quietly, no expression on his face that David could read. He swallowed hard, looking around the library for something to say.

"I'm curious, though," David continued, walking around Sam and the desk, stopping behind the light once more. "What, exactly, are your intentions with my daughter?"

"Uh, intentions?"

"Yes. Intentions. What do you want from her?"

"Nothing, sir."

"Sam, come on." David waited, crossing his arms over his chest, stepping beside the light just enough for Sam to look up and see his protective father stance.

"I-I really like Raine," Sam looked up, "sir."

"You like her?"

"Yes, sir." Sam gulped again then, with a deep breath, found his strength. "I like her, and she's told me she isn't allowed to date until she is sixteen, so we won't date until then, sir. If it is okay with you."

"You want to date my fifteen-year-old daughter? And how old are you, Sam?"

"I just turned sixteen."

"A whole year older than Raine."

"Yes, sir. Almost a year, but I understand. I'll respect the rules and won't ask her on a date until October." Sam licked his dry, pale lips. "I promise."

"Well, Sam," David said, taking a more relaxed position seated behind the desk, "I suppose that will be fine. In October."

"Yes, sir." Neither said anything for a moment. David shuffled papers on his desk, pretending to look for something, but really wanting to see what Sam said next. "Would it be all right if I, um, hang out with her sometimes? Not like a date…"

"Hang out?"

"Yes, sir, like at school. Or… I don't know. I just like being with her. She's really special."

"Yes, she is very special." David picked up a pencil and tapped it on the desk. "I tell ya what, Sam. I don't want to ever find out you and Raine were alone in this house. Do you understand?"

Sam's face lifted, and his shoulders rose, finally seeing this situation turning around for him. "Yes, sir. I'd… I'd like that, to see her, I mean. No date, just as friends?"

"As friends?" David leaned back in the chair, considering how to approach the subject further. "Sam, have you kissed my daughter?"

Sam's shoulders sank, his mouth dry, his breathing shallow. "Um, well…"

"So, you did?"

"It was… It was my first kiss. Hers too. Just once. I swear!"

David spun around in the chair, turning towards the shelves. He didn't want Sam to see him trying to control his laughter at the whole interrogation, the absurdity of expecting his daughter wouldn't like a great kid like Sam. He was handsome, even David could see that, and if there was any boy she'd like, David was grateful it was Sam Hudson and not one of the other goons in town. Composing himself and putting on the stern father face, he turned back to see Sam, still a kid, for all practical matters, literally shaking in his shoes.

"I'm so sorry, sir. I didn't mean to do anything wrong."

"I get it, Sam. I was sixteen once too, which is why I am so concerned for my daughter." David stood, moving the lamp back to the normal position. "I tell you what, Sam. No dating, but you are welcome to visit her here at the house, when I am in the house, or when Raine's grandmother is in the house."

"Really? Thank you, sir. I won't disappoint you. I promise."

"You may kiss her once, only once, each visit, only when you leave, and only if she wants you to kiss her. Remember, I will be watching, and I have eyes all over this town."

"Yes, sir. I promise I'll respect her. I wouldn't do anything to hurt her."

"I'd hope not," David said. Looking at the tax papers on his desk, it occurred to him that Sam's father was a professor of finance, and his grandfather was an accountant of some kind. "Sam, does your father prepare taxes?"

"No, he's a teacher, but my mother is working with my grandfather at his firm. She's an accountant."

"Yes, she has been a great help to me with taxes year."

"Yes. She'd talked to her cousin about working at the bank, but she likes doing taxes. I think she's going to keep working for my grandfather."

"She doesn't want to work at the bank?" David recalled when Liam used his cousin to make Ashlyne jealous. He smiled at how pitiful that seemed, to use your own cousin as a stand-in date.

"No. Grandpa and her uncle don't get along so well."

"What about you? Are you going to be an accountant?"

"No sir. I want to work in a rehab facility."

"Rehab? That's an unusual occupation for a young man."

"Physical therapy has come a long way lately. I think it would be a good career, and besides, I really like helping people."

"I see." David nodded, considering this. "Sam, I can see why Raine likes you, and of all the young boys in town, I suppose I am happy you like her too."

"Yes, sir. Thank you." Sam nodded, finally able to take a deep breath and smile.

Maggie knocked once before opening the library doors, sent in by Bryce to rescue Sam from David's questioning of teenage romance. "David, get out here! It's your party and you two are locked up in the library."

"We're done in here," David said. "Thank you, Sam. Oh, and I appreciate your discretion in what we discussed."

"Of course, Mr. Sommer. Thank you."

Sam nodded and scurried past Maggie, thankful for the opportunity to escape the third degree from David. Maggie gave David the look only a sister could give, adding, "What did you do to him, David Sommer? Did you put the light on him like Pa did to Bryce?"

"Now, why would I do that?"

Uncle Ed arrived, taking the seat on the sofa next to Bryce, who patiently listened to tales of years past. Ed was full of stories going back to his childhood, growing up on the same street where Lorraine, Melinda, and Petra lived.

"Hey, Bryce."

"I'm listening, Ed."

"What did the ocean say to the beach?"

"Um, I don't know."

"I know!" Linda recently turned nine and loved Uncle Ed's jokes. "It said, I'm going to get you all wet!"

"No," Uncle Ed grinned, "it didn't say anything. It waved."

"It waved?"

"Get it?" Uncle Ed laughed, showing his missing back teeth.

"Oooooh, now I get it!" Linda laughed, missing her front teeth. "It waved!"

In the kitchen, Ashlyne was taking orders from Lorraine, Petra, and Melinda. They schooled Ashlyne on the proper way to mix potato salad, and she listened contently, adding mayonnaise when instructed. She caught David staring and flashed him a smile that made him tingle all the way down to his toes.

The kitchen table was cleared of potato peel and cutting boards, and Melinda covered it with a clean tablecloth, plates, flatware, napkins, bread, baked beans, kale and butternut squash, and more dishes with lids. The place smelled like home should smell. Aunt Petra opened a card table while Annie opened folding chairs to accommodate the growing crowd. David noticed Mack by the porch, leaning against the door jamb.

"Tell me, Mack," David gestured towards Annie, "how'd that happen?"

"Oh, you know. She's worked at the pub for a while, and well, we spent many nights together, just talking. She's a real sweet girl."

"Yes, she sure is something." David watched Ashlyne, who was now getting a lesson on fried chicken from Lorraine. Ashlyne was beautiful, graceful, and intelligent, but it was obvious she was not comfortable at a stove or around fried chicken. "She really is something."

"Ain't' nothin' wrong with that." Mack gestured towards Ashlyne. "I think you might have found the one, David."

"No, no. There's nothing going on there." David watched her laugh, her long hair pinned up but still cascading down her back. David mumbled, "Not yet, anyhow."

When the first batch of chicken was fried, and Melinda called everyone to the table to fix a plate, David took Ashlyne by the hand and led her outside.

"Where are we going?"

"Just wait, you'll see."

They walked to the storage barn, where the small door creaked open to a dark, cavernous room with streaks of light coming in between aged wooden slats. He found the switch and two overhead lights flickered. Still dim, but he took her hand again, showed her to a large heap under a gray tarp.

"What is this?" she asked.

"Something Pa bought years ago. I found it out here while searching for things to sell at the flea market and thought it should be yours." He pulled the tarp, revealing a tall apothecary cabinet, with small drawers. "Pa bought it from your grandparents before they passed. It has the Hughes' name at the top—see?"

"Oh, my goodness… I remember this. I wondered where it had gone." She ran her hand across the top and opened one of the drawers.

"It's yours. I'll get it over to the store whenever you are ready for delivery."

"David, it's beautiful. Let me buy it from you, please."

"It's a gift," David said, taking Ashlyne's hands and stepping closer.

"It's your birthday. You should be receiving the gifts today."

"You being here is all I want for my birthday." He looked into her eyes, nervous to take things to the next step, but it was something he felt he was ready to do right then, while it felt right. He leaned forward but hesitated to kiss her before explaining how he felt. "Ashlyne, I'm not sure how—"

"David?" Maggie called, "Where are you? Ma is looking for you."

David let out the air he didn't know he was holding. His dang sister had such impeccable timing. He snickered and stepped back, shaking his head. "Be right there, sis."

Ashlyne smiled, kissed David on the cheek, and led him from the barn.

Inside, Lorraine lit the last of the candles on a large cake while the *Happy Birthday* song was sung by everyone. David blew out candles, with the help of Ben, then opened gifts. Lorraine gave him a new pair of sneakers, Maggie, work gloves, Raine, a leather, pocketed folder. He wasn't expecting such a big deal on his birthday, and having Ashlyne there made it all that much more special. She fit in so well with his friends and family, like she'd always been around.

"I have one more thing for you, Dad." Raine handed him a small sack. "It's pumpkin seeds. I thought maybe we could have a pumpkin patch this year, and we could sell the pumpkins at church, like when Grandma sells her jams."

"That's a great idea, Raine." More than that, it was something they could do together. She was growing up so fast, and after talking with Sam, David realized it wouldn't be long before she was out of the house, married, with kids of her own. It happened in a blink of an eye. A rush of emotions filled his body, stinging his eyes. He hugged her, pushing back the tears. "We'll plant these next to the barn, in the old pasture."

With the leftovers packed on Chinet plates and covered in foil, the guests carried them home for dinner. David sat on the porch swing with Ashlyne, talking about Mack and Annie, and the new sneakers Lorraine bought for his birthday gift.

"I have something for you," she said, placing a small cloth bag in the palm of his hand. He opened it, pulling out a leather strap with a gemstone attached. "It's tiger's eye, to protect you."

"That is really cool, Ashlyne. Thank you."

"The leather chain can be expanded to put on, then pull the two ends to tighten it, like that." She pulled the straps and tucked the ends under his collar, then checked that the tiger's eye hit right at his collar bones. "Perfect."

"It will protect me, huh? From what?"

"From whatever you need protection." It was cloudy and the wind picked up, as if a storm was moving in, and Ashlyne crossed her arms and rubbed her shoulders.

"You cold?" David grabbed a blanket from the chair next to him and opened it around her shoulders, then leaning back, he left his arm around her shoulders. He smiled, thinking of how Sam had his arm in the same place just a couple hours before.

"Thank you," she said and leaned into him, resting her head on his shoulder. "You are so fortunate to have such a loving family. Generations gather here to celebrate, and that is something special. Do you do this often, I mean for holidays and such?"

"We do. I guess we always have, since I was a kid." David told her about their Christmases before his grandfather died, and his Uncle Henry, who was Raymond's brother. He used to come over and fall asleep on the couch and stay for three days. After Raymond and Henry died, he swore they could still smell cigar smoke in the library. Now, the usual holiday guests were his sister's family and Lorraine's sisters. Melinda and Tim didn't usually stay long, and Petra and Ed liked to keep their visits short too. "I would think once Raine and all of Maggie's kids start their own families, the crowd will grow."

"It's nice she's so close to you—literally across the street—but also, you two seem like you have a good relationship."

"Yeah, and, man, did she pull through for us when Caroline was sick." David sighed. "It seems so long ago now, but on the first anniversary of her death, it felt like it just happened all over again."

Ashlyne nodded, thinking of Brandon and how they met at the Little Shamrock. They didn't have much time together, she'd never met his family, or visited the town where he grew up, but love was there. He went to Hawaii, where she thought he'd be safe, and was killed. "Grief does that. It changes constantly and never goes away. But when you realize it's okay to grieve, the reality that once hurt so much to think about becomes a kind, gentle memory."

"A comfort." David felt that comfort today. Although Caroline's spirit was still around, it felt natural to have Ashlyne there as well. If Caroline could meet her, she would approve. Glancing down into her eyes, he added, "She would have loved you."

"Yes? You think so?" Ashlyne studied David's blue eyes, recognizing the emotion he held back. Being an empath was somewhat of a double-edged sword with most of the men she'd dated, especially when they touched her. "I can feel her around us."

"Do you?" David laughed and looked up when the ceiling light flickered. "Do you feel Raymond too?"

"I can sense a lot of things others cannot. It's who I am, David."

"But, just to be clear, you are not a witch, right?"

"Tsk…" Ashlyne laughed, avoiding answering the question. "What's a witch, anyway? I don't own a black pointy hat, and I've never put curses on anyone if that's what you mean."

"Okay, but you didn't say no."

"If I am a witch, I'm a good witch."

David stared at her for a moment, not sure how to take that, exactly. Looking into her eyes, he could see her—all of her—and knew she was good. Slowly, he leaned in for a kiss. Soft, lingering, and fiery. He had no idea so much passion could be passed with a simple kiss, how much changed with one kiss.

Chapter Seventeen

Presentation day was coming up fast, and everyone gathered at Raine's to practice. The board was complete, with maps of Cypress Hill when Magnus received the five-thousand acres, and where it was today. The photo of the military hospital was next to drawings of Cypress Hill, and a list of facts about Colonel Sommer's time in the Confederate Army, how he supported John Bell, and how his own son fought against him with the Union. The little they discovered about Franz Sommer was included as well, fighting with the Army of the Cumberland.

"Dad took me to the library at the university, and I found newspaper articles that will change the story a bit. It seems after John Bell lost the election to Lincoln, he met with Lincoln, who said they wouldn't attack Tennessee. When they did, Bell joined the Confederate side. The colonel supported Bell, and when the Confederate Army was formed, Adalbert became a colonel."

"They supported Lincoln before?" Lucy asked.

"Yes, here, I made copies at the library."

"Let me see." Lucy snagged the papers from Sam, still wanting control of the project. "Okay, so Bell and the colonel didn't want to split the country—they wanted to keep the Union, but after Fort Sumter, he wanted to protect Tennessee should Federal forces attack, so they aligned with the Confederacy."

"And the Union Army occupied Tennessee in 1862. It says Franz fought in the Battle of Stones River, near Murfreesboro. That's when Cypress Hill was used as a hospital for Union soldiers, in early 1863."

"Where was the colonel during all of this?"

"I didn't find any information about Colonel Sommer, only about Franz Sommer who joined the Union. They have books at the library with the names of all the soldiers in the war, but nothing more about the colonel."

"That's strange," Raine said. "We know they both came back here eventually. Right?"

"Yes, the colonel is buried here, and Franz lived here after marrying Margaret. They had Henry and Raymond." Eva held up a diagram of the family tree she'd made for the presentation board. "So where did Franz go?"

"I wonder if there is anything in Adeline's diary." Everyone looked at Raine.

"You have a diary?" Sam asked. "Let's see it."

Raine brought the diary down from upstairs, and the four sat on the couch reading it together. Adeline talked about the birth of Gilbert, how he was such a quiet child, didn't cry much. She mentioned Ellen, how she would watch him, bringing her own child with her.

"Ellen? My granny?" Eva asked.

"Yes, she told us she worked here, but didn't write much about it. She called Ellen her friend."

"How about that?" Eva smiled.

"Have you read it all?"

"No, I haven't."

"Well, come on, see if there is anything about the colonel or Franz, you know, anything for the report."

Raine turned the pages one by one, reading about the vegetable garden she grew, the crops her husband oversaw, the cattle, sheep, and poultry. She wrote about buying fabric and learning how to sew from Ellen by helping her make matching dresses for Irene and her mother. "Here's something,"

I have my son, and I love him dearly, but I've always dreamed of having a daughter. At this point of my life, it doesn't seem possible. My husband and his brother are so different, and with the passing of their grandfather and his deathbed riddles about a treasure, they seem to argue more and more about who will find it first. The brothers argue, and they both argue with their father. I'm hoping it does not divide them more than the war divided Franz and Adalbert.

Franz is nearly manic about finding this mysterious treasure. I personally believe it is simply a myth. Adalbert made it all up to entertain they boys and distract them from other problems going on in the household, but they are adults now. Adalbert should have settled the matter before he died, rather than adding to the mystery.

While the farm is doing well, the cost of labor sometimes is greater than the profit of selling tobacco or corn. Franz made tough decisions regarding the business, while Adalbert granted land to former slaves, even those slaves held by other farmers, like the Lewis family.

"This is good stuff, but how do we tie it into the project?" Eva asked.

"It shows how dependent plantations were on slave labor, which may not be the point we want to make." Sam thought for a moment. "What else do we know about the Lewis family?"

"Not much," Lucy replied, "but we could go talk to them. They still live here."

"Listen to this," Raine continued reading from the diary. "This is written in 1914, after Adalbert died."

It continues, the hunt for the elusive treasure. Franz has been digging under all the trees on the property, as this was a repeated clue. 'It's under the trees,' Adalbert said. 'Look under the trees. Hidden in plain sight.' Well, every tree on the entire front hill has three-foot-deep holes around them. Rupert Slidell, Franz' closest friend, has joined the quest for treasure. They have dug every day for the past month, now digging by the cabin in the swamp.

"Why would they think it's in the swamp?" Eva asked.

"It could be there, I suppose." Sam looked at Raine. "Remember, the cabin was on dry land. It's not that swampy and probably sits on limestone bedrock. That's why the cabin hasn't sank into the swamp."

"You went there?"

"Yes, we rode the horses down a couple weeks ago." Raine shrugged. "You were babysitting, Lucy, and Eva was dancing."

"Yoo-hoo, I'm home, Raine!" Lorraine carried bags in from the grocery and set them on the table.

"Hello, Mrs. Sommer. Do you need help carrying bags?" Sam offered.

"Yes, please, Sam. There are two more in my car." Sam nodded, was out the door and back in a flash, carrying the bags. "Thank you, dear."

"Read on, Rainie. What else does it say?"

Raine read to herself, turned a page or two, then gasped. Looking at her friends with her mouth opened wide, she said, "Franz disappeared."

"Disappeared? What do you mean?"

The men have searched for three days now, and with the heavy rain today, they don't know if they will ever find Franz. Mr. Slidell has taken the men to the spot where they were digging, only to find a fresh sink hole in the ground. One of the men climbed down at least twenty feet, a rope tied to his waist, but no sign of Franz. We can only assume the worst, and Margaret Sommer is planning a memorial service for the weekend.

"This is so sad," Raine said.

It explains why Franz isn't buried in the cemetery with the rest of the family, Lucy thought, tapping her index finger on her chin. "Hey, do you all remember the last sleepover, when we played with the Ouija board?"

"You mean when you summoned the dead?" Eva gave her a tilted-head, half-smile look. "That night?"

"Yes," Lucy whispered. "I wonder if it was Franz."

"You think Franz is swarm-man?"

"There's been a ghost in this house for a long, long time," Lorraine said, poking her head around from the kitchen. "I suppose you found the Ouija in the library, right, Lucy?"

"I did, yes."

"Adeline had one, tried to talk to Raymond after he died. Her friend Saoirse told her not to use it, that it was dangerous."

"Saoirse—Granny talked about her."

"That is the older Hughes woman. Ashlyne's grandmother, maybe her great-grandmother, I think. You should ask her."

"It's amazing how all the families are connected here, at least the families that were around a hundred years ago."

"Hey, listen to this." Raine continued reading from the diary.

The memorial service for Franz was held today. The community showed up to celebrate his life, including Rupert Slidell. Unfortunately, Mr. Slidell was intoxicated and had to be escorted out of the church. There are rumors that Franz' death was not an accident, but rather caused by Mr. Slidell and Franz fighting over the treasure they found buried near the cabin. Mr. Slidell denies any wrongdoing, swears he would never hurt his friend, yet in his drunken state, he admitted they fought over a wooden box, and that is when the earth gave way, taking Franz and the treasure with him.

"What are you reading, Raine?"

"It's Adeline's diary. We found it in her room."

"What in the world are you doing going through her things?"

"Research," Lucy and Raine answered simultaneously.

"I'm pretty sure this Rupert Slidell murdered Franz, Grandma."

"I see," Lorraine said. "Well, please continue. What else does she say?"

Raine read quickly, turning several pages before speaking. "This entry is from 1916, two years after Franz went missing."

Mr. Slidell ended his own life today. He stood by his story the entire time, that Franz' death was a terrible accident, yet I have my suspicions, as does Saoirse. The holes on the hill have long been filled and the treasure never found, yet it feels so near, hiding in plain sight, just as Adalbert once said.

On a positive note, my sister, Lucille, is visiting from Virginia. Gilbert took an immediate liking to her and how I wish she would stay longer. Her husband brought her here while he takes care of business in Nashville, and then they will return to Virginia.

"I wonder if that is who I'm named after," Lucy considered.

"I remember your grandfather suggesting the name Lucille when your mother was pregnant, Lucy."

"I never knew this."

"You should include all the little, unrelated facts on your report, like an addendum. Let Mrs. Weismann know everything you girls have learned. And you too, Sam."

"Yes, ma'am."

"I think we have enough to say the colonel was a Confederate soldier, Franz was Union, and they reconciled and lived peacefully after the war."

"I agree. It seems they put the war behind them and worked together on the farm," Raine said.

"We need to check with the Lewis family, to see what they remember about the land being given to them," Lucy said. "Eva, let's go there now, and Sam, you and Raine write up the list, like Grandma suggested. For extra credit."

"You got it," Sam said, leaning back on the couch, his arm around Raine.

"I mean it, you two. Work, no playing around," Lucy said.

"Yes, Raine. Your father will be home soon." Lorraine winked.

Sam jumped up from the couch, moving to a chair to work on the paper. There was no way he would be caught with his arm around Raine in this house—he remembered the conversation with David very well.

***

Lucy and Eva knocked on the door to the old house at the end of Lewis Drive. An elderly woman answered.

"May I help you?

"Hi, I'm Lucy Mitchell, and this is Eva."

"Hello. Are you Mrs. Lewis?"

"I was Abigail Lewis, now Abigail Norton."

"Mrs. Norton, we're working on a history project for school," Eva said, "and we'd like to ask you a few questions."

Lucy and Eva talked with Mrs. Norton for an hour, leaving the house with a wealth of information and letters written by her father, Bert Lewis, and grandfather, Isaac.

"Thank you again, Mrs. Norton. We will return the letters to you in a few days."

"You girls are quite welcome. I'm so glad I've hung on to those letters—just knew that someday they would come in handy."

***

The presentation went very well. Sam and Lucy did most of the speaking, with Raine explaining the paintings she did and the maps. Eva discussed the family tree and connections within the community, including how the Lewis family were fugitive slaves, protected at Cypress Hill until after the Thirteenth Amendment was ratified.

Eva and Lucy also solved the mystery of the disappearance of Franz Sommer, although that was not included in the presentation to the class. The letters from Mrs. Norton had an eyewitness account of what happened. Bert Lewis was a young boy at the time, wandering the swamp for turtles for his mother to make turtle soup. He overheard two men arguing on the ridge and witnessed one man pulling a knife on another man holding a small wooden box. The man with the knife lunged towards the other, stabbing him in the chest, then tried to pull the box from his hands. The man with the box pulled away, held on tight to the box, and fell backwards into what Bert later realized was a large sink hole.

As was common during the time, a black man accusing a white man such as Rupert Slidell of murder was a death sentence. It wasn't long ago that four black men were lynched in Russellville, and there was no punishment for the white men who did it – the Ku Klux Klan. Bert was too young to remember, but it was a story told to all the young men in his family, so they'd understand how things were in Kentucky. It was not uncommon for black men to be beaten, tortured, and lynched for no reason, so when Bert Lewis witnessed Slidell causing the death of Franz, he kept quiet. Other than his parents, he told no one. He wrote the events down as his testimony of the events, and Isaac wrote what he knew of the event, and the letters had been stored in the family bible since. They knew someday, when the time was right, they would be found.

"It's amazing, and so tragic," Eva said, reading about the fear Bert must have experienced living back then. Four men killed, and the killers didn't need to hide the fact they did it. "If it were to happen today, things would be completely different."

"Yes, and Franz would be buried in the family cemetery, not a sink hole in the swamp." Lucy sighed, thinking of Franz, not the lynching Bert described. "I suppose after all this time, there's no point trying to bring his body back."

"Gross!" Eva said. "Let him stay there."

"Eva's right. It's been too long, and by now, the sink hole has probably grown. There's no telling if we could find him or the treasure now."

"What treasure is that?" David asked. He wasn't trying to eavesdrop on Sam, but, well, he was listening in. Like a good father should. "Find whom?"

"Hey, Dad," Raine said. "Lucy talked to Mrs. Norton, and she has letters from her grandfather who claims to have witnessed Rupert Slidell murder Franz in the swamp."

"Here, read these letters." Lucy handed him folded papers. "Says he saw Slidell stab Franz, then they fought over a wooden box and Franz fell into a sink hole up on the ridge, with the treasure."

"It doesn't say it's a treasure, Lucy. It says he had a wooden box. They were digging for the treasure."

David read the letters twice, trying to figure out which sink hole it could be. He knew Franz, Raymond, Henry, and his father searched for this treasure for decades but never found it. It was possible Franz had found it, then hid it at the old cabin until Slidell was out of the picture. He was sure Franz made a deal with Slidell to split what they found, or at least share a portion of the treasure. And if the treasure was there, it could still be there today. It could save the farm.

David folded the letters and handed them back to Lucy, a plan generating in his mind. He couldn't tell anyone, and hopefully, he could climb down into the sink holes around the cabin without being suspect. "It was under the trees, in plain sight, that's what Adalbert always said. I doubt it was in the swamp."

"It could be there, Dad."

"Did you all tell anyone about this?"

"No." Raine shook her head.

"It was on the extra credit paper for Mrs. Weismann, but we didn't talk about it during our presentation," Sam said. Then it struck him. David was going to look for the treasure. Sam had picked up on the family finances, especially after helping his mother go over the receipts when she did their taxes. David needed this treasure. "We won't say anything about it."

"Good idea. We don't want anyone snooping around the swamp." David slapped Sam on the back, trying to keep calm. Inside, his blood was pumping through his veins, the adrenaline running high as he tried to recall if he had a heavy rope to rappel into a sinkhole. It would have to be a large sinkhole, being this happened sixty years ago, unless the hole had filled up and widened, which sometimes they did. He'd need a shovel, maybe a pickaxe.

Bryce was in Louisville working at Churchill Downs with Cross Bridge. They had five horses up there this year, one a contender for the Kentucky Derby. David would have to do this alone, and without raising concerns for his mother or Raine that he was doing something dangerous. He would load tools in his truck today, then tomorrow, he'd go treasure hunting.

"I'm heading home, Raine. Mom's waiting for me to watch Ben."

"Me too. I've got rehearsal tonight," Eva added. "Don't forget my recital this weekend. I hope you all will be there."

"Definitely! Grandma is driving us to Murray. I've never been to a dance performance like this, in a real auditorium."

"Yes, I'm excited for you, Eva!"

Sam hung back with Raine, and while David went out to the barn, Lorraine was in the house to supervise them. "Raine, I have a feeling your father is up to something."

"Really? Like what?"

"I'm not sure."

Thankful it was over, Raine went back into Raymond and Adeline's room. Sam went with her, and with her heart pounding and hands shaking, she ever so gently placed the diary back into the chest under the window. No signs of Raymond, or swarm-thing, and they swiftly left the room and returned to the library.

"Glad that's done."

"Yes, and I'm sure we'll get a really good grade."

"Hey, I just thought of something."

"What's that?"

Rupert Slidell. His initials are R.S."

"Yeah, what about it?"

"When we had the Ouija board, and it spelled out murder, it kept going to R, then S. I thought it way Raymond Sommer, or maybe me. What if it was Rupert Slidell?"

"That's R. S. all right. What does it mean? Is Rupert the swarm-thing?"

"No, I don't think so, but maybe it's Franz."

"Has it been back lately?"

"Not since we cast a spell and banished it." Raine grinned, leaving that to digest with Sam.

"You… you did what?" Sam raised his eyebrows with wide eyes, mouth gaping. "What are you saying, Raine? Are you a witch?"

She ignored him.

"Raine?"

Chapter Eighteen

David took the truck down the access road as far as he could go without risking being stuck in the mud. He parked at the trailhead leading to the cabin and pulled the supplies he'd put in the back of the truck the day before. With Lorraine at work and Raine at school, he knew he'd have hours to search and still be back at the house before they got home. There was no need to worry them. No reason to give them hope if the treasure wasn't found.

He carried the ropes, shovels, and flashlights to the top of the ridge at the edge of the largest sinkhole. If the diary said they searched twenty feet down, this was most likely the sinkhole they suspected Franz had fallen into.

Rappelling down would be a challenge, he knew, mostly because of his leg, as the upper part of his leg that remained didn't have the strength it once had. It was challenging to carry everything up to the ridge, climbing down a hole will be even more of a challenge. He wished Bryce was with him. He'd be the only one he'd talk to about the treasure if he found it, and rightfully so, as half should be Maggie and Bryce's fortune.

He tied one end of a heavy rope to a solid cypress tree, at least four feet in diameter, and a second, thinner rope on the opposite side, to a sturdy sycamore. With the smaller tied around his waist, he tossed the heavy rope down into the hole, then lowered the tools down using a heavy chain hooked to a third tree.

The sinkhole was seventy, maybe eighty feet down, at least that was how far he could see it. The ropes were only a hundred feet each, so he should have plenty of extra, but just in case, he tossed another down into the hole. Once he got down there, he wasn't coming up without a treasure, not without exploring as far down as he could go.

With a deep breath, grasping the stone on the necklace from Ashlyne, he stepped to the first landing, about six feet down, and reassessed. His feet were sinking in the soft moss, with ferns and some grass growing on the narrow ledge. The next level down was a bigger jump, the one after that a few more feet. The opposite side was the deepest, straight down from the top. He was grateful for the areas on this side where he could rest, adjust the ropes, and lower his tools ahead of him.

The hole was at least twenty feet wide, and twice that long. He wouldn't expect the treasure or Franz' body to rest at the shallower end, but most likely deeper. Surely, this hole was searched when he went missing. He sat on the first landing, gave the rope a tug, and swung down to the next level, another ten feet or so. He pulled his tools with him and turned on the flashlight, looking down into the abyss. There was no end to the sinkhole that he could see, but there were more landings down farther. He drank from his canteen, looked at his watch, and thought carefully before making his next move.

The next drop was about five or six feet. He needed to see what was there before risking another, which looked to be a narrower ledge. With the shovel and pickaxe on the chain, he lowered those down, using the heavy rope to swing the tools back when needed. With the other rope still around his waist and attached to a hip harness, he rappelled down safely.

The flashlights searched the area below. It was mostly rocks and dead limbs now, so deep that sunlight could not reach. No sign of a wooden box. No bones. No sign of Franz. The ground was also loose, and when he stepped close to the edge to peer down, the rocks gave way and fell. Stepping back against the stone wall behind him, he again needed to think carefully before making his next move.

"What am I doing?" he said out loud. "Dammit, Adalbert, there had better be a treasure."

Looking up through the large opening, he felt safe. The rope was secure, and while the climb up would be challenging, he could do it. Especially if he found the treasure. To test the depth, he tossed a large stone to the opposite side, and after hitting solid matter twice, it splashed.

It shouldn't surprise him that there was water at the bottom of this sinkhole, being this close to the river and the lake. There were caves all over the place, and it could very well connect. *One more level down*, he thought. *One more level.*

Checking the ropes, lowering the tools ahead, and checking for the best place to land, he pushed off, moving to his left, for the wider spot on the ledge. His left boot wedged between two stones, and landing a few feet lower pulled the prosthesis from his knee. He reached for it and felt it slip between his fingers. It hit solid matter twice, then splashed.

***

The grades were handed out in Mrs. Weismann's class the day after presentations were done. As expected, the Cypress Hill project received the highest grade—an A plus! Faith's group also received an A for their report on Birmingham, Kentucky, while Randal's team received a C for the Mill project, and Priscilla's team a B for the Mayfield statue. No team received a grade lower than C, which assured everyone in the class a passing grade for the semester.

"We did all right, I'd say." Lucy beamed with pride. "And to think all that history of Cypress Hill has been around all this time, and we didn't know a thing about it."

"I suppose that's why preserving history is so important," Raine said. "I've never thought about it much before, but without historians to keep the history, it would be lost."

"History is written by the victors. Isn't that what Mrs. Weismann said?"

"She did say that, and wow, it has new meaning now." Raine leaned into Sam, her arm around his waist and his arm around her shoulders.

"Aren't you two so cute," Eva said, eyeing one of Sam's friends in the hall.

"Hey, Marcus." Sam nodded at him.

"Hi, Sam." Marcus stared at Eva, nodded to each of the girls. "Hello, ladies."

After introductions, they all walked over to fountain square to Pasquale's Pizza. Lucy talked nonstop about the project and how they were like detectives in researching. Sam told Marcus about how the girls did a séance to help research Cypress Hill. Eva mentioned her dance recital, then had to leave for practice. Lucy had to watch her younger siblings and headed home, leaving Raine with Sam and Marcus.

"I should be getting home too," Raine said, holding her stomach. "I don't know if the pizza settled on my stomach. I don't feel so well."

"It tasted fine to me," Sam said. "You sure it was the pizza?"

"No, I've had this funny feeling all day, really. I don't know what it is."

"Come on then, I'll walk you home."

Raine and Sam saw David's truck was gone, and Lorraine wasn't home yet, either, so they sat outside. Raine knew better than to allow Sam inside, especially after what her father had told him.

"I wonder where he went, maybe to see Ashlyne."

"We could walk back and see if he's there."

"No, I'd rather just call. Will you wait out here while I go call Ashlyne?"

"Sure." Sam knew better than to be caught inside alone with Raine too. "I'll go check in the barn, just to make sure he's not in there."

Ashlyne had not seen David all day. Raine's second call was to Mack, and David had not been there, either. The horses had not been set out to pasture, but they had been fed, as had the hens. It was nearly five when Lorraine pulled in the drive.

"Grandma, where is Dad?" Lorraine opened the trunk of her car, and Sam carried three bags of groceries inside the kitchen.

"He didn't tell me he was going anyplace, Raine. Maybe he's at the bar?"

"I've called Mack and Ashlyne."

"I'm sure he's fine, Raine. He'll be home soon."

The expression on Raine's face was more than Sam could take. He knew she was worried. "You okay, Raine?"

"Yeah, I'm fine. I'm going to go lie down for a while, maybe I'll feel better. Call me later?"

"Sure, I'll call you later." Sam had an idea of where David had gone, and he started to get a funny feeling about it too. He kissed Raine and gave her a hug. "You're father is fine, I'm sure of it."

Raine went up to her room and closed the door. It was warm, so she opened the windows for a breeze. Lying on her bed, she looked at the photo of her parents on the nightstand. They were so young when that photo was taken, and so much in love. Funny how time passes so quickly when you're happy and life is good, but when worried about someone, the seconds creep by.

She stared at the clock until after six, and her grandmother called her down for supper. She opened her bedroom door, and the same oil painting from the library fell on her foot. "Ow!"

"Are you okay, Raine?"

"Yes." She picked up the painting of trees. "This painting was outside my door again. Did you do that?"

"No, Raine, I've been in the kitchen since I got home."

"Are you sure you didn't put it there?"

"I am certain, Raine." Lorraine took the frame from her as she came downstairs. "Raymond must be trying to tell you something."

"Wish he could just use words." The phone rang, and Raine answered, "Hello?"

"Raine, it's Sam. Any word from your father?"

"No, he isn't home yet." Raine looked at her grandmother, who shrugged, seemingly not worried a bit about David. "Sam, we're getting ready to eat. We'll talk tomorrow at school."

"Sure, talk to you then."

David hadn't returned home for dinner, and while Lorraine played it cool, like there was no reason for concern, Raine heard her making calls after dinner. He wasn't at Mack's, and he wasn't with Ashlyne.

"He must have gone into Murray to buy alcohol," Lorraine said, which made sense because they did not sell packaged liquor in Cypress Grove. You could have a beer at Mack's or at the Pasquale's, but the Quick Stop only sold gasoline and snacks.

Cross the county line, and you could buy it. They called it a damp county—not a dry county, where no alcohol sales are allowed, but damp, where you could order a drink in a restaurant, but not buy it to take home.

Raine went to bed with an uneasy feeling. She knew something was wrong. She tossed and turned all night, and the next morning, Lorraine tried to put her at ease.

"He's stayed out all night before, Raine. I'm sure he's fine. Probably had too much to drink and slept in his truck."

"Or he drove off the road. Or he could be in jail—what if he got arrested?"

"He's never been locked up before, Raine. He's not stupid. He wouldn't drive if he was too drunk."

"But he hasn't been drinking lately…" Raine sighed. She could tell her grandmother was worried too, but they had to keep going. Lorraine put on her uniform for work, and Raine got dressed for school.

She found a V-neck shirt in her mother's things, burgundy with light blue and white stripes. She looked in the mirror, turned sideways, grateful to have found her mother's bras to wear. She'd never had one of her own, not a new one, but she was the exact same size as her mother was before she got sick. She cleaned her earrings with alcohol and applied clear lip gloss. With bell bottom blue-jeans and sneakers, she was ready for school.

Lorraine waited at the bottom of the hill for Lucy and Eva, who ran to the car when they saw Lorraine waiting. They jumped in the backseat, and Lorraine headed towards the school.

"Hey, Lucy, hey, Eva," Raine said.

"Raine, I love your shirt!" Eva said. "I'm so glad to see you wearing something besides baggy sweatshirts."

"Yeah, I didn't know you had boobs," Lucy said. Eva backhanded her in the arm. "Ow! What did I say?"

"It's okay, Eva. I didn't know I had boobs, either. Or maybe I did but didn't want anyone else to know."

"Well, I'm sure Sam has noticed." Eva backhanded Lucy again. "Would you stop doing that?"

"Don't listen to her, Raine. There's nothing wrong with wanting to look more… feminine." Eva scooted forward and gathered Raine's hair behind her head. "Can I braid your hair? It would look so cool, and we could see your earrings."

"Sure, go ahead."

"You okay, Raine?" Eva whispered.

"I'm not feeling so well."

Lorraine dropped the girls off at the corner, and they walked side by side in the front doors of the school. By the time they got to their lockers, Raine realized Sam wasn't there. He'd been meeting them at the lockers each morning since they started working on the project. Maybe now that the project was over, he wouldn't anymore.

It didn't make sense to Raine. She thought he was meeting *her* at the lockers, not meeting the project group. Maybe he didn't want to be her boyfriend anymore—that couldn't be it. She was not a confident person, but she was sure about one thing. Sam really cared for her.

They had different first period classes, but when he wasn't in algebra class, Raine started feeling sick to her stomach again. When the girls met before lunch, Raine was distraught. Not only was her father missing, but now Sam.

"I'm sure he's okay, probably playing hooky with his friend, Marcus." Only this theory was blown when Marcus met them at the lockers.

"Hey, have you guys seen Sam?" Marcus was speaking to Eva, who, for whatever reason, pulled her shoulder up and tilted her chin down, giving Marcus a bashful smile and batting her eyes.

"No, have you?" Eva purred.

"Uh, no. I suppose he stayed at home." Marcus shrugged it off and turned all his attention to Eva.

"That's what happens with all the making out he does with Raine." Eva giggled, and Marcus gave a half-smile, leaning against the locker next to hers.

"Hey, I'm going to the office and see if I can walk home. I'm not feeling any better."

"Okay, Raine. I hope you feel better," Eva said.

"Yeah, I'll give you a call later." Lucy closed her locker and headed to the cafeteria with Marcus and Eva.

The office secretary called Lorraine at work, who gave the okay for her to leave school early. Once home, and discovering David had not returned, Raine called Mack, who hadn't seen him. Then she called Ashlyne.

"Ashlyne? It's Raine." Her voice trembled, her breathing irregular. Hearing Ashlyne's voice brought out the fear and emotions Raine had been holding back. With a tearful explanation of her father's disappearance along with the uneasy feelings she'd had the past day, Ashlyne offered to come over to the house.

"Has he stayed away overnight before, without letting you or Lorraine know?"

"No, not that I can remember. Not even when he was at his worst, with the drinking, I mean. He's always called to let us know."

"Let's think back, see if there is anything he might have said in the past week to give us a hint."

"I can't think of anything. He's been fine—quit smoking, you know." Raine grabbed her hair, still braided, and pulled it forward down the front. "The only reason he wouldn't come home is if he was injured."

"I've noticed he hasn't been drinking much, so that's a good thing. Right?" Ashlyne asked. "Maybe he's taking some things to sell at his friend's antique store. Do you know Billy, Mack's cousin?"

"I've met him a few times, but he hasn't said anything about that, and Mack didn't mention it when I talked to him. Other than the pearl necklace I found in the attic and the paintings in the library, I'm not sure what else he planned to sell." Raine sighed. "Can I get you something to drink, Ashlyne? I'm sorry, it didn't occur to me that I called you away at lunchtime. Would you like a sandwich?"

"No, thank you, Raine. You go ahead if you are hungry."

"No, I've been nauseous all day, even yesterday. I don't know why."

"I get that way sometimes. Usually, it's my body telling me something isn't right."

"That's what it feels like. Then, with Sam not at school today, it added to this feeling. It was just too much."

"Sam wasn't in school?" Raine shook her head. "How did the presentation go, the history project?"

"Great! We got an A+, the highest grade."

"That's wonderful, Raine. I'm very proud of all of you, especially you. I'm sure it wasn't easy digging up history of the family."

"Yeah, and we figured out what happened to Franz." Raine stopped breathing, and felt every neuron in her body zap with the realization of where David had gone. "Oh my God… I know where he is, and I'll bet Sam is with him."

***

Sam's bike was not made for trails. The access road was muddy, but manageable to steer around large holes and protruding tree roots. David's truck was parked at the trailhead, confirming Sam's suspicions that he was searching for the treasure and ran into trouble along the way. With the recent rain, he could have fallen into a new sinkhole. The rain also brought out water moccasins and other venomous reptiles in the swamp. Sam said a silent prayer for David and for his rescue mission.

The trail going down to the field by the cabin was more of a slide, leaving his shoes covered in sloppy dirt. He took a fall at the end, taking a shard of tree in his right elbow. Grateful he'd thought to bring a makeshift medical kit, he pulled the large splinter from his arm and wrapped it in strips of an old bedsheet to stop the bleeding.

He left the bike at the old cabin and hiked to the top of the ridge with a duffle bag filled with rope, flashlights, water, snacks, and even needle and thread from his mother's sewing kit. He'd seen enough action movies to know a rescue might involve sutures, and he was prepared.

His heart pumped with long strides uphill, pausing at the top for a moment to take in the view. It was foggy below, but in the distance, he could see the water and the large preserve area between the two manmade lakes. The quiet was deafening. High in the sky was a solo hawk, flying out to a clearing of fog on the ridge south of where Sam stood. It was breathtaking.

The ground was mostly slippery limestone, with few trees, and Sam carefully stepped over the jagged rock, keeping an eye out for snakes, rodents, and lose ground. He stopped, observing for signs that David had been through, then moved on towards the clearing. There, he saw a rope around a tree. Then, another, with a large sinkhole between the trees.

"Mr. Sommer?" He called several times, but no answer. The thicker rope tied around the tree did not continue down into the hole. It ended about three feet from the tree. Sam picked it up, noting the sharp cut end. It didn't break—it was deliberately cut. "Hello? Mr. Sommer?"

Sam walked to the other side of the pit and found the smaller rope the same way—cut about three feet from the tree. Who would have done this? Sam reached for the rope and stopped when he spotted poison ivy surrounding the tree. No way was he getting into that, and he gave a silent thanks to his father, who made him join the Boy Scouts when he was younger. Today, was one of those days he used much of what he learned in Boy Scouts. He used a stick to pick up the rope and put on gloves before touching it.

"Mr. Sommer? It's Sam. Are you down there?"

"Sam?"

"Yes! It's me."

"I'm in a bit of a pickle down here."

"The ropes have been cut. I have one, but it's not a heavy rope." Looking at the thick rope David used, then at the rope he'd brought, he realized he needed a heavier rope. "Mr. Sommer, I'm going to lower my rope. Can you tie your heavy rope to the end, and I'll pull it up?"

This worked for both ropes, and Sam secured the ropes around the trees with a new knot, then tied to the cut rope. Sam had never climbed down into a deep, dark sinkhole before. They didn't talk about things like that when he went to Boy Scouts in Michigan, nor was it talked about on Pine Creek where his father grew up. This was definitely dangerous. His heart was pumping in his ears and he took long, purposeful breaths to slow his breathing, yet he couldn't stop the wide grin across his face as he sat on the edge with the heavy rope wrapped around his chest. With leather gloves grasping the rope, he kicked off the side of the sinkhole.

"Careful there, Sam."

"I got it. Almost there." It was only a few minutes and Sam was standing next to David, forty feet down in a hole. The ledge was narrow, but at least ten feet long. Sam looked down into the abyss. "Whoa."

"My leg is down there."

"Your leg? Oh my God, Mr. Sommer!"

"My prosthetic leg, Sam. From Vietnam."

"Oh, yeah, of course." Sam opened his backpack and pulled out a jug of water, handing it to David. "I have peanut butter and jelly sandwiches too. I thought you might be hungry."

"How the hell did you find me here?"

"We talked about Franz, and it's like I could see what was going through your mind. The treasure. Is it down here?"

"I kind of stopped looking for it when my leg fell off. Then someone threw the ropes down, and since then, I've been trying to figure out how to go up, not down."

"I don't know, sir. Going down would probably take you to the lake. You could have swum out that way." Sam tried to hold back a smile, and David started laughing.

"Too soon, Sam. Too soon."

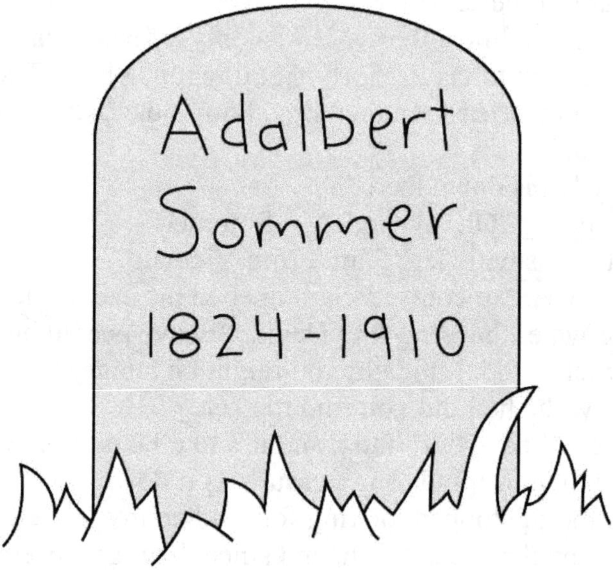
Adalbert
Sommer
1824-1910

Chapter Nineteen

Raine saddled the horses while Ashlyne left a note for Lorraine, explaining where they were going. Raine discovered the ropes that usually hung in the barn were missing, so she galloped Star to the Mitchell's barn and took their rope, just in case they needed it. If her father and Sam were in a sinkhole, it could be quite deep, especially the big one by the cabin.

"Hey, Raine Sommer, what in the world are you doing? And why aren't you in school?" Maggie stood at her back door, holding the screen open with her hip. She stirred something in a large bowl with a wooden spoon.

"I can't explain now, Aunt Maggie, but we're going to the swamp to look for Dad."

"For David? Why? Hey, what's the rope for?"

Raine rode off, meeting Ashlyne at the bottom of the hill. Maggie was home with Ben and Lisa and couldn't follow, else she'd surely be on a horse following them. Raine needed to go without Maggie. She loved her aunt but Maggie could be as bossy and controlling as Lucy. Raine trotted from the Mitchells', then walked the horses down the access road.

"They're okay, right?"

"I'm sure your father has been very careful, especially spelunking in a sinkhole. He seems like a capable man."

"Spelunking? What is that?"

"Spelunking is more of a cave diving hobby people do, to explore the underground. Maybe rappelling is something one would do in a sinkhole."

"What if Sam found Dad, tried to help, but now they are both stuck in a hole?"

"We don't know for sure they are down here at all, Raine, so let's not jump to any conclusions."

"I know, but I can't believe I didn't see this before. I should have known he would go looking for the treasure." Raine was tearing up again, but more than anything, she was just angry at herself.

"You couldn't have known, Raine."

"I just don't understand why the treasure was buried down at the cabin, when Adalbert always said it was in plain sight. It dooon't make sense." Raine reached for the necklace she wore every day, hoping that if she just held it in her hand, it would give her the answers. Her mother would send her a message, some sign to let her know David was okay.

"Are you sure the treasure was found near the cabin? Maybe Franz brought it here but found it on the hill, or shoved in the kitchen wall."

"I suppose Franz could have brought it here. I can't remember exactly what the letters said right now, but Bert Lewis wrote that he saw Franz with a wooden box, fighting with Rupert. Maybe Franz didn't find it here, but it definitely went in the hole with him. Raine smiled, adding, "I just realized something."

"What's that?"

"I'll bet Bert Lewis was named after Adalbert." She smiled, thinking about the connection. The things Adalbert did to help former slaves, giving them refuge as runaways from Memphis, then granting them land after the war.

"There's David's truck!" Ashlyne pointed down the road where the yellow pick-up was parked. "He's here."

Raine made a clicking sound and gave Star a squeeze with her knees. She went into a relaxed canter, with Freckles following suite. Ashlyne has never been on a horse since she was a teenager but was adjusting well. She held on to the saddle horn at first, then eased into the pace. Star and Freckles slowed as they neared the truck, and Raine guided them towards the path that led to the cabin.

"There's a cabin down here? This doesn't look like a good place to build a home."

"Yes, the original cabin that Magnus Sommer built when he first settled here. It's pretty much gone, aside from the stone foundation and an old metal bed frame. The cabin is built on a limestone plateau, which is why it hasn't sunk in the swamp. The big sinkhole is up on the ridge." Raine pointed up a steep limestone peak, taking a trail behind the cabin. "We'll have to go around to the other side to get to the top."

"You've been down here lately?"

"Sam and I came down a few weeks ago, but this is as far as we went. I hope he found Dad."

"Were you on bicycles? I see tire marks in the mud."

"No, we weren't. Maybe those are Sam's tracks from today." The tension in Raine's chest eased a little, knowing Sam was with her father. *If he's hurt, at least he's not alone.*

Together, they carefully followed a narrow path up the ridge, around large boulders, between cedar trees and tall grass. Raine called out for her father, then for Sam.

"David!" Ashlyne called out.

"Dad! Where are you?"

The trail was steep in places, then leveled off under a thick canopy of cypress, oak, and other native trees. The horses were careful on the rocky path, and Raine guided Star carefully on a narrow stretch with a drop-off to the right. One misstep, and horse with rider would tumble. The other side of the ridge was an easier trail, and as they neared the top, the sunshine bled through the leaves and warmed their faces.

"Dad?" Raine called out. "Sam? Are y'all up here?"

"Look, there's a rope tied to the tree."

"And another on the other side." Raine dismounted Star, tied her up to a fallen log strong enough to hold her, then tied Freckles a few feet away.

Ashlyne squatted near the heavy rope, calling down into the hole, "David? Are you okay?"

"Ashlyne? What are you doing here?" David called up.

"Raine was worried."

"Dad?"

"Raine?" Sam called. "We're okay, but we may need help pulling your father up."

"Why would he need to be pulled up if he's okay?" Raine asked Ashlyne in a hushed tone. "He must be injured."

"Raine, did you ride the horses up here?"

"Yes, Dad. We rode the horses."

"Good. Tie the heavy rope to the saddle. Pull me up with Star. She'll know what to do."

"Dad, are you hurt?"

"No, Raine, just really embarrassed." Raine let out all the air she'd held in her lungs and smiled. "Your boyfriend here came to rescue me with peanut butter sandwiches."

"And Ho-Ho's. I brought Ho-Ho's too."

"I'll get Star. You wrap the heavy rope around you good, okay?"

"Raine, have I ever told you that you are as bossy as your grandmother?"

"No, but thank you."

Ashlyne untied the rope from the tree, noticing the cut portion still there. Raine tied the end to the saddle on Star, and in a matter of minutes, David was sitting next to Ashlyne on a log.

"I've lost my leg, Raine." Ashlyne looked at Raine, not fully understanding. She hadn't realized his lower leg was amputated, and she didn't ask questions, knowing he'd explain when he was ready.

"His prosthesis, he means his prosthesis is lost. The leg was lost in Vietnam," Raine supplied.

Sam made his way up without help. Short of breath and smiling ear to ear, he said, "That was fun!"

"And you! What were you thinking, coming up here? Why didn't you tell me?"

"I thought about it after we talked last night, so early this morning, I rode my bike up here, you know, to look around. When I found your father's truck, I had a feeling he was treasure hunting."

"No treasure, I suppose?"

David and Sam shared a glance, and Sam pulled a wooden box out of his backpack.

"You found the treasure? Dad!"

He opened the box, revealing rows of rolled Cuban cigars. "Sort of…"

"What? Do you think that's the wooden box Bert saw Franz and Rupert fighting over?"

"Could be. I mean, Rupert could have thought it was gold or diamonds." Sam scratched his arms, noticing red splotches on both wrist. "Dang it! I was so careful."

"Sam, what is that?"

"There was poison ivy around one of the trees up there. I was careful not to touch it, but somehow it still got me. Seems like a small patch."

"It's everywhere up there on the ridge," David said. "Good thing you recognized it."

"Maybe it was put here to protect the treasure of cigars," Raine said, then smiled at Sam.

"Cuban cigars are a treasure of their own, princess. I know Franz and Raymond would both consider it treasure. It's something we may never know for certain."

"I'm a little angry with Adalbert. How could he call a box of cigars a treasure?" Raine crossed her arms and furrowed her brows. Her anger quickly vanished, realizing how close she came to losing her father. "And you!"

"Me?"

"Yes, you, Sam Hudson. You saved my father!" She wrapped her arms around Sam and kissed him on the lips, right there in front of her father. She didn't care. Without Sam skipping school and searching for her father, he might have died in that hole. She whispered in his ear, "Thank you."

With Sam leading the way down to the truck on his bike, David rode Freckles, with Ashlyne behind him and Raine on Star, behind them. Without his prosthesis, David couldn't drive the clutch in the truck, so Sam drove it back to the house with his bike in the back. Lorraine pulled into the driveway behind Sam, and the horses walked up from behind the house a few minutes later.

"What in the world is going on?" Lorraine stood by the porch, hands on hips and scowl on her face. "David Lars Sommer, what did you do?"

"Good to see you too, Ma." Sam helped David hop inside, and he explained to everyone his grand scheme to find the treasure. It would have been fine, had his leg not fallen off. "At least, we have the cigars."

"And your leg is gone?"

"There's no retrieving it, Ma. I'll go down to the VA tomorrow and see if they can fit me with a new one. In the meantime, Raine, can you find my crutches?"

"Who do you think cut the ropes?" Sam asked.

"The ropes were cut?"

"Yes, Ma, and there's only one person I can think of who would have done that."

"Liam Baker."

"You got it. I don't know how he knew I was up there, but that ridge is part of the land he was trying to get from us."

"Does he drive a big fancy car, like a Cadillac? Bright turquoise?" Sam asked.

"You saw him?"

"No, but Marcus and I saw the car parked down past the bridge yesterday afternoon. I thought it was odd that someone would be fishing down there so late in the day, but then again, anyone driving a car like that probably doesn't know much about fishing."

Raine found the crutches upstairs in her dad's room and brought them down. David was exhausted, dirty, and looked more alive than he had in three years. "Dad, I think you had fun doing something so dangerous."

"It's nothing compared to Sam. You should know what your boyfriend did today, Raine."

"What did he do, besides save you?"

"He absolutely saved me. We were sitting down there in the hole eating peanut butter sandwiches, then he grabbed this huge knife from his backpack and held it up over his head. I thought he was going to kill me, you know."

"Sam! You pulled a knife on Dad?"

"It wasn't for me, sweetie, and it's more like a tomahawk, I guess. Sam swung that thing and hit a copperhead coming at me, no more than three feet away." David laughed. "Chopped its head right off. It was amazing!"

"You did that?" Raine put her hand on Sam's shoulder, then hugged him.

"It was nothing," Sam blushed. "I learned to throw axes on the reservation."

"Oh my God, Dad! Copperheads are poisonous snakes! You could have died down there had Sam not been there."

"Sam has really good aim."

Raine smiled at Sam. "You really did save my dad's life. Twice!"

"Oh, I don't know about that…"

"Yes, you sure as hell did."

"Well, I'm just glad everything worked out okay." Ashlyne stood behind David, her hands gently rubbing his shoulders.

"Anybody hungry? I've got some hamburger to cook up and there's enough for everyone." Lorraine opened the refrigerator and pulled out a package of beef, then a skillet and a bag of potatoes. "But David, for God's sake, go get cleaned up before dinner. You stink!"

With a heavy sigh, he looked at Raine, nodding in silence, Sam, who shrugged, and Ashlyne, who bent down and kissed him on the lips. "Yes, please do."

***

The Saturday before Mother's Day, Lorraine took Lucy and Raine to Murray for Eva's dance recital. The girls spent the morning curling their hair and trying on dresses from Caroline's closet, which by now, had become Raine's new wardrobe. She found a green A-line dress with white silk ribbons around the neckline, waist, and sleeves. It fit perfectly, as did the strappy sandals in brown leather. Lucy chose a dark blue dress with small pink polka dots, paired with a pink scarf and blue leather shoes.

Sam and Marcus were waiting for them outside the Murray State auditorium.

"Hello, beautiful!" Sam couldn't take his eyes off Raine. She truly was a beauty, and not just with her hair fixed the way it was or the clothes she wore, but her whole being was beautiful.

"Hello, handsome!" Raine felt the same about Sam. Yes, he was tall, dark, and handsome, but he was so kind. And he'd saved her father's life. No one would ever beat that. "How is your wrist?"

"I have it wrapped in gauze, but I think the worst is about over. You don't want to see it, do you?" He kissed her on the cheek.

"No, thank you. I've seen poison ivy before."

"Sam, who is this young man with you today?"

"Mrs. Sommer, this is my friend Marcus Hardin." Sam whispered to Lorraine, "He's got a crush on Eva."

"Oh, I see."

Marcus had dressed up, and he stood there, nervously holding a bouquet of flowers to give Eva after the recital. Sam wore dress pants and a button up shirt, and with Raine on one arm and Lucy on the other, he escorted them inside. Marcus offered Lorraine his arm, causing Lorraine to look up at the six-foot tall tenth grader and grin. It'd been a while since a young man offered her his arm.

Eva was fantastic. She wore a light blue leotard and stiff nylon tutu with white tights. Her hair was pulled tight in a severe bun on top her head, and her make-up was bold, with deep red rouge cheeks and sparkly blue eyeshadow. All the dancers had a similar look, but Eva stood out as the only black dancer on stage, and the most elegant. She began with a series of pliés, her knees bending smoothly as she maintained perfect posture. Rising onto her toes, she executed a series of relevés, her legs extending gracefully as she balanced on pointe.

"She should have the lead," Lorraine whispered. "It's obvious she's a better dancer than any of the others."

"Shhhhh…." The lady sitting in front of Lorraine hushed her and shot her a mean look.

"Well, she is."

"Grandma, please!" Lucy furrowed her brows.

Eva glided across the stage with graceful ease, her movements fluid and precise. Transitioning into a pirouette, she spun effortlessly, her arms forming a perfect circle, eyes focused on a single point. She leapt into the air with a grand jeté, her legs splitting mid-flight before landing softly on the balls of her feet.

"Wow." Marcus was mesmerized. He stood and clapped when the show was over, and hooped and hollered, as did Sam.

After the recital, Lucy and Raine greeted Eva with hugs in the lobby area. "You were amazing, Eva!"

"That's the best recital I've ever seen!"

"It's the only recital you've seen, Lucy. But thanks!"

"Yes, and it was the best!"

"Hi." Marcus cautiously approached. "You were… it was… um, I mean, beautiful."

"Thank you, Marcus." He stared at her, unable to say more. "Are those for me?"

"Oh, yeah. These are for you. They're flowers. For you."

"Okay." Eva giggled. Seeing how flustered Marcus was, gave her all the more reason to like him. She stood on pointe and kissed his cheek. "They are lovely."

"Eva, where is your mother?"

Eva shrugged, not bothering to look around the crowd. "She dropped me off early this morning and wasn't sure if she'd make it back in time. Guess she didn't."

"I'm so sorry, Eva." Lorraine gave her a hug. "I'm sure if there was any way for her to be here, she would have been here."

"No. She's with her new boyfriend. Don something. He wasn't interested in coming so she went with him."

"Eva, we are all here for you, and you were the best dancer out there!" Seeing the glaze come over Eva's eyes, Raine knew she had to change the subject, else Eva would cry, and Eva wouldn't want to cry in front of everyone. "Can you call your mom and tell her you're with us? You can go with us to a Chinese restaurant! Please?"

"Chinese food? Like what?"

"Egg rolls, fried rice, chow mien, things like that." That's all Raine knew about Chinese food. She'd never had any.

"They have something called egg foo young, and moo shu," Lucy said.

"Moo shu? I'd order that just for the name," Sam said, his arm around Raine.

"You guys... you're the best friends in the world." The girls had a group hug.

"Best friends forever," Raine added.

"I know it," Lucy said. "Now, let's go eat."

Sam used the pay phone at the restaurant to let his father know where they were. It was within walking distance of campus, and his father's office was nearby. His father, Jack, arrived and introduced himself to everyone. He was tall and muscular, with a beaded necklace, and long, dark hair pulled back into a ponytail. Raine had never seen a grown man in a suit with a ponytail before. "So happy to finally meet you all. Mrs. Sommer, would it be all right if I joined you for dinner?"

"Yes, please, and call me Lorraine."

"Very well, Lorraine. Call me Jack."

"You know, your son saved my son's life the other day."

"He did?"

"He's quite the hero. He didn't tell you about it?" Jack shook his head, looking quizzically at Sam. Lorraine proceeded to relay the story of the Cypress Hill treasure, and how David went down a hole to find it. She went on and on about how Sam rescued him.

"Is this where you got the poison ivy?"

"Yes, but I never touched it. I saw it and was very careful."

"It may have been on the ropes. One thing is for sure— whoever cut those ropes probably has poison ivy on their hands and wrist too."

"That's a good point, Jack." Lorraine smiled, knowing how she could prove it was Liam who left David in that hole overnight. "I may need to visit the bank tomorrow."

"The bank?"

"Yes, I have a feeling a certain someone there will have poison ivy."

"Not Ned... Liam? You think it was Liam who cut the ropes?"

"I most certainly do, and I know he's your wife's cousin—"

"Second cousin. My father-in-law is Ned's cousin."

"Well, I'm sorry to say it, but he's not a good person."

"Liam gives me a bad feeling, Lorraine," Jack said. "He was pressing Colleen to work for them at the bank, and she refused. The following month, our mortgage payment was lost by the bank."

"Oh my." Lorraine saw the chess pieces moving, just as David had done at the bank. They had been playing a game all along, and Liam had gone too far now.

"Fortunately, Colleen got a receipt, and they corrected their mistake, but if the Bakers have some kind of vendetta against your son, I'd be very careful."

"I believe it's time we find a new bank."

Hoping to change the subject, she asked Jack about classes at the college. He taught finance, something he'd learned growing up on the reservation in Michigan. It was a small group living of Potawatomi on the reservation , but they'd done well, with a farmer's market and crafts made by the tribe members. Doing the books there began his love for numbers.

They discussed different dishes they'd like to try, and Jack ordered for everyone. Soon the waitress carried out clean plates for everyone, then dishes covered with silver lids, including moo shu pork, chicken chow mien, hon sui gai, shrimp fried rice and more, to share family style. Jack ordered a carryout for his wife as well.

After everyone ate, Jack excused himself. Raine watched him stop the waitress, then pull out his wallet and pay the bill. *Such a gentleman,* Raine thought. It must have been very expensive. He never said anything about it when he returned, until Lorraine opened her pocketbook and asked the waitress for the check.

"No, ma'am. No check. It's been taken care of," the young woman replied.

"Taken care of?" The waitress smiled, not sure what to say.

"I've taken care of it, Lorraine."

"Oh, my heavens! Thank you so much, Jack."

"Yes, thank you, Dad." Sam smiled proudly at his father, and Raine suspected Jack had heard of the Sommer family financial problems.

Who hasn't? she thought. *Everyone in town knows about the family money problems.* And for the first time, Raine wasn't embarrassed about it. She didn't care who knew the family spent every penny they could find on treatment for her mother. So what if her father's grief caused him to drink too much and not mind the fields. Things were getting better now.

Raine considered how much had changed since early March. David hadn't been drinking, and Ashlyne and he seem to be hitting it off well. She'd been a good influence on him, and David seemed happier now. The fields were plowed, tobacco and corn planted, and six small calves delivered a few days ago. Things were getting back on track now. With school out soon, Raine would be available to help more around the farm. She was ready to step up and do what she could for the family business. They wouldn't always be the poor Sommer family. She felt optimism in her bones.

Chapter Twenty

Church services the next day was all about mothers. Pastor Tim talked about Jesus' mother, how she raised him and stood by him while he was crucified. He talked about his own mother, and how his father wanted him to be a doctor or lawyer, but it was his mother who supported him when he decided to go to the seminary instead. He referenced a few mothers in church, including Sorcha, who was raising a child on her own after the war took Kayleigh's father from them. And he mentioned Caroline, who would be so proud of her daughter today.

David did not attend church, opting to finish chores early so he could spend the rest of the day with his mother. In fact, he had not left the farm since he lost his prosthetic leg, except when Maggie drove him over to the VA to be fitted for a new leg. It was not easy doing anything while using crutches, but he managed.

Lorraine had a pork butt in the oven, slow cooking with barbecue sauce; potato salad was in the refrigerator and a pot of green beans on the stove. She'd made chocolate pies with meringue topping and yeast rolls were rising on the table, ready for baking. The house would be full of friends and family to celebrate all mothers. After feeding the animals and securing part of the fence where the calves were grazing, David met Raine at the cemetery after church and they sat on the bench by Caroline's grave. Raine brought daisies and roses from the garden.

"Would it be okay if I cleaned up the rose garden by the gazebo, Dad?

"I wouldn't stop ya." He laughed.

"There are a lot of weeds there. At least, I think they're weeds."

"Yeah, you'd better check with your grandmother. Some of the things she grows look like weeds to me, but she uses them to cook. Herbs and such."

"Okay. School will be out soon, so I'm willing to help with whatever you need help with. I can ride the tractor or take over feeding the chickens for you."

"Raine, have I told you lately that you are the best daughter in the world?" David wrapped his arm around her and pulled her in tight. "You can help me plant the pumpkin patch today. How about that?"

"Okay, next to the barn?"

"Yes. It's been tilled once, but it could use another pass with the fine blades. You up to doing that for me?"

"Yes! Absolutely, Dad." She leaned into her father's chest, both holding a gentle gaze over Caroline's grave. The loss of her mother was ever-present, and the grief was ongoing, but it had changed shape, color, and texture. Where it was once a bold black, red, and yellow geometric pattern that filled every corner of every room with jagged spikes and a rough, abrasive sensation, it was now soft pastels that showed up over a specific space for a limited time. It was a sheer, fog-like rainbow, with a hint of lavender. This new grief embraced Raine when she missed her mother. It was comforting.

"Your mother is probably furious with me for climbing down a sinkhole."

"Definitely." Raine thought about how Ashlyne came when she called for help. She was worried about David too. She'd been with them at Easter, and again on David's birthday. "Dad?"

"Yes, sweet pea?"

"I like Ashlyne."

"Yeah, she really helped you with your project."

"And she pierced my ears, bought my drawings, and helped me find you and Sam."

"She's a special woman."

"Dad, just so you know, I'm okay with it if you want to, you know, date her or something."

"Date her?"

"Yeah, I mean, I know you two have gone to the flea market and stuff, but maybe take her out on a real date. Like to dinner or something."

"Huh," David thought about this for a moment, "I guess I haven't really asked her on a date, not like a proper date."

"Well, I have an idea that I think she'd like."

***

Lorraine entered the Lake Trust Bank at 9:15 on Monday morning, her head held high, with a knowing grin across her face. She approached the teller and requested to see Mr. Baker. Within minutes, she was escorted to Ned Baker's office. Liam was sitting on the sofa in front of the window. His hands were folded on his lap, and long sleeves covered his arms, but Lorraine was certain there were poison ivy patches underneath.

"Good morning, Mrs. Sommer." Ned lit a cigarette and sat behind his massive desk. "Can I offer you some coffee?"

"No, thank you."

"Well, what is it that brought you in today?" Ned was polite, perhaps a little too nice, considering their last meeting.

"I'm a little concerned for David."

"Concerned? Why is that?"

"It seems he's, well, I think the stress of the loans has been too much for him. He left the house the other day, and I'm not sure what happened after that."

"He's not been home?" Liam asked. "Since when?"

"He left the house on Wednesday morning. It's not like him to just disappear like that."

"I'm sure he's fine, Lorraine," Ned tried to reassure her, distracted by Liam jumping up from the sofa and nervously pacing the floor. "You okay, Liam?"

"Yeah, yeah, I'm fine." Liam ran a hand through his hair, and Lorraine could see gauze wrapped around his wrist. Poison ivy!

"Have either of you seen him?"

"No, I haven't. Are you sure he's not at a friend's house, or maybe he had too much to drink and got locked up?" Ned asked. Lorraine started to see the chess game, just as David had described. It seemed Ned was not an active participant in what Liam did to David on the ridge, although he certainly was aware of the attempt to foreclose on the farm.

"David hasn't been drinking for a while now. He'd solved the mystery of Cypress Hill, you know, the lost treasure Raymond and Gil talked about all the time." Lorraine's knight jumped Ned's pawn, capturing it. "He figured out where the treasure was buried."

"He did? There really was a treasure?" Ned was truly surprised. He moved his rook forward two spaces.

"David found the treasure?" Liam turned pale, leaned towards the window, and took several deep breaths. "Buried treasure?"

"Yes, the kids had some kind of project at school, and they went through all the papers in the library. They found the old maps left by Franz Sommer and a friend, Rupert Slidell. They'd spent years searching for it before Franz died." Her bishop moved three spaces. Check.

"Rupert Slidell?" Ned grinned. "How about that! Rupert Slidell was my great-grandfather." Lorraine wasn't a chess player, but she somehow visualized Ned moving his queen away from the king, leaving him vulnerable.

"Is that so?"

"Yes, indeed. I didn't know him. He died before I was born, but isn't that something how our families are connected?"

"David went to look for this treasure, you say?" Liam was very nervous.

"Yes, I just wish he'd told me where he was going." Check mate.

***

"Are you sure about this, David?" Bryce drove the 1953 Chevy pick-up down the access road, leaving it parked at the trailhead. David had asked Bryce and his friend, Sheriff Rodgers, to accompany him on a little excursion to the ridge.

"We'll see if he takes the bait."

"And you are certain he intentionally cut the ropes, knowing you were in the sinkhole?"

"I am one hundred percent certain," David said. "The problem is I can't get up there with one leg. Once you're up there, radio down to let me know we have communication with these walkie talkies, then when I see him head up, I'll let you know."

"And what will this prove?

"First, no one knows I was in that sinkhole but Sam, Raine, Ashlyne, and Ma."

"And now us," Bryce added. "Idiot. You could have waited for me, you know."

"You're right. I was foolish, but also desperate to save the farm." David shook his head, realizing the mistake he'd made. He could have died. "If Liam comes back today, it means he thinks I'm still up there in that sinkhole. I doubt he's coming to save me, either. He'll be looking for the treasure."

"How did he know you were up here to begin with?"

"That, I'm not sure. I suspect he was scoping out the property, and he happened to see me and followed me up."

"Okay, sounds reasonable to me." Sheriff Rodgers was nearly thirty years their senior but was in better shape than Bryce or David, especially without his prosthetic leg. "If what you're saying is true, I think you won't be seeing Liam Baker around town for, oh, say, eight to ten years, with good behavior."

Forty-five minutes later, David radioed Bryce that Liam was heading down the trail. David wished he could have made the trek up the ridge. Instead, he waited by his truck, holding one of two walkie-talkies. It was another thirty minutes before Bryce radioed David to report Liam had arrived at the top.

The ropes were still tied to the trees, just as they were when Liam cut them. The wooden cigar box was carefully placed on the nearest ledge, about six feet down. The second walkie-talkie was lowered into the sinkhole, and David waited for his cue.

Finally, Bryce called out, "He just called your name down the hole."

David picked up the second walkie-talkie, pressed the button, and in his weakest voice—a voice of a man who would have been in the hole for five days—said, "Help me…"

Bryce relayed, "He's called your name again, said he was sorry and he will help you."

David replied to Liam, "The treasure…"

"You have the treasure? Send it up first, David. Then I'll get you up."

"At… the top. In a wooden box."

"He's going in," Bryce said.

Bryce and the sheriff watched as Liam lowered himself into the sinkhole with a nylon rope. He was not an outdoorsy kind of guy, and his clumsiness showed in the way he crawled down to the ledge. He grunted and strained, trying to pull himself up, one hand over the edge grasping for a stone, then twisting sideways to get one foot over. He rolled up on the surface, covered in dirt and breathing heavily. The bandages on his wrist had come loose, revealing red blisters on both wrists. He knelt next to the hole with the wooden box, struggling to open the small latch, then, seeing what was in the box, he let out a gasp and shouted in joy.

"Whooooo hooo!"

David waited patiently. Ten minutes went by, and nothing from Bryce. He didn't radio to Bryce or the sheriff, else his voice might give up their location. He didn't radio the walkie-talkie in the hole, either. Fifteen minutes, then twenty went by, without a word. Then Bryce reported, "He's taken the bait."

David used the speaker in the hole and called out, "Liam! Help me, please!"

"Save yourself, David!"

Bryce radioed David, "We're bringing him down."

Half an hour later, Sheriff Rodgers led Liam up the trailhead, handcuffed and scuffed up from the hike back to the access road. "He tripped a few times along the way," Sheriff Rodgers said, a smile on his face.

"What the hell?" Liam said. "David, h-how did you get here?"

"What, Liam, did you think you left me in a sinkhole to die?"

"That's what it looks like to me," Bryce said.

"I'm not sure what the heck happened today, but he's being booked for trespassing, and for stolen property." The sheriff handed David the wooden box. "I believe this is yours."

"Yes, thank you! My treasure." David opened the box. It was filled with costume jewelry—diamonds, rubies, sapphires, gold—thanks to Mack's cousin. If only it were real, the farm would be secure, but for now, seeing Liam in handcuffs was satisfying enough.

The sheriff was not certain if the charges would result in jail time, and it would be up to the district attorney to decide if attempted murder charges were appropriate. It seemed reasonable to assume Liam would be removed from the board of Lake Trust Bank. Even if Liam was not convicted of a crime, it was clear he intended to cause harm to David and to the Sommer family. Ned might have tried to get the better of David, but even he would not support keeping his son on the board, knowing he'd abandoned David on the ridge.

Back at the house, Maggie and Lorraine waited for their return. David, Bryce, and Sheriff Rodgers joined them just as Lorraine pulled a hot brown casserole from the oven. They gathered around the kitchen table and relayed the story of Liam climbing in the hole.

"It was pitiful, watching him squirm around on the dirt trying to get up. I mean, he was taller than the ledge!" Bryce slurped his lemonade, then caught a look from Maggie before drinking more politely.

"You're telling me Liam was taller than the ledge he was standing on, where he got the fake treasure?" Lorraine laughed so hard, her entire upper torso jiggled. "I wish I could have seen him trying to climb out!"

"It was a sight to see. That boy looks like he's never gotten his hands dirty before today." Sheriff Rodgers watched as Lorraine shoveled a large helping of the hot brown on his plate, looking up and smiling at her as she tucked a napkin in the collar of his shirt. "Thank you, Mrs. Sommer."

"Call me Lorraine, please."

"Very well, if you call me Ernie."

David and Maggie noticed the interaction between their mother and the sheriff, passing a wide smile between them.

"Ma, this is really good. What's it called?" Maggie broke the awkward silence.

"It's hot brown. You've had it before."

"I guess I forgot. It's like an open-faced turkey and ham sandwich."

"It's the best damn open-faced sandwich I've ever tasted," the sheriff commented. Lorraine and Ernie held each other's gaze long enough to make Maggie uncomfortable. He seemed like a nice man, but this was her mother and she didn't want to watch.

"Where did you get all the costume jewels for the treasure box, David?" Maggie asked.

"That was Ashlyne's idea. She had a few pieces, and when she talked to Mack, he had his cousin bring some down. It all looked so real."

"Liam sure thought it was real." Bryce chuckled. "He hollered 'whoo hooo' like he'd…" Bryce covered his face with the napkin and laughed so hard, he choked himself. "Like he… he'd struck gold!"

"Sheriff," Maggie asked, "do you think there's enough to charge him with attempted murder?"

"Well, I think murder might be hard to prove." He wiped the corner of his mouth and mustache with the napkin. "Some type of negligence is likely the charge that will come. Of course, we'll need testimony from everyone involved, including the boy with the poison ivy."

"Sam? I'm sure he'd be willing to make a statement." David nodded, considering the connection of poison ivy, snickering a little. "Liam had blistered all the way up to his elbows. What a moron."

"Sam saw it, avoided it, and still got it on his wrist. How did that happen?" Maggie asked.

"I think it was on the rope, sort of like collateral damage. He's pretty much healed up now."

"You okay with him dating your daughter, seeing how he saved your ass and all?" Bryce nudged David, who nodded.

"Yep. He's an all right kid, I guess."

"What about you, David? You going to take Ashlyne out on a proper date?"

"Well, Maggie. I have an idea. Actually, it was Raine's idea, but I'll need a ride to the VA tomorrow to get a leg."

"Sure, I'll take you. That was fast. I figured it would take them months to fit a new prosthesis."

"It's a loaner. The custom fit will be ready in July, but this one I can use with the crutches. I still can't drive a clutch, so Ma, can I use your car next weekend for a date?"

Lorraine reached for her son's hand and smiled. "Nothing would make me happier."

***

Raine saddled the horses while Lorraine kept busy in the kitchen. David drove into town to pick up his date, who had specific instructions to wear jeans and old boots. She added a short-sleeved tee and sweater, with matching head scarf and dangling earrings.

"Have fun, you two!" Michael waved from the side of the store, helping Sorcha with the continued influx of tourist and college kids on a Saturday.

"I haven't been on a date like this for so long…" Ashlyne realized after saying this that David probably hadn't been on a date in even longer. "I'm really excited."

"Me too, and I have a feeling you'll like this."

"You aren't telling me where we're going?"

"Well, first, we're stopping by the farm. Then, you'll soon see. I really think you're going to enjoy this."

Raine was holding the horses by the barn when David pulled up the drive, and Lorraine carried a blanket and picnic basket from the house. Ashlyne smiled, putting it all together. "I really think I'm going to enjoy this too!"

David helped Ashlyne mount Freckles, then stood on a tree stump to mount Star from the right side, using his good leg. They rode through the farm, down the access road, into Mill Park. "This was once part of the farm. My grandfather donated it to the city to create the park when the mill was sold."

"Isn't the mill part of the park now?"

"Yes, the last owners donated the building, and the city rebuilt the water mill. They're talking about making it a national historic site or something."

"It has a great deal of history, kind of like Cypress Hill."

"Yes, Cypress Hill has a lot of history. Hopefully, I can make some repairs before the place falls down."

"I have a feeling it will all work out."

"If you know how to do that, let me know. Any psychic intuitions or premonitions, whatever it is you get."

"I wish intuition worked like that for me, David, but it doesn't. I feel things, but I can't predict the future."

"Yeah? I feel things too." David rode next to her, close enough to reach over for her hand. "How do you like this date so far?"

"So far, it's perfect."

They rode for about an hour, on trails winding around the mill, up one ridge, down over a creek, then across the creek again, over a wooden bridge where the horses had to walk single file to fit. The trail split at this point.

"We're going to the right. Left would circle back around to the farm." Soon, they were on top of a ridge, overlooking the lake.

"Wow," Ashlyne said. "This is beautiful."

"Yes, it is," David said, looking only at Ashlyne. "There's a clearing down by the lake where we can picnic, or we could stay up here."

"Let's ride down to the lake."

"Good. The bears usually stay up on the hill."

"Bears?"

"Big black bears. Ferocious beast. And elk as big as Freckles. Wolves, wild boar…"

"You're teasing me. David Sommer! You know I'm more of a city girl."

"I wouldn't bring you here if it were dangerous. Besides, I know Ma put my pistol in the picnic basket."

They spread the blanket in a clearing on a hill overlooking the lake. It was close enough, they walked down to the waterline, but far enough up that the ground was dry. David tied the horses to a tree in the shade while Ashlyne stood, looking at the lake.

"Do you remember the boys who drowned in this lake years ago?"

"I vaguely remember when it happened. They were delinquents, from what I heard."

"It's the reason my parents moved us to England. Some of the women in town thought my mother had put a curse on them because they'd stolen candy from the store and threw things at me and Sorcha."

"Is that what happened?"

"Yes, and I'd not really thought about it until we moved back. I find it hard to believe that seemingly intelligent people thought my mother—and grandmother—would kill anyone, much less kill children, by putting a hex on them. It doesn't make sense."

"I had no idea that's why y'all moved. Thought your dad got a new job over there."

"He did. It was coincidence that it came along at the same time, I suppose."

I'm sorry to say this, but my Aunt Melinda was... is one of the church ladies who goes around spreading rumors. She's mellowed with age, but she was convinced your grandmother was an evil witch."

"We're different, I realize that, but Grandmama was a healer. She didn't consider it witchcraft. Sorcha, now, she's embraced the entire witch role and likes that people have strong feelings about it one way or the other. But Grandmama? Never."

"What about you?" David pulled Ashlyne close, his lips inches from hers. "It seems you have bewitched me."

"Yes, well... that was intentional."

A large hollow tree was home to mamma racoon, and three babies watched them kiss, waiting patiently for them to open the picnic basket. They unwrapped ham and cheese sandwiches, two small cups of potato salad, and apple pie. They talked about everything from the kids' school project, the trap set for Liam, the success of Sage Sisters since the re-opening, and the grief they'd both experienced. As the sun slowly moved west, they packed up, leaving a pile of scraps for the racoons, and returned to the farm.

Chapter Twenty-One

Liam was officially charged with gross negligence, theft, and trespassing, and was released on bond. The Baker family did not attend church that Sunday, and thanks to Aunt Melinda, the news of his arrest had spread through town.

The Morgan siblings joined the Sommer family for a big meal of fried catfish, red beans and rice, and kale greens after church. Sorcha and Maggie walked Ben and Kayleigh around the barns to see chickens, calves, and horses, while Lorraine schooled Michael on gardening. Ashlyne and David were on the couch when Raine came downstairs.

"Why does this painting keep showing up outside my bedroom door?"

"What do you mean, keeps showing up?" David shook his head and grinned, figuring it was Raymond playing tricks.

"I keep finding it upstairs, then I'll put it in the library with the other painting. Can you just sell them at the flea market or something?"

"Are those the paintings Adalbert made?"

"Yes, those weird looking trees of his. He must have been a strange man, I mean… I can't believe all there was to the treasure was a box of cigars."

Ashlyne took a closer look at the painting in the library. "Do you think that's all there was? I mean, you didn't find Franz, right, David?"

"No, I have a feeling he fell to the water at the bottom, taken out to the lake."

"I wonder if that other ghost—not Raymond, but the swarm-thing ghost—do you think that could be Franz?" Raine asked.

"I haven't experienced him, but I suppose it's possible." David followed Ashlyne to the library. "How about I put these paintings in the truck, and I'll get them to Billy for the June flea market?"

"Yes, or I could put them in my store, see if anyone is interested."

"He doesn't seem malicious," Raine said. "He knocked the bible down from the shelf for us to find, and if he knew about the family bible, then he must have been family. Right?"

"Hard to say, sweetie."

David and Ashlyne sorted through books to see what else could be sold at the upcoming flea market. There were several original prints that Ashlyne thought could fetch a decent price, then she turned her attention to the painting of horses on the wall. Raine went in the living room and turned on the television but had trouble with the reception. She moved the rabbit ears around and turned the knobs, but it was just fuzz. "Ugh!"

"What do you know about this?" Ashlyne ran her fingers over the oil brush strokes of the horses, not sure if the artist was local, although it didn't appear to be a professionally trained artist. "It is very interesting."

"The colonel did most of these paintings. Traveled a bit, brought those weird looking trees back as a gift for Raymond." David shook his head and chuckled. "He may have had a touch of dementia by then."

"This woman in the portrait… David, she's wearing the necklace you showed me." Ashlyne examined it closely, nodding in realization that it was indeed the same pearl strand from the attic.

"How about that?" he said, rubbing his head. "I've seen that photo since I was a kid and not once did I notice the necklace."

"Can you fix the television, Dad? I think Raymond is messing with it again. Just like he moves the paintings."

"Moves them?"

"Yeah, he keeps putting them outside my bedroom door. It's not Grandma, she wasn't even home the last time it happened. Not sure how it got up there today."

"It wasn't me," David said. "Has to be Raymond."

They all felt the vibration under their feet, a slow rumble that somehow changed from a feeling to a sound, moving up the walls and surrounded them. Dark particles of matter formed, swirling around the room like fog before taking shape of a comet, darting between them and around them.

"Is this him, Raine?" Ashlyne asked. "Is this Raymond?"

"It's the swarm-thing!" Raine ducked under the desk, covering her head. "I don't think it's Raymond, but I don't know for sure."

"Over here." David pulled Ashlyne to the corner, behind a leather chair. He pulled her close, holding her head in his hand against his chest to protect her, his arm around her back. "You okay?"

"I'm okay."

"What is it you want from us?" Raine called out. "Why are you here?"

The swarm-thing emitted a vibrating noise, a deep, guttural moan, chilling Ashlyne to the bone. While the presence was a strong, masculine soul, Ashlyne did not sense it was one to fear. He was reckless in this form, but the spirit was not aggressive towards those it encountered. She closed her eyes and focused on the message he was sending, offering a safe conduit, should there be a message to send to the earthbound humans in the house.

The amorphous entity careened chaotically throughout the library, ricocheting from wall to ceiling to floor with relentless energy. Its erratic movement culminated in a collision with the painting of trees hanging on the wall, sending it crashing to the ground, its wooden frame splintering upon impact. And just as suddenly as it had appeared, the enigmatic swarm vanished, leaving behind a scene of devastation in its wake, with scattered debris and shattered remnants of the once serene library ambiance.

"Oh no! Why would he destroy the paintings when he's been moving them to my room?" Raine bent down, carefully moved broken shards of broken lamp from the canvas. "Both of them! Shattered frames... worthless now."

"These paintings moved, as in, on their own, Raine?"

"Yes," Raine confirmed. "I mean, I haven't seen them float through the air or anything like that. I thought Raymond was just teasing. He's been moving them to outside my room for weeks now."

"That is not Raymond... I can't believe it." David ran his hand over his head, grabbing the tresses at the nape of his neck. "He's always been so calm, playful. This is a different lost soul. He broke a lamp and paintings that could have been sold at the flea market."

Ashlyne moved the trash basket and helped Raine clean up the glass from the broken lamp. Then she saw something under the painting and carefully lifted the canvas of trees. "What is this?"

"They're just paintings Adalbert did when he was in France. He painted for a while when he was there, and they are signed by him." David picked up a chair and straightened a small table.

"No, the one underneath." Indeed, under the rudimentary painting by Adalbert, another oil painting of cypress trees was hiding. "Oh, my goodness..."

"What? What is it?"

"Oh, David. I hope this is what I think it is." Ashlyne gave a wide smile, then carefully lifted the two broken frames and paintings to the desk. "You've mentioned Adalbert went to France?"

"Yes, sometimes around 1889, maybe 1890s." David joined Ashlyne at the desk, as did Raine. They carefully removed the painting by Adalbert and, underneath, was a second painting, also of trees, with swirling brushstrokes and cloudy blue skies. The second painting was uncovered, this one of deep purple irises.

"These paintings... they are the treasure under the trees."

"Why would he cover up one painting with another?"

"Ashlyne, are these what I think they are?"

"Yes, Raine. I believe so. If these are genuine, David, these are extremely valuable."

"What do you mean?" David sat in the chair behind the desk and leaned back.

"Yes, what do you mean, because I doubt Adalbert's paintings are the treasure." Lorraine walked in, looked at Adalbert's paintings again, picking up the broken frame and putting it in the trashcan.

"Does that signature say… Vincent?" Raine gently touched the swirls of blue sky, the wisps of green of the trees. "Oh my God, Dad…"

"Will someone tell me what is going on?" David looked but couldn't figure out why they were amazed at his great-great-grandfather's paintings.

"These might be the work of Vincent Van Gogh, and if it is…" Ashlyne gave an open-mouthed smile and tossed her head back with a raspy laugh. "David, these paintings are worth a fortune."

"It's the treasure," Raine said. "We found the treasure, Dad!"

"Under the trees, in plain sight."

***

David carried a flashlight into the attic, taking one more look around before Ashlyne and Raine return from shopping. Girl stuff. He supposed he forgot his daughter needed a woman to take her shopping. They'd never had money to shop before now, so they had some catching up to do. Everything had changed, and for the better. While grateful that Ashlyne offered to take her, there was still a loss that her own mother was not there to go with them.

He checked boxes on the shelves, looking for a pair of Caroline's earrings that matched the crescent moon necklace Raine always wore. The room took on a glow, a warmth emitting from behind him. Slowly, he turned, and Caroline stood in front of him, dressed in a white dress she'd once worn to a Fourth of July party at Maggie and Bryce's. She was just as beautiful as an apparition as she'd been when alive and still looked at him the way she did the day they were married.

"Caroline… it's really you."

"Yes. Remember, I promised I'd keep an eye on you and Raine."

"You did say that. But how… am I hallucinating?" David asked.

"You are not, David. It's really me."

"You're not lost, are you? You're not a ghost, like Raymond?"

"No, David. Raymond chose to remain in the house to watch over it, but I assure you I have found heaven."

"There's another ghost… a swarm-like ghost. He found the Van Gogh paintings."

"His name is Isaac Lewis, a son of an escaped slave from Memphis who took shelter here during the war. He was Adalbert's personal servant after the war, and they became friends, even traveled together throughout Europe. Isaac knew Adalbert better than anyone and was dedicated to caring for him until his death. Isaac took the secret of the paintings to the grave with him but made it right, by seeing that you found them before the farm was lost."

"And he's been a… ghost here, all along?"

"Well, I may have pulled him forward when Lucy held her séance. I knew he could help, but he isn't able to communicate well from this side."

"I miss you so much, Caroline."

"I miss you too, David. We had a lot of good years together; it just didn't last as long as we hoped it would."

"It was supposed to last forever."

"No, it was till death do we part. Remember? I'm dead. You are not, David, and you have a chance to be with a wonderful woman. A distant cousin of mine, no less."

"Cousin?"

"Yes, Ashlyne and Sorcha's great-grandmother is my great-grandmother. Saoirse Cromwell."

"How about that…" David mumbled, finding it unbelievable that he'd fall in love with Caroline's long-lost cousin.

"She loves you as much as I do, David, and she loves our daughter. Raine needs her in her life, not to replace me, but to stand in when Raine misses me. This is a good thing."

"You think she loves me?"

"I know she does. Go to her, David. Tell her how you feel."

"Will I see you again?"

"Perhaps. I will be here, whether you see me or not. I'll always be close by."

David heard Ashlyne's car pull in and turned to the window to confirm. "They're here, Caroline. Raine will want to see you…" But the apparition was gone. "Caroline? Come back!"

Standing alone in the attic, David felt the room grow darker without Caroline's light to brighten it. He expected he would feel great loss, just as he had when she died three years prior, but instead, he felt peace. He was at peace with everything.

***

David came down the creaky stairs wearing a new blue suit, tie, and dress shoes. He was clean shaven and carried the leather portfolio from Raine. "Ready, Ma?"

"Oh, I am so ready for this!" Lorraine wore a new deep rose pant suit, heeled shoes, and the strand of pearls found in the attic. "David, you are so handsome. Your father would be so proud. And his father, and all the Sommer family before him."

As it turned out, the treasure was under Adalbert's paintings all along, in plain sight. Two Van Gogh oils—one of cypress trees and the other of irises, as well as some sketches in pencil found in the attic. David decided to keep the cypress painting, having it currently on loan with the New York Metropolitan Museum of Art. The iris painting was sold, providing enough money to pay off all loans and an extensive renovation of Cypress Hill to convert the home into a bed and breakfast. Lorraine retired, and if David planned well, money would never be an issue for his family again.

"We got lucky, Ma. I did nothing."

"Was it just luck? You sure your new girlfriend didn't wave her fingers here or drop some herbs on the door or something?"

"I'll admit, she is pretty magical, but you know magic doesn't work like that."

"You sure about that?" Lorraine grabbed her purse, and they walked out to the driveway. "Either way, I can't wait to see the look on Ned's face. I'll bet he turns three shades of crimson when he learns you opened an account at the Farmer's Credit Union. They were so happy when you deposited the check from Sotheby's."

Raine stepped out of Ashlyne's car and hugged her father. "You look good, Dad. Are you all going to see Ned at the bank, to pay off the mortgage?"

"Today is the day! It's funny, we haven't heard a thing from the bank since Liam's arrest."

"They should forgive our loans for compensation of Liam trying to kill you," Lorraine said. "Still, it does feel good that we can walk in there and pay off the loan. And Raine is right, David. You do look very nice today."

"Yes, Mr. Sommer. You are quite handsome, as always." Ashlyne grasped the lapel of his suit and pulled David towards her for a quick kiss. "I have something for you."

"You do?"

"Come see." Ashlyne opened the back of her car and pulled out two newly framed paintings by Adalbert, the same paintings of trees from the library. "I am so happy you didn't sell these at the flea market."

"How about that." David grinned and kissed her on the cheek. "It's all because of Isaac's lost soul bouncing around the house, knocking things over."

"Isaac?"

"I'll explain later."

"Whoever it was, he did the best he could to help you."

"These paintings will always hold a special place in Cypress Hill, don't you think, Raine?"

"Yes! We need to hang them in the library, side by side."

"That would be a great place for them. Why don't you take them inside and we'll hang them tonight. Your grandma and I will be back in a couple hours."

"Okay, I'd better carry them one at a time. They're so heavy!"

"Cyrus Dillinger might stop by to get the measurements for the new kitchen. He shouldn't need anything—just letting you know in case you see someone snooping around the house."

"All right, I won't bother him."

"I may hang out with Raine for a bit if that's okay."

"She would love that, Ashlyne. I'll see you when we get home."

David opened the door of his new red Chevrolet pick-up truck with an automatic transmission, and Lorraine climbed in. It felt good, he thought, and as he walked around, he looked up at the trees where the sun was streaking through. From the attic window, a silhouette of a woman watched as David opened the drivers' side door and waved. "Thank you, Caroline."

Chapter Twenty-Two

Fall transformed Cypress Hill into a breathtaking spectacle. The brilliance of golden cypress and red maple leaves set against the backdrop of a bright blue sky created a stunning visual. The festivities kicked off with a 4-H horse show at Mitchell Farms on Saturday morning. It was the first time Maggie and Bryce had hosted a horse show, and with the new four-row seating on both sides of the riding ring, there was plenty of space for spectators.

Bryce assisted by directing cars and horse trailers to the front field—and the most level field—for parking. Directly across the street, was the entrance to the farmer's market and first annual Fall Flea Market at Cypress Hill, headed up by Billy MacKenzie. More than thirty booths were set up on the north side, between the cobblestone drive and the gazebo, next to the rose garden, including Sage Sisters, Roadside Antiques from Murray, Days Past from Mayfield, and Billy's own store.

Raine and Sam established a table near the pumpkin patch, Eva aided kids in finding their perfect pumpkins, and Lucy took charge of the corn maze behind the barn. Raine noticed that Lorraine was making a fuss over the sheriff, feeding him apple turnovers with ice cream and caramel syrup, and this made her heart sing. Then, a taxi pulled up to the front of the house and dropped off a tall, thin woman with two large suitcases.

"Who is that?" Sam asked, pointing to the woman.

"Nana!" Raine shouted and ran to greet her.

"Happy Birthday, Raine." Ilene Hopkins gave Raine a long hug, rocking her back and forth while gently rubbing her back. "I've missed you so much!"

"I've missed you too, Nana!"

Caroline's mother, Ilene Hopkins, was visiting from Louisville. She hadn't been back to Cypress Grove since her daughter's funeral, although Raine spent two weeks with her in July, giving them a chance to connect in a way they hadn't before. Like Raine, Ilene resembled Caroline, with freckles and thick, auburn tresses down to her waist.

"So much has change around this place, wouldn't you say?"

"You have no idea. Come on, let me help with your bags and get you settled inside."

"When will the inn open?"

"Dad is hoping our first guest can check in by spring, but I think a lot depends on the contractors. He's been working on things himself."

David waved from the side garden where booths were set up. Ashlyne stood next to him. Adorned with tasteful, mystical accessories, she radiated a subtle elegance.

"Who's the woman he's with?"

"That's Ashlyne. You have to meet her! She has been such a good influence on Dad, and I have a hunch something big is going to happen this weekend."

"Something big?"

"Yes, it's a secret, and I've been sworn to not tell a soul."

Ilene nodded, a knowing smile across her lips. The lively ambiance was enhanced by the sound of a string band in the distance who had set up on an updated and freshly painted gazebo, adding a musical touch to the autumn festivities.

"David, my man!" Cyrus Dillinger called out. "Good to see you again. Thank you for allowing me to set up here today."

"I'm happy to help. You've done so much with the remodeling, and the place looks amazing. You deserve the recognition."

"Yes, Cyrus. I love the new pillars on the house. They look identical to the original woodwork." Ashlyne gestured towards the house. "It's absolutely beautiful."

"It's only cosmetic work on the outside, besides the new roof and window trim, I mean. It's the inside that is going to take some time."

"I completely understand." New wiring and plumbing would be time consuming work, and Cyrus anticipated a full year would be needed for indoor renovations. Construction on the new kitchen addition was almost completed, and the solarium repairs had begun. "Without the other indoor updates, do you feel the place will be ready for outdoor weddings in the spring?"

"It's possible." Cyrus scratched his chin, thinking about the question. "There are two restrooms on the kitchen addition, and if the event was held in the solarium and outdoors, yes. You can begin booking weddings in the spring."

"Thank you, Cyrus."

David waved to Ilene. "Ashlyne, do you have a moment? I'd like you to meet someone."

"Sure," she said. They joined Ilene and Raine on the patio by the kitchen, and David helped carry the suitcases inside.

"Ilene, so good to see you." David gave her a quick hug. "I'd like to introduce Ashlyne Morgan."

"Ashlyne Morgan… how do I know that name?" Ilene tilted her head sideways, then looked Ashlyne in the eyes. "Oh, my…"

"Ashlyne is Saoirse Cromwell's great-granddaughter," David said.

"Hello, so nice to meet you, Ilene. David tells me you are Saoirse Cromwell's granddaughter."

"Heavens to Betsy, it's true! I can see the family resemblance in your eyes. My grandmother had golden eyes just like you."

"Wait a minute," Raine said. "Does this mean Ashlyne is related to Mom?"

"Your father figured it out, yes. We're distant cousins."

Raine hugged Ashlyne around the waist and squeezed tight. "I knew there was something about you I really liked!"

The flea market was a hit, as was the farmer's market, horse show, corn maze, and pumpkin patch. Saturday at dusk, Lorraine, Melinda, and Petra sat on the screened porch with a notebook, thinking of ways to improve the event next year. The corn maze and pumpkin patch could continue the entire month of October, every weekend. They could have an art show one weekend, the flea market another, a music festival, and the weekend before Halloween, a costume contest. They could add hayrides and a haunted house.

"Do we really need to make a haunted house?" Petru asked. "Everyone knows Cypress Hill is haunted."

"Oh, I mean one for the kids. Maybe use the barn and add skeletons or monsters to jump out at them. It's just an idea!"

The vendors packed up and everyone had gone home by dark. Raine and Lucy had fallen asleep on the couch, and Ilene settled into Caroline's room upstairs. It was just David and Ashlyne sitting on the porch swing, listening to crickets in the cool autumn air.

"I wish you could stay tonight," David said. "It's so late for you to drive home."

"I've done it before. Besides, we've talked about this. I don't think your mother would appreciate you having your girlfriend sleep over, especially when Raine's grandmother is visiting."

"You can be such an old-fashioned girl, you know?"

"You could say that." Ashlyne smiled. "Isn't that one of the things you love about me?"

"One of the many things I love about you."

"Will I see you at church tomorrow?"

"Yes, I plan to get chores done early. Ilene will expect me to go, that's for sure." Ashlyne stood, got her purse and keys from inside, and David walked her to her car. "Ma's got a feast planned for tomorrow."

"She always has a feast on Sunday."

"Yeah, but tomorrow is special."

"Raine's birthday? I thought Raine celebrated at Pasquale's with her friends on Wednesday."

"She did. It's not Raine's birthday we're celebrating. It's life." David grinned, kissed Ashlyne goodnight, and watched her drive away.

***

David was up early. Raine joined him in feeding the chickens, cattle, horses, and now sheep. Everyone was dressed and ready for church when David pulled Ilene into the library to talk about his plans. Ilene was ecstatic and hugged David, to share the happiness in her heart.

"I wasn't sure how you'd feel about this, Ilene."

"Of course, that's understandable. I see so many good things happening in this house, and call it a feeling, but this is the right thing to do."

By the time others arrived, Lorraine and her sisters were in the kitchen bickering about how to know when a pork chop was fried to perfection. Michael and Sorcha came, as did the sheriff, Uncle Ed, Pastor Tim, Mack and Annie, Sam, Eva, and the rest of the family.

"Hey, Michael," Ed said, poking Michael in the arm.

"Hi, Ed. Good to see you."

"Michael, why did the clown go to the doctor?"

"Um, I don't know. Why did the clown go to the doctor?"

"He was feeling a little funny." Ed gave a wide-mouthed laugh at his joke. "Get it?"

"Ah, that's funny, Ed. The clown was feeling funny!"

"How do you remember all these jokes, Ed?" Sorcha asked him. "You've got one for every occasion."

Ashlyne looked around at all who gathered in the Sommer's home. Not everyone was blood related, but it was family. They had accepted the Morgan siblings into their nest. Even Aunt Melinda was smiling, despite her suspicions she was a witch. Ashlyne tried not to read others, but a quick look into Melinda's soul showed someone who truly wanted the best for others. There was no maliciousness, nothing to suggest fear of the unknown or beliefs that shouting at boys would lead to their untimely deaths. It was in the past if it was there at all.

After the meal was devoured and cake was being served, David asked Ashlyne to walk with him to the gazebo. They walked down the cobblestone drive, listening to a train rumbling past the mill, the horn sounding in the distance. Cypress Hill was incredibly peaceful, especially at night. The booths had been broken down, with only flattened grassy areas where hundreds of attendees had walked the day before, shopping for antiques or produce from the farmer's market.

The gazebo was lit with golden lights, something added when repairs were made. Bales of straw and stalks of corn remained from festival decoration, and as they stood looking over the town of Cypress Grove, Ashlyne realized why the gazebo was built in this location. The town square and shops were visible from the hill, with the gas lights lit around the fountain in the center. Sage Sisters, Pasquale's, and the thrift shop were all visible, like something in a Norman Rockwell painting.

"What a year this has been," he said. "To think it's been more than six months since we met, or met again, is nuts. I feel like I've known you my whole life, Ashlyne."

"A lot has happened since you came in for aspirin."

"I'm so glad I had a hangover that day." He took her hands, then turned to face her. "Ashlyne, you are the best thing that has happened to me in a very long time. I was at such a low point in my life, and after I met you, things started changing. I found myself again. I found strength, courage to do what needed to be done."

"It was in you all along."

"Maybe, but I couldn't see in myself what you knew was there. It's like you brought out the best in me, or maybe meeting you has made me want to be a better man. It's you, Ashlyne. You are the reason I came back to life, and I want you in my life."

"I'm not going anywhere."

"Good." With a deep breath, David shook the nervousness he felt trailing down his arms. "I spoke to your father this week."

"My father?" This surprised Ashlyne, as her father hadn't returned to Cypress Grove since her grandmother's funeral. She hadn't talked to him for weeks herself. "What on earth for?"

David knelt on his right knee, reached into his shirt pocket, and pulled out a ring. "I asked for his blessing, and he gave it. I want to spend the rest of my life with you. Ashlyne, will you do me the honor of becoming my wife?"

"David… yes! Yes!" Ashlyne's heart pounded, completely blindsided by David's declaration of love and proposal. He slipped the ring on her finger and stood. As he wrapped his arms around her, they kissed. "You really called my father?"

A crowd applauded from the cobblestone drive, where everyone came out to watch David propose. Ashlyne turned, tears in her eyes, laughing at the sight of her siblings, Raine, the entire Sommer family, and their friends, cheering them on.

"She said yes!" David shouted.

About the Author

Laura Litkea was born and raised in Louisville, Kentucky. She wrote her first story at age five and made her own chapter book at age seven. More than 50 years later, her debut novel is ready for the world to read. When she is not writing or working as a registered nurse, she spends time with her two grown children, her dog, cats, and many backyard chickens.

www.ingramcontent.com/pod-product-compliance
Lightning Source LLC
Chambersburg PA
CBHW051336020726
47501CB00007B/2117